DARK ALLEY

DARK ALLEY

A Hidden Manhattan Mystery

Evan Marshall

This first world edition published 2009
in Great Britain and 2010 in the USA by
SEVERN HOUSE PUBLISHERS LTD of
9–15 High Street, Sutton, Surrey, England, SM1 1DF.

British Library Cataloguing in Publication Data

Marshall, Evan, 1956-
  Dark Alley. – (The hidden Manhattan mysteries)
  1. Winthrop, Anna (Fictitious character)–Fiction.
  2. Sanitation workers–New York (State)–New York–
  Fiction. 3. Serial murders–New York (State)–New York–
  Fiction. 4. Manhattan (New York, N.Y.)–Social
  conditions–Fiction. 5. Detective and mystery stories.
  I. Title II. Series
  813.5'4-dc22

ISBN-13: 978-0-7278-6835-0   (cased)

All Severn House titles are printed on acid-free paper.

Severn House Publishers support The Forest Stewardship Council [FSC],
the leading international forest certification organisation. All our titles that
are printed on Greenpeace-approved FSC-certified paper carry the FSC logo.

Mixed Sources
Product group from well-managed
forests and other controlled sources
www.fsc.org Cert no. SA-COC-1565
© 1996 Forest Stewardship Council
FSC

Typeset by Palimpsest Book Production Ltd.,
Grangemouth, Stirlingshire, Scotland.
Printed and bound in Great Britain by
MPG Books Ltd., Bodmin, Cornwall.

*To Claire Marshall and Arthur
Fleishman, with love*

ACKNOWLEDGMENTS

Loving thanks as always to my wife, Martha Jewett; to my sons, Justin and Warren; and to all my friends for their continuing support.

I am grateful to my agent, Maureen Walters at Curtis Brown, and to Edwin Buckhalter, Amanda Stewart, Rachel Simpson Hutchens, Piers Tilbury, and the rest of the staff at Severn House for being such a pleasure to work with.

'Men are not punished for their sins, but by them.'
Kin Hubbard

It was no secret that Kelly and Garry were dating. Two and a half years ago, before Garry enlisted in the army and was deployed to Iraq, Kelly had had a crush on him. By the time he returned she had decided life was too short and quickly made her move, letting him know in no uncertain terms that she was attracted to him.

But while Garry was gone, Ernesto had started flirting with Kelly. He'd never stopped.

'Garry's just being protective of me,' Kelly said, following Anna back to her office.

At her door, Anna turned. 'He can be protective without trying to kill Ernesto. What's going on with Garry, anyway? Lately he's been so . . . dark.'

Kelly gave a troubled nod. 'You noticed it, too, huh? I don't know. Something's bothering him, but he won't say what. He says maybe some day he can tell me, but not now.'

Anna returned to her desk. She knew she should write up Garry and Ernesto, but she wouldn't. Fortunately, neither Hal Redmond nor Gerry Licari, the garage's other two section supervisors, had witnessed the fight – not to mention Allen Schiff, the district super-intendent. It wasn't that Anna had a soft spot for Ernesto, who was rarely anything but sour and unfriendly. But poor Garry had done not one but two tours of duty in Iraq, a total of thirty months. Wouldn't anyone be troubled after that? Yes, she would definitely cut him some slack.

She had finished with her review of the previous month's summonses and was starting on some tonnage reports when her phone rang. It was her older brother, Will.

'Hey, kiddo,' he said. 'How's the trash biz?'

She smiled. 'Oh, you know. I'm always dealing with a lot of garbage.'

'Yeah, me too!' he said with a laugh. Will was an investment banker. 'You OK?'

'Yeah, I'm fine. How about Lisa and Nina?' Lisa was Will's wife; Nina, their daughter.

'Fine. Nina's decided she's the kindergarten teacher.'

'A woman after my own heart. So what's up?'

'Have you talked to Mom and Dad lately?' he asked, sounding uncomfortable.

'Not for about a week, actually. I should give them a call.'

'You're going to have make two calls.'

'Come again?'

ONE

Anna Winthrop, a section supervisor at the New York City Department of Sanitation's Manhattan Central District 13 garage, was in her office reviewing the number and types of violations summonses issued the previous month, when Kelly Moore, a member of her crew, suddenly appeared in her office doorway. She was breathless, her vivid blue eyes flashing. 'Anna, you'd better get out here. Garry and Ernesto are fighting.' And she was gone.

As Anna stepped into the cinder-block corridor where all of the garage's offices were located, she saw the two men struggling on the concrete floor in front of a parked collection truck. Garry, grimacing, had Ernesto Balcazar in a chokehold. A few sanitation workers who had not yet started on their routes watched from a safe distance.

Anna marched straight toward the two men and grabbed Garry by the back of his shirt collar. 'Let him go.'

Garry looked up at her in surprise but didn't let go.

'You're both one minute from losing your jobs,' Anna said, and at this Garry loosened his hold on Ernesto, who gasped and scrambled free.

'You're crazy, man!' Ernesto spat, breathing hard, his short, solidly built body poised for more fighting.

But Garry just stood silently, staring down at the floor.

'Now what was this about?' Anna demanded, running her fingers back through her shoulder-length ash-blonde hair. Neither man responded. 'You two ought to be ashamed of yourselves. You're acting like children. Now get going on your routes. You're late.'

Ernesto scowled and headed for the truck where his collection partner, quiet gray-haired Pablo Rodriguez, stood waiting.

Garry turned to Anna, his gray eyes intense, the expression on his handsome face saying he wanted to tell her something. But whatever it was, he thought better of it, shaking his head as he walked toward his own partner, Terrence King.

When Anna turned to go back to her office, Kelly was still standing there. 'Don't be too hard on Garry, Anna,' she pleaded.

'They've had a tremendous fight, the biggest yet. I called last night and Mom answered. She said Dad had done something unforgivable but wouldn't say any more.'

'What could he have done?'

'No idea. Will you come out to Greenwich with me on Sunday?'

'Do you really think that's a good idea?'

'I do. Mom needs some help. I could hear it in her voice. Maybe we can make peace.'

Anna and her boyfriend, midtown patrol officer Santos Reyes, had planned to go to a crafts fair in Tribeca on Sunday. 'Would it be OK if Santos came along? If he wants to, of course.'

'Sure . . . though I don't know that he'll want to. It's liable to get pretty ugly.'

'That's OK. He's a cop. It can't be worse than what he's seen.'

'I suppose not,' Will said, not sounding too sure. 'I'd pick you up, but I've got a meeting with a client that morning, not far from Mom and Dad's. Can I meet you at the house? Say, ten o'clock?'

'Sure. See you then.'

She returned to her tonnage reports. A few minutes later her phone rang. It was Allen Schiff. 'Anna, can you come out to the entrance area, please?'

She found Allen at the front gate with a sturdily built young man who looked around thirty. He had light-brown hair in a buzz cut and startlingly blue eyes that he turned searchingly on Anna.

'This is Ron Carson,' Allen told her. 'He's looking for Garry.'

'I'm Garry's supervisor. He's out on his route now. I don't expect him back for a while.'

'When?'

'Probably around one. Do you want to come back then?'

Uneasily Ron looked up and down the street. 'Maybe. Can you do me a favor? Tell him I was looking for him, ask him to call me?' He took a matchbook from his pocket and jotted down a phone number.

'Sure, no problem,' Anna said to Ron, who turned and walked away. She and Allen both watched him until he turned the corner and was out of sight.

'My guess is they knew each other in the army,' Allen said. 'You see that haircut? The way he walked?'

Anna nodded thoughtfully. 'Why do you think he was acting so spooky?'

'Who knows?' Allen turned to re-enter the garage. 'These poor kids, it's a wonder they can function at all after what they've been through.'

Inside, Kelly was waiting to speak to Anna. 'Who was that?'

'Ron Carson. He's looking for Garry, wanted to talk to him. I told him Garry would be back from his route around one.'

'What did he want?'

'He didn't say. He just asked me to tell Garry he was here and to call him.'

Anna returned to her office. After half an hour she had finished her tonnage reports and was turning her attention to a possible revision of cleaning and collection routes when her phone rang again.

'Anna, it's Terrence.'

'What's up?'

'Can you come over to New Amsterdam Mews?'

'Why? What's going on?'

'I'd rather tell you when you get here.'

She sighed. If he wasted her time he'd be sorry. In the corridor she passed Hal Redmond and told him she'd be right back. Then she got into her white department car and left the garage through the chain-link gate on to West Forty-Third Street. She drove four blocks west, north on Twelfth Avenue, and right on to West Forty-Eighth Street. There was Terrence and Garry's truck, parked halfway down the block on the right. She pulled up behind it. Terrence was standing on the sidewalk waiting for her.

'So what's going on?' she said, getting out.

At fifty-four, Terrence was the oldest worker on Anna's crew and also the most senior. He'd seen a lot, yet he always maintained a deadpan, inscrutable expression. Now, for the first time in Anna's memory, he looked worried.

He came up to her, one gloved hand gripping the other. 'It's the weirdest thing. Come on, I'll show you.'

She followed him across the street to the entrance of New Amsterdam Mews, a narrow brick courtyard that ran perpendicular to the street. On the right stood a row of stables converted long ago into quaint, one-story apartments; on the left, the blank side of a nine-story apartment building. Terrence walked to the end of the shady courtyard, stopping at the back of the apartment building and pointing to something.

Anna looked. On the patchy grass behind the building sat four full garbage bags.

'What?' she said, losing patience. 'Terrence, what is it?'

'Garry came back here, Anna. I figure these are the first bags he grabbed.' Against the back of the building was a large heap of more full garbage bags.

Something on the ground caught Anna's eye. She bent to pick it up. It was the face of a little girl, carefully cut from a photograph. She turned it over. On the back someone had written HLBC. Absently she put it in her pocket. 'All right,' she said to Terrence, playing along. 'So where is he?'

He shrugged. 'He's gone.'

'What do you mean, gone?'

He threw out his hands in a helpless shrug. 'Gone! He got off the truck, ran in here . . . and never came out.'

She glared at him. 'Oh, for Pete's sake. That's what you called me over here to tell me? Of course he came out. He's having a smoke around the corner, or he had to use the bathroom and popped into a Dunkin' Donuts, or maybe his grandmother called him and he had to help her with something.' Garry lived with his grandmother.

'Well, if he went for a smoke or had to use the bathroom, wouldn't he be back by now? This was twenty minutes ago. And I never saw him leave. I called his cell phone. He doesn't answer.'

'Then it's got to be his grandmother. Hold on.' She brought out her cell and called Kelly. 'Have you got a number for Garry's grandmother?'

'Why?' Kelly asked. 'Is something wrong?'

'No,' Anna said impatiently, 'I just want her number. Do you have it or not?'

'Yes, sure. Hold on.' She gave it to Anna. 'Her name is Evelyn.'

'Thanks,' Anna said, and dialed Evelyn Thomason.

'Hello?' came a weak, high-pitched voice.

'Mrs Thomason, this is Anna Winthrop. I'm Garry's supervisor at the garage. Is he there, please?'

'Here?' Evelyn sounded bewildered. 'Garry's at work with you. Why would he be here?'

'He . . . seems to have . . . left. We thought maybe you needed him.'

'No . . . I'm fine.'

'Were you aware that he had any appointments today?' It was far-fetched, Anna knew, but possible.

'Appointments? No. Like I said, he's working.'

'All right, Mrs Thomason. Thank you.'

'When you find him, ask him to call me, will you?' Evelyn said.

'Of course. Thanks again, ma'am.'

Terrence was staring at her. 'So now what do we do?'

'There's nothing we can do. But I'll tell you this. When he decides to reappear he's going to have some major explaining to do. He's on thin ice already today.'

That was it, she thought – the fight with Ernesto. Garry's disappearance had to be related to that. After she had told Terrence to continue on his own – an order met with a dark glower – she got back in the car and called Ernesto.

'Yeah, Anna.'

'Ernesto, have you seen Garry?'

'Garry? *Me?*'

'Yes. Have you seen him or not?'

'No, not since I left the garage. Why?'

'Never mind.'

When she got back to the garage, Kelly was waiting for her. 'Anna, what's going on? Why did you want to talk to Garry's grandmother?'

'I thought she might know where he is.'

Kelly gave a baffled frown. '*Where he is?* He's on his route, that's where he is.'

'No, he's not. Terrence says he went into New Amsterdam Mews to collect the trash bags and never came out. The bags are lying there on the ground, as if he just vanished.'

Kelly's expression made it clear she thought this was ridiculous. 'Of course he didn't vanish. Obviously he had to go somewhere.'

'OK. Where?'

'I don't know – maybe he needed to go to the bathroom, or went to buy something to eat, or . . . I don't know, maybe he wasn't feeling well.'

'Then why didn't Terrence see him come out of the mews, why didn't he tell Terrence where he was going, and why doesn't he answer his cell?'

Kelly tried the number herself. After a while she switched off her phone. 'I'm sure there's a perfectly reasonable explanation.'

'I hope so. You were just telling me he hasn't been himself lately.'

Kelly laughed. 'I said he hasn't been himself, not that he's Houdini.'

By the end of Anna's shift at two o'clock, Garry had still not reappeared, nor had he called. As Anna passed through the garage's entrance area, Kelly emerged from the door leading upstairs to the break room, locker rooms, and showers. Their gazes met. Anna smiled. Kelly smiled back, but there was worry in her eyes.

As Anna finished telling Santos about Garry's disappearance, Santos took a sip of wine, then set down his glass. 'You tried the hospitals?'

She looked at him. 'I never thought of that. Of course! He's hurt himself. He's in the hospital and can't communicate with us. You're so smart.'

The waiter brought their pasta. They were in a little Italian café they liked on Ninth Avenue, around the corner from Anna's apartment.

'Where did you say he and Terrence were again?'

'West Forty-Eighth Street, between Eleventh and Twelfth avenues.'

He thought for a moment. 'Let's see . . . the closest hospital is St Luke's Roosevelt. Why don't you see if he's there?'

She did. He wasn't. 'Now what?' she said, closing her phone.

'Just give it time,' he said, and his handsome face broke into a smile. 'Don't be such a mother hen.'

'He's on my crew. It's my job to make sure he's all right.'

He nodded in concession. 'How's he been lately? You know, his mood.'

'Bad. Something has definitely been bothering him. And this morning he and Ernesto got into a wrestling match.'

'Over Kelly?' He knew about Ernesto's flirting.

She nodded. 'Had to be.'

He shrugged, shook his head. 'What it needs is time, Anna. It will all sort itself out. People don't just . . . vanish.'

After dinner he walked her to her apartment building on West Forty-Third Street between Ninth and Tenth avenues. At the steps, they kissed. A *tsk*ing noise came from the direction of the building. When they looked up, Iris Dovner, Anna's difficult downstairs neighbor, stood in the open doorway, scowling. She wore a voluminous yellow muumuu. Her fluffy white hair was tied up in a matching yellow kerchief. 'You should know better,' she said to Santos, taking in his uniform. Then she turned and went back inside.

They burst out laughing.

'If she only knew you were staying over,' Anna said as they entered the foyer and started up the long stairway to the second floor.

'You think she doesn't know?' Santos said, and in response came the sound of Mrs Dovner's apartment door slamming.

They were still laughing as Anna closed the apartment door and put her arms around his neck, drawing him down to kiss her. But midway through the kiss he drew back. 'Hello? Anna, are you in there? I think I lost you.'

Her face was worried. 'I'm sorry, I just can't stop thinking about Garry.'

'Let me try St Luke's again,' he said, 'see if there's been any sign of him. While I do that, you can try his grandmother again.'

Evelyn Thomason told Anna that Garry had never come home. Anna promised to call her with any news. When Santos hung up the phone, he was shaking his head. 'Nothing yet. I'll try again later.'

'Santos. Santos, wake up.' Anna trailed a fingernail lightly across his smooth, muscular chest.

His eyes popped open. 'What is it?' he said with a slow smile. 'You feeling frisky?'

'No,' she replied, and his smile turned into a frown of disappointment. 'You said you would make some calls again in the morning. About Garry. It's five o'clock.'

'Oh, yeah, right.' He sat up, rubbing his eyes, then reached for his cell phone on the night table.

While he was calling, she went into the kitchen and made coffee. When she carried it into the bedroom ten minutes later, he was putting down the phone receiver with a grave expression.

'What is it?'

'The body of a young man has been found.' He met her gaze. 'In New Amsterdam Mews.'

TWO

They walked the few blocks from Anna's building to the mews. A police patrol car and an unmarked were parked at the curb in front of the open wrought-iron gate, where a uniformed cop stood guard. He greeted Santos with a curt nod and stood back slightly to allow him and Anna to enter.

The crime scene techs and the medical examiner were huddled over something lying in the middle of the brick courtyard. The ME looked up and spoke to the two detectives standing nearby. Inwardly Anna groaned. She had met the detectives before.

Detective Elena Rinaldi was a petite woman in her early to mid-thirties, with olive skin and exotically beautiful, slanted almond-shaped eyes. She looked the way Anna imagined Cleopatra might have looked – if she had been five feet tall. Rinaldi clearly made every effort to conceal her beauty, perhaps to be taken seriously by her male colleagues. Her clothes were always a little too big, hiding the curves underneath. Her mass of glossy black hair she kept rolled up and pinned to her head. She was frowning at the ME. 'Heller, what did you say?' she said incredulously.

Heller, a glum-faced man around sixty, gave a single nod. 'A piece of mirror. Driven through the eye socket into his brain.'

Anna drew in her breath, fought a wave of nausea. Beside her, Santos was craning his neck to see past the techs. 'Don't look,' he quickly told Anna, but it was too late. She'd seen it all. Garry lay sprawled on his back in his spruce-green Sanitation uniform. From what had been his left eye protruded a long, irregularly shaped shard of glass – mirror – though its reflective surface was covered almost entirely with Garry's blood.

While Rinaldi pondered this with a frown, her partner, Homicide Detective Sean Roche, happened to look in Anna and Santos's direction. Spotting them, he gave Rinaldi a nudge. She looked over. 'Well, if it isn't the garbage detective,' she said in a deadpan tone.

Anna felt Santos tense and instinctively move forward. She placed a restraining hand on his forearm. 'Let it go,' she whispered, and felt him relax slightly.

'Reyes,' Rinaldi called to Santos. 'What's she doing here?'

'She's with me,' he shot back, challenge in his eyes.

Rinaldi, her face expressionless, glanced from him to Anna and then back to Heller, who was crouched over Garry.

Roche, nearly a foot taller than his partner, slowly shifted his lanky frame and smoothed his red hair. 'You want me to get rid of them?'

'Try it,' Santos said before Rinaldi could answer.

Now Rinaldi turned all the way to face Santos and Anna. 'Look, you two,' she said in a low voice. 'This isn't a game. A man's been murdered here. If you want to help keep people out at the gate, great. Otherwise, take a hike.'

Anna took a step forward. 'Garry is – was – on my crew. Maybe I can help you.'

'I know he was on your crew,' Rinaldi said. 'Don't think we weren't going to talk to you – and the rest of your "crew." But while you're here, when was the last time you saw him?' She cocked her head to one side to signal that they should move farther from the body.

'Yesterday,' Anna replied, 'when he left the garage to go out on his route. His partner called me from here, asked me to come over.'

'And why was that?'

'He said Garry had come in here to collect the trash but hadn't come out.'

Rinaldi gave a skeptical frown. 'What do you mean, "hadn't come out"?'

'Just what I said. He ran in and never came back.'

Without responding, Rinaldi strode to the end of the courtyard and took in the narrow backyard. Anna came up beside her. Roche came up on Rinaldi's other side. 'The bags were sitting right there,' Anna said.

A ten-foot chain-link fence ran along the back of the yard. To the left, against the fence, stood an old wooden shed with a rusty padlock on its door. 'Open it,' she told Roche. While he complied, she turned back to Anna. 'So he comes back here and doesn't come out. Then what happened?'

'He didn't answer his cell phone,' Anna said. 'We called his grandmother – he lives with her – but she had no idea where he was. As the day passed, we kept thinking – hoping – he would show up, but he never did.'

With a frown Rinaldi cast her gaze about the mews, taking in the quaint facade of the apartments that had once been stables, the old twisted locust trees that cast the courtyard mostly in shadow, the blank wall of the apartment building on the other side.

Heller stood and came over. 'He wasn't killed there,' he told Rinaldi.

'What do you mean?' Rinaldi said.

Heller looked at her as if she were mentally deficient. 'Just what I said. He was killed somewhere else and then brought here and dumped.'

'Where was he killed?' Rinaldi asked.

'How do I know? I *can* tell you his body wasn't dragged. The killer carried him somehow and dropped him here.'

Anna and Santos exchanged baffled glances.

Roche came over from the shed. 'Full of rusty tools, an old lawn-mower, a rake. Looks like the shed hasn't been opened for years.'

Rinaldi turned back to Anna. 'What time was it when his partner called you?'

'Around seven.'

'Is there anything else you can tell me?'

'No . . . I don't think so.'

'Who found him?' Santos asked.

'A man in one of these apartments,' Roche said, pointing to the mews. 'Name of Wendell Chandler. He came out around five this morning to catch a cab to LaGuardia for an early flight.'

Rinaldi said to Anna, 'We'll be coming to the garage in a little while, so don't go out to play in your trashmobile.'

Roche let out a single wheezy laugh.

Santos drew Anna away and they left the mews. An ambulance had pulled up behind the two police cars to take Garry's body away. Across the street, a small crowd had gathered on the sidewalk.

Anna and Santos started toward Eleventh Avenue. Before Anna knew what was happening, she was crying. Santos put his arm around her shoulders and squeezed her to him.

'I knew it was something bad,' she said. 'How am I going to tell Kelly?'

Santos was silent for a moment. Then he said, 'I'll help you.'

When they reached the garage, the sanitation workers on Anna's crew were of course still out on their collection rounds. Anna called Kelly and asked her to return to the depot. Then she and Santos sat in her office, she behind her desk, he in the guest chair, waiting.

When Kelly finally appeared, she looked as if she had already been told, her mouth pressed shut, her pretty face a ghastly white. Anna indicated the lemon-yellow love seat – a treasure someone in Anna's section had thrown out – and Kelly promptly sat. She stared at Anna, waiting.

'Kelly, Garry's dead,' Anna said gently, without preamble.

'I know,' Kelly said softly.

'How did you know?' Santos asked. 'Who told you?'

'No one. I just knew. He would never have just vanished like that without calling me, telling me what was going on.' Kelly looked from Anna to Santos. 'How?'

Anna swallowed. 'I don't think you—'

'I do want to know. Tell me.'

Santos spoke up. 'A piece of glass – mirror – was driven through his eye socket into his brain. It happened when he went behind the apartment building next to New Amsterdam Mews to get the trash. That's why he disappeared. However, we don't yet know where he was between that time and the time his body was found.'

For a few moments Kelly just stared at him, as if he had spoken in a foreign language. Then she fell back against the back of the love seat, clapping a hand to her forehead and closing her eyes.

'Are you all right?' Anna asked, leaning toward her.

'I . . . I feel a little faint,' Kelly said.

Santos had already jumped up and left the office. He came back a moment later with a cup of water. He handed it to Kelly and she took a sip.

'You know,' she said, after she had partially recovered, 'I knew something bad was going to happen. I told you Garry hadn't been himself lately.'

'I don't see how the two are connected,' Anna said.

'I don't know how they are, but they are. There was something going on – something bad – that Garry wouldn't tell me about. He said he would tell me some day, but not now, not until it was all resolved – that's how he put it, "resolved".'

'Do you think it had something to do with his grandmother?' Santos asked.

Kelly shrugged. 'It may have. I have no idea. All I know is that something bad was happening with *someone*, and now that someone has killed Garry.'

There was a knock on Anna's open door. Allen stood in the doorway, his face grim. 'I just heard.' He shook his head. 'Horrible. Two detectives are here to see you, Anna.'

She nodded and Allen went off to get them.

'I really should get to work,' Santos said. 'Will you two be OK?'

They both nodded. 'I'll talk to you later,' Anna told him, and he was off.

Allen returned with Rinaldi and Roche, who walked into the tiny office without an invitation.

'I'd better be going,' Kelly said, rising.

'Not so fast,' Rinaldi said. 'Who are you?'

'Kelly Moore.'

'You're on her –' Rinaldi cocked her head in Anna's direction – '"crew"?'

Kelly nodded. 'And Garry was my boyfriend.'

Rinaldi and Roche looked at her with new interest. 'That so?' Rinaldi said. 'When did you see him last?'

'Yesterday morning before he went out on his route.'

'And how did that go? Did he say anything to you?'

'No. He was mad. He and Ernesto—' She stopped, unsure, and looked at Anna.

'What?' Rinaldi said. 'Who's Ernesto?'

'Another sanitation worker in my section,' Anna told her. 'He and Garry had a fight yesterday morning.'

'Over what?'

'Over me,' Kelly said. 'Garry caught Ernesto flirting with me. It was nothing.'

Rinaldi turned to her with an expression that said she'd been impertinent. 'I think we're capable of deciding what's nothing.' She turned to Anna. 'What's this Ernesto's last name?'

'Balcazar.'

'Where is he?'

'On his route.'

'Get him. We'll talk to him first, then the others.' Rinaldi turned to Roche. 'I also want to speak to the workers in the other two sections.' To Anna: 'Who supervises those?'

'Hal Redmond and Gerry Licari.'

'You got that?' Rinaldi said to Roche, who was already scribbling on a pad. He nodded and left the room.

Rinaldi turned back to Kelly. 'So . . . Garry was your boyfriend. He must have told you things.'

'What kind of things?'

'Like if he was having a fight with anybody – in addition to this Ernesto. If anybody was mad at him. Things like that.'

'I knew something was bothering him,' Kelly said, 'but when I asked him what it was, he wouldn't say. He said some day he would explain it all to me.'

Rinaldi considered this. 'Who else did Garry have in his life? Besides you.'

'His grandmother. He lives – lived with her. Her name is Evelyn, Evelyn Thomason.'

Since Roche was gone, Rinaldi grabbed a sheet of paper and a pen from Anna's desk without asking and wrote down the name. 'Who else?'

Kelly thought a moment, then shrugged. 'He really didn't have any friends, at least not any he told me about. He'd only been back two months.'

'Back from where?'

'Iraq.'

'Ah. Did he ever mention anything that happened over there? I mean, anything about people who might have it in for him?'

'No.'

'How long was he over there?'

'Two and a half years. He did two tours of duty.'

Rinaldi shook her head. 'Heck of a thing.' She looked up as Roche reappeared with Ernesto. 'Come in, sit down.'

Ernesto's face bore its usual sour expression. His brown eyes flashed around the room as if looking for the reason he was there.

'I understand you and Garry had a fight yesterday morning,' Rinaldi said to him.

Ernesto gave Anna a look that said traitor. 'I guess,' he replied.

'You guess?' Roche said. 'Either you did or you didn't.'

'All right, so we did. So what?'

'Watch yourself, sonny,' Rinaldi warned him. 'We'll ask the questions. What was the fight about?'

Kelly said, 'I already told y—'

'Quiet,' Rinaldi said. 'I want *his* answer.' She looked at Ernesto.

He pursed his lips tightly, then said, 'I . . . said something about Kelly.'

'And what was that?'

Ernesto muttered something.

'Speak up, I can't hear you.'

'I said she had a nice booty.'

Rinaldi smirked and shot a glance at Kelly, who looked embarrassed. 'I see. Then what happened?'

'Garry heard it and he came over and punched me. I punched him back and then he grabbed me and we fell on the floor.'

'Just like high school,' Rinaldi said. 'And that was it? Nothing else was said?'

'No,' Ernesto replied. 'Anna came out and broke up the fight. Then we went on our routes.'

'And that's where you were all morning yesterday? On your route?'

'That's right, and my partner Pablo – Pablo Rodriguez – he can vouch for me.'

Rinaldi gave one nod. 'All right, go. You, too,' she told Kelly. 'Roche – get this Pablo.'

When Pablo appeared, his good-looking face was wary, his disconcertingly light eyes moving from Anna to Rinaldi to Roche. Without being invited he sat down on the love seat.

'That's right,' Rinaldi said, 'make yourself at home. Now. I understand Ernesto Balcazar is your partner.'

'That's right.'

'And yesterday morning you and he did your route as usual?'

He nodded.

'He was with you the whole time?'

'Of course he was with me. We were doing our route.'

'He never left? Not even for a moment?'

'No.'

'Are you and Ernesto close?'

'Close?'

'Friends?'

Pablo considered this. 'No, not really. I mean, we get along, we're a good team. I like him OK, but I wouldn't say we're friends.'

'All right,' Rinaldi said, and dismissed him. 'Now,' she said to Anna, 'you said Garry's partner called you yesterday morning after Garry didn't come back out of the mews.'

'That's right. His name is Terrence King.'

'Get him in here.'

When Roche returned with Terrence, it was clear he had heard about Garry. There was deep shock in his eyes and he kept shaking his head in disbelief.

'Have a seat,' Rinaldi instructed him, and he dropped on to the love seat. 'Now, you were with Garry when he disappeared yesterday.'

'Yes, ma'am.'

'Just yes will do. You're almost old enough to be my father. Tell me what happened.'

Terrence told her what he had told Anna the day before.

Rinaldi said, 'Now, you claim you never saw him come back out of the mews, but the truth is you weren't watching the mews entrance every second, isn't that correct? You couldn't have. You were collecting trash on the other side of the street.'

'True,' Terrence said. 'But when we're collectin', everything happens very fast. I keep comin' back to the truck – I woulda seen him come out.'

'Maybe,' was all Rinaldi would give him. 'Did you and Garry get along?'

'Sure,' Terrence replied. 'We joked around, laughed sometimes. I mean, I'm not sayin' we was buddies or nothin', but we got along all right.'

'Never any problems?'

'No.' Terrence's eyes bulged. 'What, you think *I* killed Garry?'

'I didn't say that. I understand something had been troubling Garry lately, that he had something on his mind. Did this seem the case to you?'

'Yeah, I would say so.'

Rinaldi waited.

'He was real quiet, moody. Sometimes I'd look over and he'd be thinkin' real hard, like he was trying to figure somethin' out.'

'Did he ever tell you anything about what was bothering him? Anything that gave you a hint?'

'No.'

Rinaldi thought for a moment, her eyes wandering, then glanced over at Roche. 'All right, you can go,' she told Terrence, and turned to Anna. 'Now I want to talk to all the others. You'll arrange that for us.' It was a statement, not a request.

Anna went out to round up the remaining members of her own crew, and asked Hal and Gerry to do the same with theirs. Rinaldi and Roche set up shop in the break room upstairs, which suited Anna fine because she had work to catch up on and, more importantly, she wanted to talk to Santos. She called him.

'How's it going?' he asked.

'All right. They're up in the break room talking to the other sanitation workers. Have you heard any more about Garry?'

'Not yet, but I'm sure I will. I'll come by for you at the end of your shift. We can grab a bite.'

'Sounds good. See you then.'

Three hours later, Rinaldi and Roche returned to Anna's office.

'Anything useful?' she asked them.

'None of your business,' Rinaldi said. 'I want you to open Garry's locker for me.'

Anna got the master key from her desk and led them back upstairs and into the men's locker room.

There wasn't much in Garry's locker, just a set of street clothes and a can of deodorant. At the back left corner were some folded pieces of newspaper.

'What's that?' Rinaldi said.

Anna picked them up and opened them. 'Two newspaper articles.'

'About what?'

'The headline on one of them is US SOLDIER CHARGED WITH RAPE AND MURDER. The second one is SOLDIER CHARGED WITH RAPE AND MURDER FOUND DEAD.'

'Let me see those.' Rinaldi took and read them. 'They're about Iraq,' she said with a scowl.

'As Kelly told you, he was there two and a half years.'

Rinaldi shrugged and dropped the clippings on to the bench behind her.

Roche spoke up. 'Anyplace else he might have kept his stuff?'

'No.'

Rinaldi sighed. 'OK, then,' she said to Roche, 'let's go speak to the grandmother.'

On an impulse, when no one was looking, Anna quickly picked up the two newspaper articles and stuffed them into her pocket. Then she followed Rinaldi and Roche down the stairs and out to the garage's entrance area. The detectives went left toward the street and Anna went right, heading for her office.

'Anna—'

She turned. Terrence was coming toward her.

'Can I speak to you for a minute?'

'Of course,' she said. 'In my office.'

She closed the door and got behind her desk while Terrence took the guest chair.

'What's up?'

'I just remembered somethin' that happened last week – Friday, it was – and I thought I should tell you. I don't know if it has anything to do with what happened to Garry. It probably doesn't, but I still think you should know everything.'

She nodded, waiting.

'We were on our route, on West Forty-Sixth Street between Eleventh and Twelfth. I stopped the truck and Garry and I hopped off. I grabbed some bags, threw them into the hopper, and got back behind the wheel, ready to move on, but then I realized Garry hadn't come back to the truck.'

'Where was he?'

'Down the street, about half a block away. He was talking to somebody.'

'Who?'

'A man. Young, I think, but I'm not sure of that. He was too far away and he was in the shadow of a tree.'

'So what happened?'

'Nothing. They talked.'

'And that's it?' She frowned. 'I imagine there are lots of times sanitation workers speak to the public.'

'Sure, I know that. That wasn't it. It was how Garry looked afterward. He was white as a sheet, like he'd seen a ghost or somethin'. I've never seen him like that.'

'Did you ask him about it?'

'Of course. I said, "Hey, who was that guy?" but he didn't answer me. He just kept looking down and shaking his head. I said, "You all right?" and he looked up at me, kind of startled like, and said, "Yeah, yeah, let's get going."'

'And that was that?'

He nodded. 'Like I said, I don't know if it has to do with anything, but it was real strange and I wanted you to know.'

Her eyes narrowed. 'You had already remembered this incident when you spoke to the detectives, hadn't you?'

'Yes,' he admitted.

'Then why didn't you tell them?'

'I thought she would laugh at me, say it wasn't important. But I knew you would listen.'

She watched him go.

The incident Terrence described had taken place only two blocks from where Garry was murdered. Was that significant? Who was that man, and what had he said to upset Garry so?

Sitting at her desk, thinking about Garry, she suddenly remembered the two newspaper articles from his locker and brought them out again to read them. The date on the first article was November 6, 2009, about eight months earlier. The date on the second article was November 12, 2009.

US SOLDIER CHARGED WITH RAPE AND MURDER

BAGHDAD, IRAQ – A US soldier was charged on Friday with raping and murdering an Iraqi teenager, the military said in a statement.

Pfc Travis Brown was apprehended after being seen fleeing the isolated farmhouse where Neda Majeed, 17, lived with her parents 23 miles south-east of Baghdad. The young woman was alone at the time. Brown apparently acted alone.

He is being held at Camp Liberty, the largest American base in Iraq.

SOLDIER CHARGED WITH RAPE AND MURDER FOUND DEAD

BAGHDAD, IRAQ – A US soldier who was being held for the rape and murder of a young Iraqi woman has been found dead in his one-person cell, according to military sources.

Pfc Travis Brown had been arrested four days earlier and charged with raping and murdering 17-year-old Neda Majeed in her family's farmhouse outside of Baghdad.

Brown had been shot through the stomach at close range. He was being held at Camp Liberty, a large complex of American military bases where thousands of soldiers are stationed.

As of yet, no one has been charged in Brown's murder. Typically, soldiers who are not on duty are required to remove the ammunition from their weapons while at American military facilities in Iraq.

Had Garry somehow been connected to this man Travis Brown? Anna went in search of Kelly and found her in the women's locker room, changing into her street clothes. She looked up inquiringly.

'Did Garry ever mention anyone by the name of Travis Brown?'

Kelly's gaze wandered as she searched her memory. 'Travis Brown . . . No, I don't think so . . . though that name is familiar for some reason.'

'He was an American soldier in Iraq who was charged with raping and murdering a young Iraqi woman.'

'Right! But a few days after he was arrested, somebody murdered him, right?'

'That's right.'

'Did Garry have some connection to him?' Kelly asked.

'That's what I'm trying to find out. There were two newspaper articles about the case at the bottom of his locker.'

'Maybe they were friends?' Kelly shrugged. 'Sorry, no idea.'

When Anna's shift ended at two o'clock that afternoon, she emerged from the garage entrance and saw Santos walking down the street toward her, his face grim. 'Let's go back to the mews,' he said. 'I want to show you something.'

THREE

The entrance to New Amsterdam Mews had been taped off as a crime scene. A different uniformed cop stood guard. The crowd across the street was gone, but a TV news crew pulled up in a van and immediately began taping Anna and Santos approaching the mews. Santos and the cop exchanged a few words. Then he and Anna ducked under the tape.

The air was cool and fresh here under the locust trees that now cast dappled shadows over the low mews apartments. It was hard to believe violence could ever occur here. As Anna and Santos reached the middle of the courtyard, one of the apartment doors opened and a wizened little man emerged. 'Have you learned anything?' he asked Santos.

'No, sir,' Santos replied, and Anna realized he would have replied that way even if the police *had* learned anything. The man wandered away toward the street.

Santos, a few steps ahead of her, was heading for the back of the courtyard. She caught up with him. 'What is it?'

'Over here,' he said, crossing the place where Garry had dropped the four bags of garbage. Beyond it, against the chain-link fence at the back of the yard, stood the wooden storage shed. In front of it stood another uniformed cop. He nodded to Santos.

To Anna's surprise, Santos was walking around to the back of the shed. 'Have a look,' he said, and stood back so she could see.

Now she saw bright yellow crime-scene tape stretched across a gap about a yard wide between the back of the shed and the chain-link fence. She looked but saw only matted grass and weeds.

'This is where he was killed,' Santos said.

She looked at him sharply. 'How do you know?'

'They found traces of Garry's blood.'

'Did they find anything else?'

'You mean that might suggest who did this to him? Unfortunately, no.'

She gazed down at the lonely space. Through the fence she could see the backyard of a building on West Forty-Ninth Street.

'This is where he was . . . stabbed,' Santos said, breaking into her thoughts. 'Then his body was carried out to the courtyard and dropped there.'

She looked at him. 'But why? Why not just kill him and leave him here?'

'Well,' he said pensively, 'let's think about it. Obviously the killer grabbed Garry and dragged him back here. Why not just kill him and run? Two possible reasons, I think. First, the killer wanted to wait until dark to leave here. The only way out is back through the courtyard to the street, and in daylight there would have been a good chance he would be seen. So he may have hidden back here all day. Second, he didn't just want Garry dead. He wanted to dump his body in the middle of the mews. He would need to wait for darkness to do *that*, too.'

'But why?' she said again. 'If killing Garry was the objective, why bother carrying him out there?'

He looked at her. 'That's the question, isn't it? Of course,' he went on, 'there's another way this might have gone down. The perp grabs Garry and drags him back here, kills him, leaves the body for now and goes into one of the mews apartments or the apartment building, because he *lives* there.'

'You canvassed the residents?'

'Of course. No indication that one of them did this, but that doesn't mean anything. No one claims to have seen anything suspicious.'

They wandered back to the open courtyard, stood near the spot where Garry's body had lain.

'The ME says he died around seven thirty yesterday morning.'

'Seven thirty . . . That's when I was standing right here speaking to Terrence.' She put her hand to her mouth and shot a glance at the shed. 'We were standing here while – while—' She couldn't say it. She began to cry. Santos put his arm around her and pressed her to him. She gazed up at him. 'Who would do such a thing? What could Garry possibly have done to deserve to die, and to die like that?'

'That's exactly what the police are trying to find out,' he said gently.

'And while they do . . .' She looked up at him, new conviction in her voice. 'I'll be trying, too.'

At 2:45 the following afternoon, Anna and Kelly came up out of the 168th Street subway station in Washington Heights, in the northern tip of the borough of Manhattan. Evelyn Thomason's seven-story apartment building was on 168th itself, just off Amsterdam Avenue. In the small vestibule, Kelly pressed the intercom button for Evelyn's apartment and she buzzed them in.

The lobby was spacious, suggesting grandeur in another era, but now it was barren of furniture and someone had spray-painted *cuero malo!* in green on the elevator doors.

'She's on four,' Kelly said, and pressed the elevator call button.

'You've been here?' Anna asked.

Kelly nodded. 'Once. Garry wanted me to meet her.' Her eyes welled with tears and she looked down.

When they stepped off the elevator Evelyn was waiting in her doorway at the end of a long corridor. Slim and straight-backed, with sharp features and short-cropped hair dyed a severe black, she looked to Anna to be in her early to mid-seventies. She looked them up and down, taking in their green Sanitation uniforms. There was an awkward moment when Kelly stepped forward to embrace her and the older woman took a step back. Instead they exchanged cheek kisses.

'Mrs Thomason,' Kelly said, 'I'd like you to meet Anna Winthrop.'

Evelyn gave a small smile. 'Garry talked about you,' she said in her high-pitched voice. 'He said you were good to him. Come in.'

Anna had thought she would never find an apartment more loaded with knick-knacks than Mrs Dovner's, but now she had. Figurines and small bowls and an extensive thimble collection occupied every available horizontal surface. Yet Anna saw no dust. The apartment was immaculate, the sofa and chairs in the living room meticulously arranged, the throw pillows perfectly aligned. Large windows with elaborate drapes and shears looked out on the street.

A tray with coffee and tea things sat on a large ottoman. Anna and Kelly sat down on the sofa, Evelyn in an armchair facing them.

'I don't know what I can tell you,' she said quietly as she poured them coffee. 'I've told the police all I know, and heaven knows I was in no condition to talk after they made me identify my Garry's body.' From her face Anna could tell she was remembering what she'd seen. She took a crumpled tissue from her pocket and pressed it to her nose, sniffing.

Kelly's face reflected the pain she felt for the older woman. 'We're not just here to ask you questions, Mrs Thomason. We also wanted to tell you how very sorry we are.'

The slight smile again. 'That's very kind.'

'Mrs Thomason,' Anna said, leaning forward, 'I'm sure you've been asked this, but is there anyone you can think of who might have wanted to . . . hurt Garry?'

Evelyn shook her head. 'He'd barely been home two months from the service! He didn't have time to make any enemies.'

Obviously untrue, Anna thought, but kept it to herself.

'What about friends? Did he have a lot of friends?'

'No. He told me he wasn't going to be friends with any of the people he was friends with before he enlisted. He was starting over.'

Anna frowned. 'Why?'

Evelyn gave a little shrug. 'Those people were bringing him down, he said. He was going to be friends with a better class of people.' She looked at Kelly. 'Like you, dear.'

Kelly smiled sadly.

Evelyn went on. 'He was hoping to make some friends at work. He liked everyone, liked Terrence, his partner.'

Kelly said, 'What about these people from his past, the ones he didn't want to be friends with any more. Can you think of anyone who might have clashed with Garry before he went to Iraq?'

'I didn't know his friends, but he never said anything about problems with any of them.' Evelyn's eyes narrowed as she shifted her gaze from Kelly to Anna. 'Garry didn't have time for trouble. He always worked hard, wanted to make something of himself. Went to George Washington High School on 193rd and got good marks in his classes. After high school he did odd jobs until he decided to take the civil service exam and apply for a job at the Sanitation Department.'

Anna set down her empty coffee cup on the tray. 'If you don't mind my asking, how long had Garry lived with you?'

'All his life, since he was a baby. My daughter, Roberta −' she pointed to a framed photo on a side table of a dark-haired woman with pretty, delicate features − 'died in a car accident.'

Both Anna and Kelly said that they were sorry.

'And Garry's father?' Kelly asked.

Evelyn cast her eyes upward. 'No father. I mean, he was never around, left even before Garry was born. So it was up to me. I'd lost Roberta but I had Garry. I loved him so much. Now . . .' She put the tissue to her nose, her eyes. 'Now I've got no one.' Silently her slight shoulders rose and fell.

Anna and Kelly exchanged a sad look and rose.

'Mrs Thomason, thank you for seeing us,' Anna said, 'and please accept our deepest sympathy. Garry was a pleasure to work with, and we'll all miss him.'

Wordlessly the older woman saw them out.

'Oh.' Anna turned to her and fished a card out of her pocket. 'Here's my cell phone number in case anything occurs to you. If you think of someone who might have wanted to hurt Garry.'

Evelyn took the card and nodded as she closed the door.

'Phew,' Kelly said, waving her hand next to her face. 'Poor thing. She puts twenty-seven years into raising Garry like her own son and then one day he's gone. It's not fair.'

'No, it's definitely not fair,' Anna agreed as they started down the corridor toward the elevator.

The door to the apartment next to Evelyn's opened and a tall, thin, elderly man emerged. 'You here to see Evelyn?' he said. 'I see you both work for the Sanitation Department like Garry.'

'That's right. I'm Anna Winthrop, Garry's supervisor, and this is Kelly Moore, his girlfriend. And you are . . .?'

'Syd Goldblum. My condolences,' he said to Kelly. Then he shot a glance at Evelyn's door. 'It's awful when someone dies and you haven't – you know – patched things up, made things right.'

'What do you mean?' Kelly asked.

'I guess she didn't tell you,' said Syd, who it was clear knew perfectly well that whatever he had to say, Evelyn Thomason hadn't told them. 'Monday night she and Garry had a horrendous fight. Horrendous. I heard them shouting.'

'Really?' Anna pictured Syd with a wine glass pressed against the wall, listening. 'What do you think the fight was about?'

'I don't know,' Syd said, obviously unhappy about it, 'but Garry was real mad, I can tell you that. "Half my life!" he kept screaming at Evelyn. "Half my life!"'

Kelly frowned in puzzlement. '"Half my life"? What does that mean?'

'Not a clue. But whatever it meant, he was sure upset about it.' Behind Syd, a kettle whistled. 'Better run. Ladies.' He closed the door.

They continued down the corridor.

'*Pssst!*'

The sound had come from behind them. They turned. The door of the apartment beyond Evelyn Thomason's was ajar. It opened wide and a plump face topped with a silver bouffant poked out. The woman gestured for them to come to her.

'Police again,' she said in a low voice, looking them over.

'Actually,' Kelly said, 'we're with the—'

Anna jabbed her with her elbow. Then she gave the woman a reassuring smile. 'Just checking on Mrs Thomason, seeing if there's anything we can do.'

'Really?' the woman said in a wheezy voice. 'That's really nice. Oh – I'm Imogene. Imogene Small. Evelyn and I are old friends.'

'Ms Small,' Anna said, 'we understand Garry and his grandmother had an argument on Monday night. Did Evelyn happen to mention it . . .?'

At that moment Evelyn Thomason's door opened. The three women turned to look. When Evelyn saw them her face darkened. 'I really don't think there's anything she can tell you.'

Anna looked back at Imogene, whose eyes were huge.

'I was just telling them how sorry I am about Garry,' she said.

'I'll bet,' Evelyn said. 'Close your door, Imogene, and let these people get back to work.'

Cowed, Imogene withdrew into her apartment like a turtle into its shell. Evelyn remained in her doorway, her gaze fixed on Anna and Kelly. They walked over to her.

'She's a terrible gossip,' Evelyn said, watching them carefully.

'Did you and Garry have an argument on Monday night?' Anna said.

'That's none of her business,' Evelyn said, 'and none of yours, if you'll forgive my saying so.' She walked into her apartment and firmly shut the door.

'That was weird,' Anna said in the elevator.

'Yes, it was. For some reason Evelyn didn't like the idea of Imogene telling us about that argument. But why? I can't see how it could be related to Garry's murder.'

The doors slid open and they started across the lobby. 'It's probably not,' Anna said. 'But that doesn't mean she wouldn't want us to know about it. You know, private family business. Maybe Garry was telling her she'd deprived him of something for half his life . . . though I can't imagine what that could be. Money?'

Kelly shrugged. 'Whatever it was, as Syd said, I hope they patched things up before Garry died.'

Anna entered New Amsterdam Mews and walked down the row of picturesque apartments running along the right side. She found number 7 and rang the bell.

The door was opened by a man who looked to be in his early forties. He was of medium height and slim, with small features and thinning brown hair, probably dyed. He wore khakis and a blue polo shirt. He smiled. 'Yes?'

'Mr Chandler, my name is Anna Winthrop. I'm a section supervisor at Manhattan Central District Thirteen sanitation garage. I worked with Garry Thomason.'

Abruptly his expression grew wary. 'Yes . . .?'

'I wonder if I could speak with you.'

He hesitated, then reluctantly stepped back so that she could enter.

'In here,' he said, indicating the living room on the left. It was a small, charming room, decorated in the colonial style, with expensive-looking antiques and Oriental carpets. A large vase of magnificent pink and blue hydrangeas sat in the center of the cocktail table.

Anna sat on the sofa. Chandler took a love seat facing her. 'What is it?'

His brusqueness surprised her. 'I want to talk to you about Garry Thomason, about what happened,' she said, referring to his discovery of Garry's body.

'Look,' he said, and stopped abruptly when a young man who looked around twenty entered the room from a hallway at the back. Tall and slim, he had refined, handsome features and fair hair cut close to his head. He wore jeans and an athletic undershirt.

Suspiciously he looked Anna up and down. 'Who's she?'

'No one. Go in the other room.'

The young man paused, then turned and left.

Chandler waited a moment, then said, 'I can't pay any more, and I want the cut-outs.'

Anna blinked. 'Excuse me? I'm afraid I don't know what you're talking about.'

Chandler's eyes had grown large. 'I'm so sorry. I thought you were talking about that charity.'

'What charity?'

'For the Sanitation Department. I've already donated as much as I can afford.'

'What charity?' she repeated. 'I'm not aware of any charity connected to the Sanitation Department.'

'No, no, I should have been clearer. It was for the union that the sanitation workers belong to. The Teamsters, isn't that it?'

'Yes, that's right.'

'Well, someone from the Sanitation Department came to the door, asking for a donation for the union. I gave him ten dollars.'

'I see. What did you mean when you said you wanted the cut-outs?'

Chandler drew in his breath. 'The man I gave the money to said donors would receive a collection of special die-cut postcards honoring the Sanitation Department. I'd like to have that. For my son, Danny. He's interested in things like that, how the city works, you know.'

'I see,' she said, though she didn't. 'Who was it exactly who asked for this donation?'

'Why, this Garry Thomason, of course – though I didn't know his name then. That's why it was especially shocking when I found him dead in the courtyard. When he came for the union he was with another man I assumed was his partner. Now,' he said, leaning back, 'what *did* you come to talk to me about?'

'About Garry, as I said. I'm doing what I can to help find out who killed him. I'd like to hear from you exactly what happened when you found him.'

He looked uncomfortable. 'I have told all this to those two police detectives, and I hardly think it's appropriate for you to conduct your own investigation, but –' he shrugged – 'I guess I don't mind telling you. It's really quite simple. I had to leave very early that morning to catch a plane. I went out and there he was, lying on the ground. It was horrible. I called the police.'

'Do you mind if I ask what kind of work you do?'

'I own a computer consulting firm. We work with large stores around the world to set up point-of-sale software.'

'How interesting,' she lied. 'You must be quite successful.'

He smiled modestly. 'One of the leading companies in the field.'

'And ten dollars was all you could afford to give to the Teamsters?'

'Listen, Miss Winthrop, what I can and can't afford is none of your concern. I think we're done here.' He rose.

'Thank you for your time,' she said at the door. He made no reply. 'Oh, I almost forgot. I need your phone number.'

'Why?'

'I'm going to find out about those die-cut postcards and give you a call.'

For a moment he glared at her. Then he gave her his number. She wrote it down on a slip of paper from her purse.

As she crossed the mews she waited for the sound of his door closing, but it never came. She turned. He stood in the doorway watching her, his expression inscrutable.

From the mews she walked to the garage, even though her shift was over for the day. She went in search of Terrence and found him coming out of the break room, heading for the men's locker room. 'I need to speak to you,' she said.

'Oh, hey, Anna. Can it wait till I'm done showering? I stink.'

'No, it can't wait. Come with me.'

In her office she closed the door and turned on him. He sat on the love seat, eyes wide.

'Terrence,' she said, sitting down behind her desk, 'I understand you and Garry have been soliciting donations for the Teamsters.'

He looked confused. 'What? Who told you that?'

'Wendell Chandler, the man in New Amsterdam Mews who found Garry's body.'

'Oh, yeah . . .' he said, nodding. 'Sure. That's right. Garry and me, we were collecting money for the union.'

She shook her head, not understanding. 'What do you mean, "for the union"?'

'You know, to support the things it does.'

She slammed her hands down on the desk. He jumped. 'How many people did you do this with?'

'Only him, Anna, I swear. It was Garry's idea. He said he needed money and asked if I did, too, and I said, "Sure, who doesn't?" He said he had this idea to go up to the people on our route and tell them we were looking for donations for the union.'

'Why would you only have asked Chandler?'

'Because of the way he reacted. He got all weird and suspicious. He gave us some money, but Garry and me realized it wasn't going to work.'

'How much money did he give you?'

He stared at her. 'Gosh, Anna, I don't remember. Whatever it was, Garry gave me half and I stuffed it into my wallet. Are you going to report me?'

'No, at least not yet.'

'Not yet?'

'I want to know what you were really up to before I do that.'

'Anna, I swear,' he said, leaning forward, 'that's all it was.'

'Go take your shower. You're right. You stink.'

Looking like a chastened little boy, he rose and walked out.

FOUR

'Unbelievable,' Santos said as he pulled on to a long, winding brick drive and Anna's parents' home came into view: a seven-bedroom, seven-and-a-half-bath, 15,000-square-foot fieldstone mansion covered in ivy. He had come along for moral support.

'What's unbelievable?' Anna asked.

He pulled up in front of the house and switched off the ignition. Gazing across the lawn at the six-car garage adjacent to the house, he said, 'That two people with this much money could ever be unhappy.'

She looked at him askance. 'You're not serious. Money has nothing to do with it. It's a relationship, period. Besides, my parents may be rich but they don't think of themselves that way. It's just how they live, what they are.'

'They weren't always this rich,' he said.

'True,' she conceded. Years earlier, Jeffrey Winthrop and a partner had founded Winthrop & Carnes Medical Products, which they sold years later to Johnson & Johnson. Jeffrey was now a billionaire. 'But you get used to it awfully fast.'

Will's red Porsche appeared on the drive and pulled up behind them. They got out. Will, tall and handsome in khakis and a navy polo shirt, gave Anna a hug and a kiss, then shook Santos's hand. 'Well,' he said with a sigh, 'let's see what's going on, shall we?'

As they entered the vast foyer with its sweeping double stairway the house seemed empty. It was that quiet.

'Hello!' Will called. 'Anybody home?'

For several moments there was no response. Then they heard the sound of a door opening on the second floor and footsteps. Tildy appeared at the railing, her pretty face set in a frown. 'What are you doing here?'

'Well, that's some welcome, Mother,' Will said.

Tildy waited. Anna started up the stairs and the two men followed.

'Mother,' Will began, kissing her on the cheek, 'what's going on with you and Dad?'

'Going on?' Tildy said, clearly irritated. 'I told you quite clearly on the telephone. Your father and I have had a . . . disagreement. We're certainly capable of handling our private business without people showing up uninvited.'

'Uninvited!' Anna said with a laugh. 'I wasn't aware we needed an invitation to come here.'

Tildy's face softened and her lower lip trembled slightly. 'I'm sorry, dear. That was an awful thing to say. Come.'

She turned and led them down the wide corridor. She wore jeans and a T-shirt that Anna now realized was smeared with paint in bright colors. They followed her all the way to the end of the corridor, where she opened a door that led to another wing of the house that ran at a right angle to this one.

'Where are we going?' Anna asked.

Without replying, Tildy walked to the end of this corridor, finally opening a door on the right. A large, bright room had been set up as an artist's studio, with a large easel in the center and a still life of colored glass bottles set up near the window. Tildy's painting was well under way, a clever abstract composite of the bottles' jewel-like colors.

'What do you think?' Tildy asked them.

'Beautiful,' Santos said solemnly.

Anna shot an impatient glance from him to her mother. 'We're not here to see your art, Mother. What exactly is going on with you and Dad? We're not leaving until you tell us.'

Tildy gave Santos a sweet smile. 'Thank you for the compliment.' She turned to her daughter and son. 'All right. If you must know, last week your father and I were at a garden party at the Holtons' in honor of their son and daughter-in-law who are moving to Dubai. The son is something in oil, I think . . .'

'We don't care about that,' Anna said. 'What happened?'

'Your father got stinking drunk, that's what happened.'

'Forgive me, Mother,' Will broke in, 'but that's hardly anything new.'

'No, it isn't, is it?' Tildy said angrily. 'Except that this time it was worse than ever. Your father had already had several drinks and his face was bright red. He came up to me and asked if I wanted a drink because he was heading over to the bar. I told him no, thank you, and that I thought he'd had quite enough.

'Well, that face got even redder and he said, "That's not what I asked you, Mathilda. Do you want a drink or not?"' Her eyes welled with tears. 'I can't remember the last time he called me Mathilda

– probably before we were married. He was so . . . cold. Well, I can be just as cold. "I don't care what you asked me," I said softly. "You've had enough." That's when he started to roar.'

'Roar?' Anna said.

'Yes, roar. It's not necessary for you to know exactly what he said – I won't use those words. He said I was controlling and judgmental and that I'd been a thorn in his side for longer than he could remember, and if he wanted a drink he was jolly well going to have one. As you can imagine, everyone at the party – and there were hundreds – was watching us. It was like a bad dream. I've never been so embarrassed and ashamed in my life.'

'Then what happened?' Will asked.

'What do you think happened? I walked out.'

'Daddy drove you home?'

'No! I wasn't going to ride with him. He was in no condition to drive, anyway. If he wanted to kill himself, let him. He wasn't going to kill me. I called Ethel,' she said, referring to her secretary, 'and asked her to come and get me.'

'What did Daddy say to you?'

'Say to me? Why, nothing. He *can't* say anything to me because I've been living in this part of the house ever since. I've told the servants to let him know in no uncertain terms that he is not welcome here.'

Anna and Will exchanged glances. 'And where is Dad?' Will asked.

'I don't know,' Tildy said airily, taking up a large paintbrush, 'and I don't care. It's over.'

'Over!' Anna cried.

'Yes, dear,' Tildy said, applying a sweep of cobalt blue down the edge of a bottle, 'people do get divorced, you know.'

'Not you and Daddy,' Anna said firmly. 'What is it you want from him? An apology?'

'No. There's really nothing I want from your father . . . except that he leave.'

'Is that really fair?' Will asked, walking around the easel to look at her. 'Doesn't he deserve at least a conversation? A chance to tell you he's sorry? It's all so . . . abrupt.'

Tildy looked at him. 'You don't know everything, William. For the past seven years I've been attending Al-Anon,' she said, referring to the support group for family and friends of alcoholics.

'Does he know?' Anna asked.

Tildy nodded simply. 'When he found out, he was shocked, wanted to know why I was doing it. I told him it was because of his drinking problem, that if he didn't want to get help for himself, that was his business, but I needed help dealing with *his* problem. And do you know what he said? That his drinking wasn't his problem – it was *my* problem.'

They were silent as she worked on her painting. Anna tilted her head in the direction of the door, and Will and Santos nodded.

'Goodbye, Mother,' Anna said, kissing her on the cheek. The two men did the same.

'Goodbye,' Tildy said cheerily, concentrating on her painting.

'We'll come back again soon,' Anna said.

Tildy turned to her. 'That's nice, dear, but I can't guarantee I'll still be here.'

When they had walked back down the corridor and through the door to the front wing of the house, Anna blew out her breath. 'You were right,' she said to Will. 'This is the worst ever.'

'What are we going to do?' he asked.

'We're going to talk to Daddy,' Anna said, and led the way.

They found him at the extreme opposite end of the U-shaped house, in the wing parallel to the one in which Tildy had sought refuge. He was in a library Anna couldn't remember ever seeing before, sitting in an oversized leather armchair, engrossed in a book. On a table beside him was a plate with the remains of a meal on it. Hearing them come in, he looked up and smiled brightly. 'Company!' he said, rising.

Will gave him a one-sided arm hug, and Santos shook his hand. 'How are you, Mr Winthrop?'

'Jeff,' he said with a smile. 'I've told you, please call me Jeff.'

Santos smiled and nodded. Anna gave her father a hug and a kiss. 'Oh, Daddy,' she said, 'what have you done?'

'Done?' He looked bewildered. 'What do you mean?'

Anna frowned in exasperation. 'Mother is ready to leave you, that's what I mean. Daddy, you've got to do something about your drinking.'

'Oh, that,' he said with a dismissive roll of his brilliant-blue eyes.

'Yes, that,' she said, and ran her hand affectionately over his close-cropped white hair.

'Your mother is overreacting, don't you think?'

'No, Daddy. She told me what happened and I don't think she's overreacting at all.'

Jeff looked to Will and Santos for support. They both looked down.

'So what do you suggest I do?' Jeff asked Anna.

'I think it's pretty clear. You need to get some help.'

'*Help?*'

She nodded. 'Daddy, let's face it. You're an alcoholic. And you're getting worse. You need to do this not just for Mother but for yourself.'

There was a sound at the door and they all looked up to see one of the maids coming in with a tray. She smiled at them. 'Can I get you some dessert, Mr Winthrop?' she asked, taking the dirty plate. 'There's some nice blueberry pie.'

'No, thank you. I really shouldn't,' he said, patting his flat, muscular stomach. 'Which reminds me, I haven't worked out yet today. Would you folks care to join me?'

Anna glared at him in disbelief, while the two men just shook their heads politely.

'All right,' Anna said with a sigh. 'Pretend it's not happening. But don't say we didn't warn you.' She turned to Will and Santos and cocked her head in the direction of the door.

There was nothing more to be said.

'What do you think?' Will asked Anna and Santos once they were outside.

'Daddy's in total denial,' Anna replied. 'If he doesn't get help soon, he's going to lose Mother.' When both men looked surprised, she continued. 'She's been putting up with his drinking for a long time – longer than she's been letting on. I really think she's had it.'

Will gave a nod. 'We'll have to try again with him.'

But none of them looked hopeful.

'By the way,' Will said as he walked his sister and Santos to Anna's car, 'I heard about that young man on your crew. I'm sorry.'

Anna smiled warmly at her brother. 'Thank you.'

Will shifted his gaze to Santos. 'Have the police got any leads?'

Santos hesitated, clearly uncomfortable discussing the case, but Anna spoke up. 'Not one.'

'Strangest thing,' Will said. 'Is it true he went behind that building to get the trash and disappeared? Then his body was found there in the courtyard in the morning?'

'That's right,' she said, but knew not to talk about the discovery of the gap between the shed and the fence where Garry was killed.

Will, obviously sensing their reluctance to discuss Garry's murder, said, 'Well, as I told you, I'm sorry. This isn't your first tragedy.'

It was true. About a year earlier a female member of Anna's crew had been found murdered in a courtyard adjacent to the garage.

Will said, 'This man Garry wasn't even thirty, I read.'

'Yes,' Anna said. 'Just back from Iraq and apparently trying to turn his life around.'

Will frowned. 'From what?'

Anna met his gaze, shifted it to Santos. 'That's the question, isn't it?'

Anna and Santos entered the foyer of Anna's building, arms loaded with groceries. They had decided to make dinner and watch a movie they'd picked up at the video store. Anna, entering first, let out a low groan. Mrs Dovner stood in her doorway, talking to a man Anna had never seen before. The older woman looked up as they came in. 'Oh, Anna,' she said.

'Hello, Mrs Dovner.'

The man turned. He was short – five feet two inches at the most – and slight, with a small bald head and a shifty look in his eyes as he took them both in. Anna disliked him on sight, though she wouldn't have been able to say why.

'Anna,' Mrs Dovner said, 'this is Mr Herman. He's moved into the apartment above yours.'

That apartment had been vacant since its occupant, a doctor, had moved to Toronto a few weeks earlier.

Mr Herman gave Anna a tight smile and put out a limp hand. 'How do you do?' he said. 'Lionel Herman.'

'And this is my boyfriend, Santos Reyes,' Anna said, and the two men shook hands.

'He's a cop,' Mrs Dovner said dryly.

'Ah,' Mr Herman said, his expression unchanging. 'Well, I look forward to being your neighbor, Anna.' A twinkle came into his eye. 'I promise not to make too much noise.'

Anna eyed Mrs Dovner suspiciously. One of her ongoing complaints was that Anna made too much noise. Had she told this to Mr Herman?

'I'm sure you won't,' Anna said sweetly, and started up the stairs, Santos close behind. 'That was interesting,' she said as they entered her apartment.

Santos lowered his groceries on to the kitchen counter. 'What do you mean?'

'It's completely out of character for Mrs Dovner to have introduced me to that man.'

'Why? He's your new neighbor.'

'Doesn't matter. She hates me. She made a point of calling us over to introduce him.'

'So what's your explanation?' Santos asked, placing the butter in the fridge.

'I think,' Anna said, putting away a box of crackers, 'she was showing him off.'

He looked puzzled. 'I don't follow.'

'I think she's interested in him.'

'You mean – romantically?'

'I know, it's amazing. But there's got to be a heart in there somewhere. You remember how she helped me that time.'

'True.'

'Wow,' she said, gazing across the room. 'Mrs Dovner's got a boyfriend.'

'I didn't like the look of him.'

'Neither did I. But she does, obviously. As they say, there's a lid for every pot.'

Anna stopped, frowning, as she turned the corner of West Forty-Third Street the following morning and the garage came into view. A good-size crowd had gathered around something on the sidewalk, a few yards from the building's entrance.

Coffee cup in hand, she walked up to the back of the crowd, craning her neck to see. 'What's going on?' she asked a young woman.

'It's so cool,' the young woman said, stepping back. 'Take a look.'

Anna stood on tiptoes and shifted to the right to see what everyone was looking at. A man who looked around fifty stood with his back to the group as he worked on something, shoulders hunched. After a moment he stepped back, revealing what appeared to be a pile of junk. On the ground lay a large commercial truck tire which he had filled with aluminum soda cans. Now he began placing empty plastic Coke bottles in a ring around the tire. Suddenly he turned and addressed the crowd with a smile. 'Now what else can you give me? Something you were going to throw away.'

He was good-looking, with regular, dark features and a mop of glossy black hair. He smiled, revealing even white teeth.

'Here's something,' a woman at the front of the crowd said, and handed him a Styrofoam burger box.

'Perfect!' the man said, taking it from her. He began carefully tearing it into irregular strips, which he pressed on to the tire in an attractive diagonal criss-cross pattern. The crowd applauded. Now Anna noticed a plastic bucket on the sidewalk near him, into which people were dropping coins and a few bills before moving on. 'Thank you, thank you,' the man said with a gracious nod of his head before returning to his creation. 'Now, what else have we got?'

Anna moved forward, working her way to the open circle. She approached the man, who now had his back to her. 'Excuse me,' she said. 'What's going on?'

The man turned and smiled, eyebrows raised. He took in her uniform. 'Ah.' He put out his hand. 'I'm Clive Beatty.'

She gave a little frown. 'That doesn't answer my question. What are you doing?'

He laughed. 'I would think that's obvious. I'm creating art.'

'Art?'

'That's right. I'm a street artist. Trash artist, to be more accurate.' He gestured grandly to his assembled refuse. 'And this is my art today.'

'And why are you doing this?' she asked, playing along.

'Why? Because, dear lady, that's what I do. I take things the world doesn't want and turn them into things of beauty.'

Anna thought that was highly debatable, but didn't comment.

'It's my statement,' Clive went on. 'Most of what we throw away should be used for something else. This would be a far more beautiful world if we did.'

'Hardly a new idea,' Anna said.

He looked a little hurt. 'That may be, but this is my humble way of expressing it.'

A man came forward and dropped a dollar bill into the bucket. 'Aw, leave him alone, lady,' he said, and sauntered off.

Clive looked at Anna as if waiting for her response to that.

'Yeah! Find someone else to bother,' a young man called to her, and others in the crowd muttered in agreement.

Anna's gaze darted from Clive to the crowd to his 'art.' Then, saying nothing, she turned and walked into the garage.

Allen Schiff was making his way toward her, a scowl on his face. 'What's going on out there?'

'A street artist.'

He groaned.

'He's pretty harmless, I'd say.'

'Would you?' He shook his head as if wondering about her grip on reality. 'Do you think a crowd just outside the gate is harmless? For one thing, it's dangerous.'

'True.'

'But when you try to move these people you're automatically the villain. What kind of "artist" is it, anyway?'

'A trash artist. He's making a statement about how much we throw away.'

'Oh, great! A statement! It's pretty clear who the villain is with this guy. Us!' When Anna frowned, he said, 'Think about it. What makes it possible for New York City to throw so much away, more than any other city in the world? The New York City Department of Sanitation, that's who.'

Anna considered this. 'So you want me to get rid of him?'

'No! We've got to be careful here, or we'll have a public-relations nightmare on our hands. I can just see the headline. DSNY SILENCES ARTIST WORKING TO CLEAN UP CITY. No,' he repeated, shaking his head. 'I'll take care of him . . . when I've figured out how.' He started to walk away, then turned. 'Will you be here for the next hour or so?'

She nodded.

'Good. Garry's replacement is starting today.'

She blinked. 'Someone's been hired?' When he nodded, she said, 'And why wasn't I involved in this process?'

Rather than looking sorry, he looked annoyed. 'Anna, in a perfect world I would have brought you into the loop, but we needed someone fast, this young man fit the bill, so I hired him. I'll bring him in to meet you.'

Without responding she turned and headed back to her office. As she walked, her irritation was replaced by deep sadness. Garry hadn't even been gone a week and his replacement was here, simple as that. But life had to go on, she supposed.

She sipped her coffee and puttered at her desk, unable to focus. She realized she was nervous about meeting Garry's replacement but couldn't have said why. She thought about Clive out front and, on impulse, googled his name. The only Clive Beatty of any renown was a lion tamer who died in 1965. She scrolled down. No, no mention of an artist, street or otherwise, with that name. Perhaps he was only known in New York City.

Ten minutes later Allen knocked on her door accompanied by a good-looking young man with sandy hair and dark, brooding eyes. 'Anna Winthrop, I'd like you to meet Damian Porter.'

Damian put out his hand, and as Anna took it those stormy eyes locked on to hers. She wrested her gaze away.

'You'll be in Anna's section,' Allen explained.

'Happy to meet you, Anna,' Damian said, his voice as smoky as his eyes. 'I'm sorry about what happened. I realize this is a difficult situation for you.'

'You mean that you're replacing Garry? Thank you, but no,' she said, smiling kindly. 'One thing has nothing to do with the other. Welcome. I hope you enjoy working here.'

'Well,' Allen said briskly, 'I'll leave you two to it,' and he walked away.

'Right,' Anna said, and turned back to Damian. 'Your partner's name is Terrence King. He's the most senior worker in my section. He's a really nice guy, easy to get along with. He's already out on his route, of course. I'll take you to him – I'm sure he'll be relieved to have help again.'

She led the way to her department car. As she got in she happened to glance across the roof of the vehicle and was startled to find Damian staring at her. 'Is something wrong?' she asked.

He gave her a thin-lipped smile. 'Nothing at all,' he said, and got in.

When she returned from introducing Damian to Terrence and leaving them to finish their route, Kelly was waiting for her near the door to her office. She was holding a folded newspaper.

'You're back early today,' Anna said brightly, and Kelly followed her in and sat down. She had a dark expression.

'What's up?' Anna asked.

Kelly stood and laid the newspaper across Anna's desk so she could read an article Kelly had circled. Accompanying the piece was a photograph of a man.

'Look familiar?' Kelly asked.

Anna studied the picture. It was of a young man with a buzz haircut and light eyes. She looked up. 'He does look familiar, but I can't place him.'

'It's that guy who came looking for Garry the day he . . . was killed. Ron Carson.'

'Of course.' Anna looked more closely at the article Kelly had circled.

IRAQ WAR VETERAN MISSING

STATEN ISLAND, NY – Police are looking for a 28-year-old man who has been reported missing by his wife.

Ronald Holmes Carson, 28, a veteran of the Iraq war who recently returned home after two tours of duty, was last seen late Sunday evening near a tool shed behind his home in the West Brighton area of Staten Island, said Sgt Mullane, police spokeswoman.

Carson's cell phone and keys were found on the ground near the shed, Mullane said in a press release.

His wife told police that his absence was 'not at all like him,' Mullane said.

He is a Caucasian male, stands about 6-feet-1-inch tall and weighs about 200 pounds. He has short light-brown hair and blue eyes.

Mullane said he is possibly wearing jeans, a New York Yankees T-shirt and running shoes.

The article ended by providing a police telephone number that anyone with information could call.

When Anna looked up from the newspaper, Kelly was staring at her. 'He went missing three days after Garry was killed. Too much of a coincidence, don't you think?'

'What is?'

'That Garry is murdered, and now this man who was looking for Garry is murdered.'

'Who said he was murdered? It just says he's missing.'

'Oh, come on, Anna. You know how these things go. How often does a story like this end up that the guy is found alive?'

Anna didn't respond, just swallowed. 'So what are you suggesting?'

'I don't know . . . But something's going on.'

'I suppose it's worth looking into. But I don't think the police in Staten Island are going to be willing to speak to me.'

'Who said anything about speaking to the police?'

'You mean the wife?'

Kelly nodded.

'Wait a minute,' Anna said suddenly, and yanked open the middle drawer of her desk. She lifted a plastic organizer full of paper clips and rubber bands, rummaged among a number of pieces of paper, and finally pulled one out. 'This is the number Ron asked me to give Garry. I forgot all about it.'

'I bet it's his cell phone.'

'Which was found on the ground,' Anna said. 'The cops would have looked through the call records on it and then given it back to his wife.'

'Are you going to call it?'

'Of course I am. But not yet. I want to think about what I'm going to say.'

'OK. But when you go out to Staten Island to see her, I'd like to come along.'

Anna called the number that afternoon from her apartment. It rang for so long that she was about to hang up when finally the call was answered and a woman's voice said a cautious hello.

'Mrs Carson?'

'Who is this?'

'My name is Anna Winthrop. I work for the New York Department of Sanitation—'

'What do you want? Why are you calling me?' A note of mild hysteria had crept into Mrs Carson's voice.

Anna realized she had better quickly state her reason for calling, or lose her chance. 'I'm calling about your husband. Last week he came to the garage where I work, looking for a man on my crew who has since been murdered.'

'Garry Thomason?'

'Yes, how did you know?'

'My husband saw in the paper that Garry had been killed and told me he and Garry were in Iraq together. I didn't know Ron went to see Garry.'

'He never did see him. The morning he came was the morning Garry was killed.'

'You're not saying Ron killed Garry?'

'No, nothing like that. I . . .' Where to begin? 'Mrs Carson, would it be all right if I came to see you? It's complicated, but I think we might be able to help each other.'

There was a long silence on the line. 'All right,' Mrs Carson said at last. 'When can you come?'

'I could come now.'

'Now?' Another silence. 'I suppose it's all right if you come soon. I have the children . . .'

'I completely understand. I'll come immediately. I'd like to bring someone with me, a young woman also on my crew who was Garry's girlfriend. Would that be all right?'

Mrs Carson said it was. She gave Anna her address.

FIVE

The fastest way was to take the car. Anna picked Kelly up in Brooklyn and they drove to Staten Island.

The Carsons lived in a little box of a house with dented gray aluminum siding and a scruffy strip of grass in front. A doll's baby carriage sat on the bottom of the concrete stairs leading up to the front door.

The door opened before Anna's finger reached the doorbell. Mrs Carson stood holding the hand of a little boy who looked around three. Behind them in the shadows stood a little girl who looked five or six. Without speaking, she ushered them into a small living room cluttered with toys and children's books, and motioned for them to sit on the sofa. She sat on a threadbare ottoman and told the children to go play. Once they were gone, Anna introduced Kelly. Mrs Carson didn't offer them coffee or anything. Anna hadn't expected her to.

'Now what is this about?' Mrs Carson asked.

'Mrs Carson—'

'You can call me Julie.'

'Julie. As I told you on the phone, your husband came looking for Garry at our garage on Wednesday morning – the morning Garry was killed. You've told me your husband said he and Garry were in Iraq together.'

'Yes, they were friends, he said.'

'I see. When we opened Garry's locker, we found these two newspaper articles relating to Iraq.' Anna handed them to Julie, who carefully read them, a hand pressed to her forehead as she concentrated.

At last she looked up and handed the clippings back to Anna. 'I know what this is about. At least, some of it.'

Anna's eyes widened and she shot a glance at Kelly. They waited.

'When Ron came home from Iraq, he was different. Quiet. Not the man I knew.'

'If you'll excuse me,' Kelly said, 'isn't that to be expected with a soldier?'

Julie quickly shook her head. 'It wasn't just that. I know Ron better than he knows himself. Yes, of course he was troubled by things he'd seen in Iraq. But this was something more. Something was bothering him, eating at him.'

'Did he tell you what it was?' Kelly asked.

'Not for a long time. But it was getting worse and worse. It was always there, always weighing on his mind. Finally I told him I couldn't take it any more, that he'd better do something – get some help – or our marriage was going to suffer.'

'What did he say?' Anna asked.

Julie looked down. 'The first thing he did was fall into a chair and start to cry.' Her gaze wandered as she remembered. 'Then he told me . . . but only some of it, as I said.

'He said he and three other men, also from the New York City area, had been close friends in Iraq. They were all assigned to the same base, Camp Liberty in Baghdad. One of these men was Garry. Another was Travis Brown, the man accused of murdering and raping that Iraqi girl, Neda Majeed.'

'And who was later murdered himself in prison.'

'That's right.'

'Who was the fourth man?'

Julie looked from Anna to Kelly. 'Ron wouldn't tell me his name. But let me back up a little. Ron told me about what happened to that Neda . . . but Travis Brown didn't do it.'

'Then who did?' Anna asked.

'The fourth man. Ron didn't say why, but this man had it out for Neda. She had done something to him, humiliated him somehow, and he wanted revenge. He told Ron and Garry and Travis that he knew where she lived. He was going to put a scare into her, he said.

'Apparently this Neda was a nasty piece of business, and the other three men had seen evidence of that. So they were willing to help their friend get his revenge on her.

'Ron said they made up a story for their superiors. They said they had good reason to believe Neda's parents were hiding explosives in their farmhouse. They were given permission to go and investigate.

'The fourth man – I don't know what else to call him – knew Neda would be alone in the house. He'd been watching, knew the family's schedule. He told the other three that he was going to burst into the house and scare the girl, *and that's all*. Garry stood at a nearby checkpoint as a lookout, and Ron and Travis stood guard at the front door. The fourth man went inside.'

'And what happened?' Anna asked.

'Nothing at first. It was quiet. Then Ron said the girl started shrieking. It was horrible, so horrible Ron knew immediately that the fourth man was doing more than just scaring the girl. Ron said they should go in. But Travis had a funny look on his face, and Ron suddenly knew Travis had known all along whatever it was the fourth man had planned to do. Travis wouldn't move. So Ron ran into the house alone.'

Julie started to cry, at the same time that her little girl ran in with a Tupperware container full of crayons for her mother to open. Julie popped it open. 'Here you go, honey.'

'Mommy, why are you crying?'

'I'm not, sweetie. Go play with your brother, OK?'

The girl ran off.

Julie continued. 'The fourth man was gone. Neda was on the kitchen floor. Her pants were down around her ankles. There was a knife in her neck and blood everywhere.

'The back door was open. Ron knew the fourth man had run out that way. Ron knew he'd better do the same. As he did, he heard a man at the front of the house order Travis not to move.'

Julie tilted her chin in the direction of the articles in Anna's hands. 'As you read there, they blamed Travis. They thought he'd acted alone, that he'd just done it and was leaving the house. He was arrested and put in a cell on the base.'

'Did he tell them what had really happened?' Kelly asked.

Julie gave a disgusted smile. 'No, he didn't.'

'Why not?'

'Because, as Ron put it, they were the Four Musketeers. All for one and one for all, and all that nonsense.'

Kelly looked amazed. 'So he was going to take the blame for something he didn't do?'

Julie simply nodded. Then her face darkened. 'But it didn't go very far, did it? Because someone got into the prison with a loaded gun and shot him.'

'Who?' Anna wondered aloud.

'Who do you think?' Julie said.

Anna's eyes widened. 'The fourth man?'

'Of course. Why do you think Ron wouldn't tell me his name? Because if this man was capable of killing Travis, he was certainly capable of killing Ron and Garry.'

'But Ron didn't tell the authorities the truth, did he?'

'No, of course not. But neither had Travis. Obviously, the fourth man wasn't absolutely sure about that "all for one and one for all" thing. He wasn't taking any chances.' Julie met Anna's gaze. 'No chances at all.'

Anna said, 'So you think . . .?'

'That the fourth man killed Garry? Of course; Garry knew the truth. And now he's killed my Ron.'

'But your husband is missing, Julie,' Kelly said, 'not dead.'

Julie shook her head impatiently. 'He's missing *and* dead. Ron said it was only a matter of time unless he and Garry went to the police.'

'Then why didn't they?'

'Why do you think Ron was looking for him? But he was too late.'

For several moments the three women sat in silence. The setting sun cast a bleak glow over the small room.

'Who is this man?' Kelly asked in a low voice, nearly a whisper.

Julie looked at her. 'Don't. Don't try. No good can come of it. He'll kill anyone who knows the truth.'

Anna looked up at her sharply. 'You know who it is, don't you?' It was a statement, not a question. 'Ron did tell you his name.'

Julie shook her head. 'He didn't, I swear it.'

'Aren't you worried he's going to come after *you*?' Kelly asked.

Julie gave a little shrug. 'I don't think so. I don't think he would have expected Ron to tell me what happened.'

As if on cue, a wail came from the other room. 'Mommy!' The little girl came running in, eyes wide. 'Brendan ate a crayon.'

'You'll have to excuse me,' Julie Carson said, and hurried from the room.

Anna and Kelly let themselves out.

Allen was right about Clive Beatty bringing trouble. He brought it the next day.

Anna was nearly finished with an inspection of the garage's perimeter and of the vehicles in her section when Gerry Licari ran up to her. 'All hands on deck,' he said. 'Trouble out front.'

He jogged toward the garage entrance and she followed him. As she emerged on to the sidewalk she heard shouting coming from the crowd around Clive. Allen Schiff was already shoving his way in. People stepped to each side, affording Anna a view of the activity at the circle's center.

Clive stood frowning darkly, his arms folded, as a man with a bright red face kicked and grabbed at his sculpture. Bottles and Styrofoam strips and cans flew everywhere, causing some people in the crowd to duck.

'What's going on here?' Allen demanded.

Clive opened his hand in the direction of the other man, indicating that Allen should ask him.

Suddenly the man turned on Allen. 'What's the matter with you people?' he shouted, bent forward at the waist. 'Why haven't you driven this nut away?'

'May I ask who you are, sir?' Allen asked.

'Yes, you may ask,' the man replied sarcastically. 'I'm Barry Hazen and I live a few doors down. It's bad enough living with the noise and the stench from your garage without having to deal with this circus every day. I can't even get by!'

'Sir, I understand your frustration,' Allen said. 'Give us a little time and we'll work this out.'

Hazen looked from Allen to Clive, then suddenly grabbed another plastic bottle and hurled it over the heads of the crowd into the street before loping away.

Allen turned to the audience. 'OK, folks, show's over. Please move along.'

The crowd quickly dispersed. Clive stood with his arms folded, waiting.

'Mr Beatty,' Allen said with a forced smile, 'I'm sorry this happened. I assure you it doesn't represent the sentiments of the Department of Sanitation.'

'Just what are your sentiments?' Clive asked.

'We can't allow you to build your . . . sculpture here on the sidewalk. But I do have a solution that I hope you'll find to your liking.' Allen moved closer to Clive and, voice lowered, began to explain.

Anna returned to her office. At lunchtime she headed for the stairs to the break room. As she approached the door, Clive walked past her from behind and went out to the street. Frowning, Anna watched him go.

'Have you heard?'

Anna turned. It was Brianna, back from her route.

'Allen gave "the artist" the courtyard.'

'What do you mean, "gave him the courtyard"?'

'Told him he could build his sculpture there.'

Brianna was referring to a small walled courtyard adjacent to the garage. Anna lowered her brows in puzzlement. 'And then what?'

'That's what Clive wanted to know. How were people going to see his sculpture if he's stuck back there in the courtyard?'

'And what did Allen say?'

'That he would find a way.'

Clive appeared from the street, carrying a laundry basket full of plastic Coke bottles. He nodded a greeting to the two women. They smiled at him.

'You won't catch me going back there,' Brianna said. 'Not ever.'

Anna knew what she meant. Brianna had once run screaming from that courtyard, saying she had found a corpse. 'But that's the only place you're allowed to smoke,' Anna pointed out.

'I can wait,' Brianna said, and headed for the break room. 'You comin'?'

'Mm,' Anna said thoughtfully, and followed.

Anna was peeling a banana in the break room when her cell phone rang. It was Allen. 'Get down here. Two of your boys are at it again.'

This time it was Ernesto and Damian. By the time she got downstairs it was all over. Ernesto stood not far from the stairway, nursing his jaw. Damian was stalking away. Anna would deal with him later. She approached Ernesto.

'Before you say anything, Anna, this time it wasn't my fault.'

She waited.

'Damian said Kelly would never be interested in me because I'm a little Spanish sourpuss.'

Anna had to repress a smile. 'You're not Spanish.'

'And I'm not a little sourpuss!'

To this she made no response. *Sour* was a word she would definitely use to describe Ernesto most of the time. 'Now, why would Damian have commented on whether Kelly would be interested in you, I wonder?'

He lowered his gaze. Finally he said, 'I guess I . . . said something.'

'And what was that?'

At that moment, as if from nowhere, Kelly appeared, an angry stare fixed on Ernesto. 'He said he could light my fire like Garry never could.'

Anna turned to Ernesto, feeling more and more like a school-teacher. 'Is that true?'

Reluctantly he nodded.

'I've told you to leave her alone. I'm writing you up.'

Ernesto didn't even try to argue, instead lowering his head and walking slowly away. As Anna turned to go back to her office, she spotted Damian standing by a stack of orange safety cones, watching her. She went up to him.

'Not getting off to a very good start, are we?'

He didn't reply, simply continued watching her.

'Is something wrong?' she asked. When he looked confused, she said, 'Why do you keep staring at me?'

'I'm not staring at you,' he drawled. 'Maybe it's you who's lookin' at me a lot.'

She quickly shook her head. 'Listen. Play by the rules or you're out. There are plenty of people who would gladly take your job.'

'What rules do you mean?'

'Keep your comments to yourself. Mind your own business. Just do your work.'

'All right, Anna,' he said with a nod, and turned and strolled away. She watched him go, then directed her gaze elsewhere for fear he would turn around and see her looking at him.

Back in her office, she placed her cell phone on the desk and realized she had a new voice message. It was Santos.

'Anna, call me. There's been another murder, and I think it's connected to Garry's.'

On East Forty-Ninth Street between Second and Third avenues, Santos pulled up to the curb behind three other police cars and he and Anna got out. They were parked in front of a building whose first floor was of bright white stone, the three floors above of red brick.

They approached an archway in the building with black wrought-iron gates standing open. Above the archway were the words AMSTER YARD, and above these words the brilliant red and yellow flag of Spain hung from a flagpole.

Santos saw Anna looking at the flag. 'This is the Cervantes Institute,' he explained. 'It's a Spanish cultural center – lectures, exhibits, readings, classes, that kind of thing. I came here once when my brother Hector's wife was in a dance production.' His face had grown sad at the memory. Hector's wife, Carla, had died of breast cancer two years earlier. 'This way.' He led the way through the archway and along a short corridor that turned into an arcade, with an entrance to the Institute on the left and an open courtyard on the right. Taking it in, Anna felt as if she'd been transported into Europe of another century.

Small nineteenth-century brick buildings of one to four stories enclosed a picturesque courtyard garden landscaped with flowers, trees, and shrubbery. On one of the buildings, touches of black wrought iron embellished a gray mansard roof, quaintly shingled. On a large flagstone terrace sat green metal tables and chairs.

'It's beautiful,' Anna said, her voice full of wonder as she took in the quiet sanctuary. 'A world within a world. But where is everybody? Isn't this where you said . . .?'

Preoccupied, Santos had stridden ahead. Anna followed and realized the courtyard was in fact an L-shaped cul-de-sac. Now a bustle of police and crime-scene technicians came into view. In the center of the verdant space, several figures knelt over the corpse. Anna recognized Heller, the ME from New Amsterdam Mews.

Santos headed toward the body and Anna reluctantly followed. The victim was a young woman – in her mid- to late twenties, Anna guessed – with shoulder-length hair of a dark strawberry blonde, and pretty, delicate features. On those features was a look of exquisite pain. From the center of her pale-green silk blouse protruded what appeared to be the slender wooden handle of a knife.

A few yards to Anna and Santos's left, a petite woman and a tall red-haired man with their backs to them were talking to a plump brown-haired young woman who was crying. The woman with her back to them turned. It was Rinaldi. She saw Anna and Santos and rolled her eyes but turned back to the young woman. After a few moments Roche ambled over. 'What are two you doing here?'

'I'm a cop,' Santos said. 'Like you.'

'But you're not a detective. And she's not a cop at all,' Roche said, his gaze shifting to Anna and back to Santos.

'I brought her here because she may be able to help us with this case,' Santos said.

Suddenly Rinaldi was there. 'Help "us"? And how is that?'

'Garry Thomason was—'

'Yeah, I know, on her crew,' Rinaldi said.

Santos continued, 'And since this young woman's murder appears to be linked to Garry's . . .'

Rinaldi blinked hard and shook her head. 'Whoa, stop right there. Who said the two murders are related?'

'Isn't it obvious?' Santos said. 'Both bodies have been found in courtyards.'

Rinaldi shifted her hip and put her hand on it. 'Listen, friend, why don't you let us be the ones who decide what's linked to what? As far as I'm concerned, there's no pattern. Two similar things don't make a pattern. Three – now *that's* a pattern.'

Santos shook his head impatiently. 'Let's not argue about that. Who is she?'

Rinaldi paused as if deciding whether to tell him. 'Young woman, name of Yvette Ronson. Whoever dumped her here didn't even bother to take her purse or even go through it, far as we can tell. Lived on West Forty-Sixth Street.'

'"Dumped her here," did you say?' Santos asked.

'That's right.'

Heller came up to them. He'd overheard their conversation and was nodding glumly. 'She wasn't killed here. Creep killed her somewhere else – stabbed her in the heart with a steak knife – and brought her here.'

'Sounds like a pattern to me,' Anna said, and four sets of eyes clamped on to her.

Santos gave his head an infinitesimal shake to signal that she shouldn't speak. But the words were already out. Rinaldi turned to her. 'Like I just said, Ms Winthrop, we'll decide what's a pattern.'

'Who found her?' Heller asked Rinaldi and Roche.

'Helene Freundlich,' Rinaldi told him. 'She's a librarian at the Institute. She got to work around ten this morning, saw something on the ground through her office window, came out and found the body.' She paused, thinking. 'I guess it could have been dumped any time.'

'No, that's not true,' Santos said, and everyone turned to him. 'This place is open Monday through Friday, nine a.m. to nine p.m. Otherwise those gates are locked.'

It was clear from Rinaldi's expression that she hadn't known this. 'So the body was dumped either before nine last night or after nine this morning.'

'Which gets us nowhere,' said Roche, ever loyal to Rinaldi.

But even Rinaldi knew he was wrong. 'No, we'll talk to people who were around at those times. Freundlich couldn't have been the first to get here this morning. Maybe someone else saw something. We'll also show everyone Yvette's photo. Helene says Yvette had nothing to do with the Institute, but she can't know everything.'

'My guess is she was killed last night,' Heller said, walking away, 'but I'll know more later.'

Rinaldi walked off toward where the techs were still working on Yvette. Roche followed. Left alone, Anna and Santos met each other's gaze, then turned and left the courtyard. A few minutes later, Santos pulled up in front of the garage and Anna got out.

'Keep me posted?' she said. With a faint smile he nodded and drove off.

In the middle of the afternoon, he called to tell her more. 'Heller's confirmed that Yvette was killed last night. She was stabbed in the heart with a cheap steak knife. No prints anywhere. You want to grab a bite?'

'Can't. I'm going to talk to Helene Freundlich.'

'Why?'

'Because in spite of what Rinaldi says, I do think there's a pattern here. I'm going to pursue this further than the police will.'

'Rinaldi said she didn't think there was a pattern *yet*.'

'So we should wait for the third? I'm leaving now. Catch you later.'

Before heading out to the street, Anna suddenly remembered Clive and decided to look in on him. Leaving her office she walked to the garage's extreme right-hand wall and through the doorway to the outdoor walled space. Clive was at the far left. He looked up with a friendly smile. 'You didn't tell me this place was haunted.'

She blinked. 'Come again?'

'I understand a woman was murdered here.'

'Yes,' Anna replied, uncomfortable. 'Last year. A worker on my crew.'

'Like this young man who just got killed.' He shook his head. 'Looks like you're bad luck.'

Anger rose in her. 'I don't think that's funny.'

His eyes grew wide. 'I'm so sorry! I was only kidding.'

'It's not something I'll ever be able to kid about.'

'Really, please forgive me. Sometimes my sense of humor is a bit offbeat.'

More than a bit, she thought, eager to change the subject. 'So, how's it going?' She took in his sculpture, which he appeared to have started over again: currently it consisted simply of a platform roughly five feet square, made of cinder blocks.

'This is the base, not surprisingly. Now I'm ready to start creating.'

'Still using trash?'

'Oh, absolutely. I'm *in* the sanitation garage now. How could I not?'

She wished him a good afternoon and left.

Helene Freundlich gazed down at a photo of Garry Thomason on her desk. 'He's really cute,' she said, looking up, 'but I've never seen him before. Who is he?'

'He was a sanitation worker in my section at the garage.' Anna had explained to Helene that she worked for the Sanitation Department.

'*Was?*' Helene said.

Anna nodded. 'He's dead. His body was found in New Amsterdam Mews on West Forty-Eighth Street.'

Helene frowned. 'But what has that got to do with this Yvette?'

'Maybe nothing. Or maybe the fact that both bodies were left in mews.'

Helene nodded, though she still looked a little confused. 'The police didn't show me this picture.'

'Because they're not willing to see a pattern yet. I think it's worth pursuing. Do me a favor,' Anna said, pushing the photo back toward Helene. 'Show this photo to everyone else who works here, see if anyone recognizes him.'

'The police have already done that with Yvette's photo. I told them no one here would know her and I was right. I'm sure no one will know this Garry, either.'

'Humor me,' Anna said with a smile. She placed her business card near the photo. 'Let me know what you find out. Oh, and don't mention this to the detectives if they come back, OK?'

'OK,' Helene said, gazing down again at Garry's handsome face.

'One more thing,' Anna said. 'Do you know if anyone here saw anything suspicious in the courtyard either late last night or early this morning?'

'The police asked us that, too.' Helene shook her head. 'The yard is open to the public from nine to nine, so we get all kinds of people – tourists, office workers at lunch, people who just want to sit and read. But no one saw anything out of the ordinary . . . though I'm not sure what that would be.'

'How about dumping a body,' Anna said, half facetiously.

Helene frowned, shaking her head. 'How could anyone do that without being seen?'

'That's the question, isn't it?' Anna rose. 'I'll be in touch. Thanks.'

It was nearly three thirty when she emerged from the Institute. On the street she called her father.

'You're not calling to nag me about going to rehab, are you?' was the first thing he said.

'No, Dad.'

'That's good, because both of your sisters have already done that, twice.'

'I'm calling about something else. Do you know any experts on the architectural history of New York City?'

'I don't think so. Why would I?'

'I don't know, you've got so many connections.'

'Not one like that, I'm afraid. Why are you looking for such a person?'

'It's complicated, has to do with this young man on my crew who was murdered.'

'Ah, yes, horrible thing,' her father said solemnly. Then, 'Here's an idea. Give my friend Henry Burton a call.' Burton was an Egyptologist affiliated with the Metropolitan Museum of Art who had helped Anna in the past. 'He's bound to know the kind of person you're looking for.'

'Great idea, Dad. Thanks.'

She still had Burton's number.

'Anna! So nice to hear from you. How are your parents?'

How to answer that? 'As well as can be expected, thank you.'

'Hmm, I'm not sure what to make of that answer.'

She laughed. 'Bickering at the moment, but otherwise fine.'

'Good, good. Now, what can I do for you?'

'I'm looking for an expert on the architectural history of New York City.'

'May I ask why?'

'It has to do with a young man on my sanitation crew who was murdered.'

'Yes, I read about that. I'm terribly sorry. Let me see . . .'

He set down the receiver. She was grateful he hadn't pressed her for details.

'Turns out you've come to the right place,' he said, coming back on the line. 'I do know a marvelous woman, Euphemia Black. She's a freelance journalist, has written for *The Times*, the *New Yorker*, you name it. That's her specialty, the architectural history of New York. No one knows this city's past like she does. Hold on, I've got her number here somewhere.'

SIX

T he pale light of dusk had begun to descend on Amster Yard when Anna entered the leafy enclave carrying two coffee cups. There was no one else about. She made her way over to the gray flagstone terrace and sat down on one of the green metal chairs. Looking to her right she saw the large mullioned windows of the Institute's library. Surprisingly, Helene was still at her desk, typing on a computer. She happened to look up and, seeing Anna, frowned in puzzlement. Then she rose and came out.

She approached Anna. 'Why are you here?'

Anna gave her a mild smile. 'I'm meeting someone.'

'I've already told you everything I can.'

'I know that. This isn't about you.' Anna gestured toward the yard's gated entrance. 'Open to the public, right?'

Helene hesitated a moment, looking down, then thought of something. 'I showed everyone that guy's picture. Nobody knew him, like I told you.'

'Then you *hadn't* told me everything,' Anna pointed out pleasantly.

'Now I have,' Helene said, and turned and went back into the office. As the door closed, there was movement in the periphery of Anna's vision. She turned to see a very tall, very thin woman in jeans and a white long-sleeve men's shirt making her way toward her. The woman's features were tight, her face wrinkle-free, due not to youth but to extensive plastic surgery. There was something handsome yet grotesque about her. She reminded Anna of one of the tall, spindly people in a Tim Burton film. It was impossible to tell how old this woman was.

'Anna?' she said in a throaty voice, and when Anna nodded and rose, the woman's lips parted in a beautiful smile. She took Anna's hand. 'Euphemia Black.'

'I'm very happy to meet you. I appreciate your coming at such short notice.'

Euphemia waved it away. 'Don't be silly. Henry is one of my oldest friends, and I live just around the corner from here.'

'I brought you some coffee.' Anna pushed one of the cups toward her.

'Aren't you a doll.'

'I didn't know how you like it, of course. Took a chance and put in some cream and Splenda – that's what I like.'

'I like coffee any way. Very kind.' Euphemia sat down at the table and took a careful sip through the hole in the cup's spill-proof lid. 'Now, what can I do for you, my dear?'

Sitting also, Anna frowned, unsure of the best way to begin.

'Henry said it had to do with a murder,' Euphemia said helpfully.

'Two murders, actually,' Anna said, and told her about Garry and Yvette.

When Anna was finished, Euphemia was nodding, her eyes narrowed thoughtfully. 'So you're thinking that if these murders *are* linked, if it was no coincidence that these bodies were found in courtyards – in other words, that Garry and Yvette were killed by the same person – then learning about these places might shed some light on the psychology of the murderer. A kind of profiling.'

Anna nodded. 'It's a long shot, I know.'

Euphemia took another sip of coffee and put down the cup, her gaze wandering. 'Mews, courtyards . . . Well,' she began, looking back at Anna, 'there are a number of them in the city. Each has its own story. You say this young man Garry was found in New Amsterdam Mews?' When Anna nodded, Euphemia made a spluttering dismissive sound. 'A fake.'

'Excuse me?'

'It's new, built in the seventies, but meant to look old and charming. There are a number of these. Keep in mind, it's considered prestigious to live in a mews. A sign of social status.'

'Why?'

'Because they afford a privacy not found elsewhere in a city. That's highly desirable.'

'How would you define a mews, exactly?'

'It's a street, usually private, lined with buildings that were originally stables but have been renovated as dwellings – apartments, condos, co-ops, town houses.' Euphemia indicated the yard around them. 'This isn't a mews. It's a courtyard.

'At any rate, as I said, New Amsterdam Mews is a faux mews. Previously there was an apartment building on that lot. So if your killer *is* intentionally dumping his victims in mews or courtyards, he's not particular about their architectural authenticity.'

Anna considered this. 'Why,' she wondered aloud, 'would a person dump a body in a mews?'

Euphemia gave a small shrug. 'Someone who wants to spoil its sense of tranquility, its privacy? Someone who wants to bring ugliness in?'

'Yes,' Anna said, nodding thoughtfully, 'that makes sense.'

'Now, it was the young lady, Yvette, who was left here, you said.'

'That's right.' Anna pointed to the spot where Yvette had been found.

Euphemia nodded. 'Now Amster Yard . . . its story is completely different from that of New Amsterdam Mews. But bottom line –' she looked at Anna – 'it's a fake, too.'

Anna raised her brows in surprise.

'Let me start at the beginning. It's really very interesting,' Euphemia said, leaning forward in her obvious excitement. 'This site's history goes way back – bottles, pieces of marble, and horse skulls found here indicate people were using it as far back as 1620. We know that by 1830 it was the terminal stop of the Boston stage-coach on the Eastern Post Road. That road was abandoned between 1839 and 1844, when the city's current street grid was laid out. But it wasn't until 1870 that the first house was built here.'

Euphemia sipped her coffee. 'By the 1940s there were several old, crumbling tenement houses, some run-down brownstones, a boarding house, some dilapidated shacks including a carpenter's workshop, and the home of an elderly woman with thirty-five cats. Over the years an alley between the buildings had become filled with refuse and debris. It was a mess.

'Then a well-known designer named James Amster came along. He bought up all the lots and transformed them into Amster Yard, a beautiful courtyard surrounded by offices, stores, and apartments. He made a point of attracting tenants connected with art and design. Billy Baldwin, the famous decorator, lived in the largest of the apartments for ten years. There was also the sculptor Isamu Noguchi, who created some pieces just for this garden, and the fashion designer Normal Norell. A design firm called Swid Powell was here, and Amster himself lived and worked here. Later there was an advertising agency, a Greek Island handicraft store where Jackie Kennedy liked to shop, some computer consultants.

'In 1966 the yard was declared a New York City Landmark, but over time it deteriorated. By 1992 the last resident had moved out. The place was a mess again.

'In 1999 the Cervantes Institute bought the yard as its New York City headquarters. Their renovation plan was to replace the least historically significant of the buildings with a new, three-story building, while partially demolishing the remaining buildings and restoring them and the courtyard to their 1949 appearance.

'Then they looked closer at the buildings. When they removed the drywall, they realized the interiors of the buildings were in far worse shape than they'd thought. Some of the walls had huge cracks running from top to bottom. Other walls were only the thickness of a single brick. Chimney flues had burned through many of the wood joists.

'Renovation, they decided, was not the way to go. Not only because of the cost but also the safety aspect. So in the middle of the night, without having informed anyone, they demolished it.'

'Demolished it?'

Euphemia nodded. 'The courtyard, buildings, trees, walkways . . . Razed it to the ground.'

'How did people react?'

'The neighbors were shocked, outraged. A private group called the New York Landmarks Conservancy held a preservation easement on the yard, which gave it the right to approve any changes to the property. They had known nothing about the demolition and had thought the yard was going to be restored.'

'So what happened?'

'The Institute was forced to re-create the yard from scratch. I must say they did an excellent job,' Euphemia said, gazing about her. 'But it's not what it seems. Directly below us is a 40-by-40-foot auditorium that seats over a hundred people. To build that, they had to dig down nineteen feet, which entailed drilling, splitting, and carting out 4,500 cubic yards of hard Manhattan schist bedrock – all through that six-foot-wide gate. Also hidden behind that quaint facade are a state-of-the-art library, classrooms, a large art gallery, and a wine-tasting room.

'Certain elements were salvaged from the original buildings and returned to their original places – iron awnings, plaques, light fixtures, balcony detailing. The front gate is also original. Otherwise, it's a replica, a reproduction. To preservationists like me, it's as fake as New Amsterdam Mews.'

'Maybe that's the point,' Anna said.

'I don't follow you.'

'Maybe the killer is angry about what happened to the original yard, and killing someone and dumping her body here is his way of expressing his anger.'

'Maybe,' Euphemia said, 'but how would that tie in with New Amsterdam Mews?'

'As you said, it's also a fake. A person who loves authentic mews and courtyards might be outraged at the idea of fakes.'

'Yes, I see. But who? Someone who lived in one of them? How could you ever hope to check into all those people?'

'I can't. Which means I'm going to need to see more of the pattern if I'm going to have any hope of solving this.'

Euphemia's gaze met Anna's as she realized what she was saying. 'Well,' she said, crossing her arms as if suddenly cold, 'if that happens, don't hesitate to call me.'

'Thanks,' Anna said, and the two women rose and walked in the direction of the gate.

Birds chirped loudly in the trees overhead as they do when the sun has nearly set. 'I feel as if I haven't been much help to you,' Euphemia said.

'That's not true. Without you I wouldn't have known that New Amsterdam Mews and Amster Yard are fakes, as you put it.'

'True,' Euphemia said as they emerged on to East Forty-Ninth Street. 'The next site the killer chooses – the next piece of the pattern – may tell you more . . . though I dearly hope this is the end of it.'

'Amen to that,' Anna said, but the look the two women exchanged was decidedly uneasy.

Anna walked home along the darkening streets of midtown. The air had grown chill and she wished she had a sweater. As she turned on to her block she was surprised to see Santos standing near the stairs to her apartment building, his back to her, holding his cell phone to his ear.

Her cell phone rang. It was Santos. 'Where are you?' he asked.

'Walking straight toward you.'

He turned, closed his phone.

'This is a nice surprise,' she said, kissing him.

'Let's go upstairs,' he said.

'Ooh,' she said, smiling. 'Eager.'

He shook his head. 'I've got some things to tell you.'

She knew it was about the murders. In her apartment she made coffee while he sat on a stool at her breakfast counter.

'We've shown Yvette's photo to everyone living in New Amsterdam Mews and the apartment building next door. No one recognized her.'

'Or *said* they recognized her.'

'Right.'

'That's what you had to tell me?' she said, placing a steaming mug of coffee before him.

'No, there's a lot more. First let me finish with Yvette. There was nothing helpful in her pocketbook, but a search of her apartment turned up a few things. She was from New Market, Minnesota. Came to New York last month after graduating from Minnesota State.'

'Just out of college and she had her own apartment?'

'Barely. It's a tiny studio, just a room, really. I'll tell you more about that in a minute. She worked at a daycare center on East Thirty-Ninth Street called Step by Step. We spoke to the director. She said Yvette had only worked there for a few weeks and no one there knew much about her. They all agreed she was "a nice girl." Anyway, a search of her apartment turned up something interesting. She had a collection of snow globes. You know, those round glass things you shake and the snow—'

'I know what they are. But why is that interesting?'

'Because she had one of Times Square with the words "With Love from Trent" written on the bottom, dated last week.'

'Who's Trent?'

He shrugged. 'That's what we're trying to find out. No one at the daycare center had ever heard her mention the name.'

'Was there anything else of interest in the apartment?'

'Other than a zillion romance novels and an extensive collection of books about mythology?' Santos laughed. 'No.'

Anna settled on the stool next to Santos and shook her head. 'Dead ends, it sounds like to me.'

'I'm not finished yet. We found the place where she was killed.'

Anna looked up sharply.

'From what we can piece together, the killer was waiting for her in a dark stairwell beside the steps to her brownstone. He must have jumped out and grabbed her as she went into the building. He dragged her into the dark and stabbed her – we found her blood.

However, there's no evidence of the body having been dragged out. For whatever reason, this lunatic somehow transported her body all the way across town in order to dump it in Amster Yard.'

'Like Garry. Killed behind the shed and then carried to the middle of New Amsterdam Mews.'

Santos nodded. 'There's more. I've saved the best for last.'

She waited.

'An anonymous tip came in today, a guy – sounded young – who said the man who killed Garry Thomason and Yvette Ronson is one Jared Roberts at an address on Bank Street in Princeton, New Jersey.'

Anna's eyes were wide. 'Who's Jared Roberts? Did the police go to the address?'

'Roche and Rinaldi did, sure – in cooperation with the Princeton police, of course.' He looked at her. 'The address turned out to be a single apartment in a converted stable.'

'A mews . . .'

'You got it. Courtyard and all. The place was real secluded, no other houses nearby.'

'Was this man Roberts there?'

Santos shook his head. 'He'd flown the coop – and wiped the entire place clean of fingerprints. He'd definitely been expecting the cops.

'None of his neighbors knew him. If they had ever seen him, they weren't aware of it. Seems this man gave new meaning to keeping to yourself. The owner of the building purchased it only recently and had never met his tenant. He showed the cops Roberts's lease, dated twenty-six years ago. There was no previous address or any other information that might have been helpful. The building's previous owner, the man who'd originally rented the apartment to Roberts, is dead. Roberts always paid his rent in cash. He always left it in an envelope in the owner's mailbox.'

'What about telephone, utilities?'

'All in the name of J. Roberts at the Bank Street address. He paid all his bills in cash. There have never been any credit cards in his name.' Santos shook his head in wonder. 'It's clear this man has worked very hard to remain anonymous . . . and succeeded.'

'Was a national check done for the name?'

He nodded. 'There are people with that name, sure, but they all check out satisfactorily.'

'All dead ends,' Anna said.

'Until the cops showed the neighbors Garry's and Yvette's photos. No one recognized Yvette, but one of the neighbors, the one who lived nearest, recognized Garry. He said he'd once seen him going through the gate at the entrance to the mews. But the neighbor had never met Garry and didn't know his name.'

'What was Garry's connection to this Roberts?' Anna wondered aloud.

'And who,' Santos said, 'is the tipster?'

MEWS MURDERER ON THE LOOSE! screamed the headline of the *New York Post* the following morning as Anna walked past a newsstand. Apparently she wasn't the only one who felt Garry's and Yvette's murders could be linked. The *Daily News*, not to be outdone, read SERIAL KILLER 'COURTS' MURDER. Anna let out a sigh and walked on.

At the corner of Ninth Avenue and West Forty-Third Street she stopped in at her favorite grocery store, owned by Mr and Mrs Carlucci. Mr Carlucci was outside, arranging a display of peaches and pears. Ordinarily Anna would call out something in light-hearted fun and he would respond in kind. Today when he turned to her his expression was anything but light-hearted, which was fine with Anna because all she had on her mind at the moment was murder.

'Morning, Mr Carlucci,' she said, approaching him.

He nodded gravely. 'Anna, I haven't seen you since . . . well, I heard what happened to that young man who worked for you. I'm so sorry.'

She gave him a little smile and thanked him.

'Tell me,' he said, 'have the police made any progress in catching who did this?'

'Not really.' She was thinking about the tip-off that had led to the mews in Princeton – a tip she was not at liberty to talk about.

'Do you think it's true that the same person killed that poor girl, Yvette?'

She shook her head and shrugged. 'At this point there's no way to know.'

He thought for a moment, his gaze fixed on a cantaloupe. Then he turned a shrewd gaze on her. 'Is there any connection between Garry and Yvette?'

'No,' she replied, a little surprised. 'At least, no connection anyone has turned up.'

'Do you think the murders are random? You know, he waits behind New Amsterdam Mews, knowing a sanitation worker is going to come back there, and grabs whoever it is – Garry. Then he hides in the stairwell beside the entrance to Yvette's building and grabs whoever happens to come by – Yvette.'

'Both of those scenarios are quite possible. We just don't know.' She had grown uncomfortable with this conversation. 'So,' she said briskly, 'what's good today for my lunch?'

But Mr Carlucci wasn't finished. 'Anna,' he said in a low voice, coming a step closer, 'what's the story with that man who just moved into your building?'

'You mean Mr Herman?' she asked, taken aback.

He nodded. 'Iris Dovner was here with him yesterday. She introduced us and said she was showing him around the neighborhood.'

'What more is there to tell?' she asked.

'I watched them walk away. Iris took his arm.'

Was it true, then, that Mrs Dovner had a boyfriend? 'I think that's sweet,' she said, thinking *sweet* was in truth the last word she would have used in connection to her ornery downstairs neighbor.

Mr Carlucci looked troubled. 'I didn't like him at all.'

'Why?'

'There was something about him. When we shook hands he looked me up and down with this cold look in his eyes, as if he was sizing me up. And his handshake was limp. That's never a good sign.'

Anna had to laugh. 'Mrs Dovner's a big girl. I say more power to her.'

But Mr Carlucci's brows remained knit together as he suggested items for Anna's lunch.

She wasn't far from the garage but didn't want to get there too fast. She wanted to think. So she continued south on Ninth Avenue but went past Forty-Third Street, walked several blocks, then went east on West Thirty-Seventh Street.

Ahead and to the left, on the north side of the street, stood the Holy Legacy Baptist Church, a small but beautiful structure built in the neo-Gothic style. As she neared the building she noticed a free-standing dispenser near the steps. Behind the clear plastic door was a stack of brochures. Curious, she took one.

The trifold leaflet contained basic information about the church: WHO WE ARE, WHAT WE BELIEVE, WHO IS OUR PASTOR. On the front was a photograph of the church itself, with the letters HLBC in bold letters underneath.

HLBC . . . She had seen those letters before . . .

Then she remembered. They had been written in pencil on the back of the cut-out girl's face she found in New Amsterdam Mews. But what had she done with it? She concentrated. Her habit was to empty the pockets of her trousers on to her dresser each evening.

Now, instead of returning to the garage, she turned around, walked back to Ninth Avenue, and headed north toward her apartment.

The pile on her dresser had grown rather large, but eventually she found the small cut-out and this time she tucked it carefully into her purse. Then she hurried back to the church and went in.

A dark-skinned woman sat a desk in the foyer. She greeted Anna pleasantly. 'May I help you?'

Anna returned the woman's smile. 'I'm Anna Winthrop. I'm new in the neighborhood and was thinking of joining the church. But I've got a four-year-old daughter and want to find out about your children's programs.'

'Of course. I have some information here . . .' The woman opened a drawer and brought out a pink sheet, a blue sheet, and a green sheet. 'I think these will have all the information you need.'

'Thanks,' Anna said, 'but I'd really like to speak to one of your teachers. Ideally one who might have my Brittany in class.'

'Hmmm . . .' The woman frowned. 'The after-school program is going on now, but I might be able to find someone who can speak to you for a few minutes. Wait right here, please.'

The woman went through a door and returned a few minutes later with a sweet-looking young woman wearing jeans and a flowered top. 'Ms Winthrop,' the receptionist said, 'this is Melanie Green. She teaches some of our younger children.'

Melanie and Anna shook hands while the other woman returned to her place behind the desk. 'I understand you have a little one you're thinking of enrolling in one of our programs,' Melanie said.

'Is there someplace we could talk privately?' Anna asked, keeping her voice low.

Melanie looked surprised and shot a look at the woman behind the desk, who hadn't heard. 'Sure, down this hallway.'

When they were halfway along a deserted corridor, Anna said, 'Actually, there's something I need to speak to you about.'

'Excuse me?'

Anna was fishing around in her purse. She took out the face

cut-out and handed it to Melanie, who turned it over and did a double take. 'This is Carlene Edmonds. Why do you have this? Why is her face cut out like that?'

Instead of responding, Anna asked, 'Do you know if Carlene lives in New Amsterdam Mews?'

'New Amsterdam Mews . . . No, Carlene's family lives in Stuyvesant Town. But New Amsterdam Mews rings a bell for some reason. Oh, I know! A young man who volunteers as an aide in our Sunday School lives there. Danny Chandler.'

'An aide? What kinds of things would he do as an aide?'

Melanie gave a little shrug. 'All kinds of things. Bringing in art supplies, helping the kids with projects, that sort of thing.'

'What about taking photographs?'

Melanie smiled. 'Well, yes, of course. He loves doing that. He posts lots of them on the bulletin boards in the hallways.' She looked down at Carlene Edmonds' cut-out face. 'So maybe Danny took this. Though why he would cut out the face, I have no idea.'

SEVEN

On her way into the garage, Anna passed Kelly.

'Take a look at the –' Kelly made quotation marks in her air – 'sculpture.'

Curious, Anna went out to the courtyard. Clive had his back to her, busy working. Hearing her, he turned and smiled. 'I'm really sorry about yesterday. Like I said, my humor can be a bit offbeat.'

She returned his smile. 'Apology accepted.' She stepped closer to the sculpture. 'You've certainly made progress.'

He gazed proudly upon his handiwork. Atop the cinder-block platform he had placed a department store mannequin that he had cut down the middle. The two halves stood a few inches apart. Around the mannequin pieces he had arranged in a ring about a dozen empty plastic bags that had once contained rose fertilizer. Large red roses decorated the front of the bags. 'Interesting . . .' Anna commented.

His shoulders rose in a chuckle. 'You don't have to be polite. It's OK not to like it.'

'No, it's not that,' she said, quite honestly. 'The truth is, I don't know what to make of it.'

'That could be said about a lot of art. In fact, that's how art is supposed to make you feel.'

'I'm reserving judgment,' Anna said, turning to leave.

'Fair enough!' came his reply from behind her.

She crossed the garage and walked down the corridor to her office. In the doorway she stopped short. Before her sat Damian, legs crossed, tapping out a song on the arms of the chair. He looked up and grinned. 'You wanted to see me?' he said in a lazy drawl.

Without knowing why, she flushed hotly. 'No. I think there's been a mistake.'

His gaze met hers. 'Has there?' He rose, passed too close to her on his way out. 'I could have sworn you wanted to see me.' Before turning away, he winked at her.

Speechless, she stood in her doorway, watching him saunter away. Then she realized he might turn around and she closed her office door and sat down at her desk. What had that been all about? She knew perfectly well. He was coming on to her – had been from the day he started. She would have to deal with him.

But by noon she had decided to give him one more chance, to do nothing unless he pulled something like that again. She knew that was the cowardly response but she didn't care. At the moment she had bigger fish to fry.

Step by Step Daycare occupied a converted brownstone on East Thirty-Ninth Street between Lexington and Park avenues. A middle-aged receptionist looked up from a Harlequin romance. 'May I help you?'

'I'm Anna Winthrop. I called earlier. I think you were the person I spoke with.'

The woman thought a moment before the lights came on in her eyes. 'Oh, right. You wanted to talk to someone about poor Yvette.'

Anna nodded.

The woman placed her open book face down on the desk and stood. 'Just a minute.'

She went through a glass door into a room painted bright yellow. On the far wall were shelves of books and toys, on the floor a vast multicolored carpet made up of squares containing numbers, letters, animals, and shapes. Anna didn't see any children.

The receptionist reappeared. 'Dora said she can talk to you for a few minutes. This way.'

Anna followed her into the yellow room. Through a doorway

into an adjoining room she saw children lying on mats, some with
their eyes closed, some awake and fidgeting. At the front of the
room an older woman sat knitting. Rest time.

The receptionist indicated a woman sitting on a child-size chair
reading *I and Thou* by Martin Buber. She rose, putting down her
book. 'Thanks, Jean,' she said to the receptionist, who went back
to her desk.

'You're Anna,' Dora said, putting out her hand. 'Dora Pine. I'm
the director.'

She looked around twenty-five and was tall and slim in dark
jeans and a sleeveless top. She had what Anna would have called
mermaid hair: it was long and blonde and ripply and hung down
each shoulder in front. She was quite pretty, with sensuous features
in a creamy complexion.

'I appreciate your seeing me,' Anna said.

Dora smiled sadly. 'Hey, no problem. You're trying to find out
who . . . what happened to Yvette, you said.' She frowned. 'I wasn't
quite clear . . . You said you're with the Sanitation Department? No,
that couldn't be.'

'Yes, that's right.' Anna indicated the small table and chairs.
'May I sit?'

'Of course,' Dora said, and they took chairs on opposite sides.

'I'll explain,' Anna said, and told her about Garry and the possible
connection between his and Yvette's murders. 'If there is a connection, then solving Yvette's murder could solve Garry's, and vice
versa.'

'I understand, but the police have already spoken to us.'

'Yes, but they don't think there's a connection – at least, not yet
– so they would have asked different questions. For instance, had
you ever heard Garry's name before now?'

Dora shook her head.

Anna brought out Garry's photo and set it before her.

'Is that him?' Dora asked. 'He's handsome. Was, I mean. But
I've never seen him before.'

'All right. Here's a question I'm sure the police did ask. Did
Yvette ever mention anyone named Trent?'

'You're right, they did ask us that. And the answer is no. They
wouldn't say why they were asking. Who is he?'

'Maybe her boyfriend. There was something in her apartment
that he had given her.'

'No,' Dora repeated, 'but Yvette and I didn't talk much. I liked her, but we weren't friends. She'd only been working here a few weeks. Oh wait,' she said, looking up. 'I just remembered something. One day Yvette said someone was going to be coming by for her after work. She wanted to know if he could come in. We have very strict rules about things like that and I told her it would be easier all around if he just waited for her outside. That could have been the boyfriend.'

'Possibly. Are there any other things like that you can remember? Anything at all that she might have mentioned, that you might have noticed?'

Dora searched her memory and finally shook her head. 'All I know is that she was from Minnesota and had no family in New York.'

'Would it be possible for me to speak briefly to anyone else she worked with here?'

'There are only two other people besides me – Jean, the woman who brought you in here, and Cathy, who's doing rest time. Come with me.'

Dora led the way into the room where the children were resting. Cathy was a plump woman in her fifties with short salt-and-pepper hair. 'This is Cathy Roman,' Dora whispered. 'Cathy – Anna Winthrop. She's here about Yvette.'

Anna nodded. 'Is there anything you can tell me about her?' she asked Cathy.

Immediately Cathy shook her head, lowering her knitting to her lap. 'We hardly ever spoke. Not that we weren't friendly, but it's so busy here, and she and I didn't really have much in common. Courtney, stop picking your nose.'

Anna asked, 'Have you ever heard the name Garry Thomason?' She held up his photo.

Cathy shook her head. 'Never heard that name. Never saw him, either. Sorry. Have you talked to Jean at the front desk?'

'She's next,' Dora said, and led the way to the reception area.

Jean was so engrossed in her romance that she didn't hear them approach. She happened to glance up and jumped. 'Oh, you scared me.'

'Sorry,' Anna said, laughing. 'That must be some book.'

Dora said, 'Jean loves romance novels.'

'I read about one a day,' Jean said.

Dora said, 'As you know, Anna's here about Yvette.' Jean's expression darkened. 'Is there anything you can tell her?'

'Like what?'

'Anything Yvette might have told you about her life?' Anna said. 'Anything at all.'

Jean gave this some thought. 'I don't think so . . .' Her gaze dropped to her book. 'No, wait. There was one thing. One day she made a comment about how many romance books I read. She said she loved them, too – except that I like contemporary romance, and she liked historical.'

'That's it?' Dora said.

'No. We got to talking and she said she'd been reading these books since she was in junior high school, and that she'd always dreamed of meeting a man like the men in these books. She called him her hero. Then one morning she came in and said to me, "I found him." I said, "Found who?" and she said, "My hero. I've got a boyfriend."'

'Then what did she say?' Anna asked.

'That was all, because she was already late and she had to get to the children.'

'She never mentioned his name?'

Jean shook her head. 'But I was curious. Last week I asked her if she wanted to have lunch. I was going to ask her then. We made a date . . . for today.'

There was a moment's silence. Then Anna asked, 'Did Yvette ever mention anyone named Trent?'

Jean shook her head.

Anna took Garry's photo out of her purse and showed it to her. 'Have you ever seen this man?'

'No, but he's awfully cute.'

'His name is Garry Thomason. Have you ever heard that name?'

Jean frowned. 'Isn't that the name of that garbage man who got killed? I read about it in the paper.'

'Sanitation worker,' Anna corrected her. 'That's right. But had you ever heard the name before that?'

'No.' Jean looked up, eyes wide. 'Was *he* Yvette's hero?'

'No,' Anna said, resignation in her voice as she put the photo away. 'I'm afraid there was no connection between them. No connection at all.'

'So what happened?' Santos asked when Anna called him from the sidewalk outside Step by Step. 'Did you find out anything about her?'

'Yes, that she had a boyfriend, but no one knows his name.'

'It's Trent,' Santos said. 'We've got to find him. I'll bet he killed her. Intimate-partner homicide. We see it all the time. You're off tomorrow, right?'

Anna had Thursdays off. 'You know I am.'

'Got any special plans?'

'Why? You're working,' she said.

'I know. I'm just asking.'

Anna blew out some air. 'My mother called this morning. She wants to have lunch. I don't know if I'd call that special.'

'Yeah, right. Are she and your dad still fighting?'

'I don't know, but I'm sure I'll find out! Later.'

She ended the call, then blocked her number and dialed the number Wendell Chandler had given her. After six rings the call went to voicemail. 'You've reached Wendell Chandler of MerchantStar Systems. I'm unable to take your call. Please leave a message at the tone and I will call you back as soon as possible.'

She hung up before the beep. Then she took a cab to New Amsterdam Mews. She didn't have time to walk.

It was quiet in the mews, truly a sanctuary amid the chaos of the city. She knocked on the door of number 7 and waited . . . and waited. She was about to give up when the lock rattled and the door was partially opened by Wendell Chandler's son.

'Danny?'

He eyed her cautiously. 'Yeah.'

'Can I talk to you a minute?'

'Why? My dad's not here.'

'I know that. It's you I want to talk to.'

Without responding, he turned and walked into the living room. Anna followed him, closing the door behind her.

'You got those postcards for us?' he asked, falling into an armchair.

'No, I'm afraid I haven't tracked those down yet. But I do have something else for you.'

He scowled. 'What?'

She removed from her purse the cut-out of Carlene Edmonds' face and placed it on the cocktail table so that she was smiling up at him.

He froze. 'Where did you get that?'

She didn't answer.

'Do you have all the rest of them?' he asked.

Still she made no reply, simply staring at him.

'My dad told you, we're not paying any more money. We already paid. The deal was we would get back all of them. So where are they?'

'I'll bring them to you, don't worry about that. But let's talk.' She leaned forward and raised her eyebrows.

'Talk about what?' he asked warily.

'Garry and Terrence told me about what they found. Garry's dead, as you know, and as for Terrence . . . well, I'm his boss and I'm taking over now. I was wondering if maybe there was some way you and I could work together.'

He was breathing hard now, his chest rising and falling in his tight T-shirt. 'How?' he croaked.

'I don't know what you've got set up in terms of distribution, but whatever it is, I think I can do better for you.'

'The Sanitation Department?' he faltered.

'Not per se. Not under its auspices. But between uniformed workers and supervisors, and civilian workers, there are more than eight thousand people in the department. That's a network we can make very good use of.'

He was staring at her, nibbling the inside of his cheek, his chest still visibly rising and falling. 'So how would this work?'

'First we'd establish a quantity – you know, how much product you can furnish, say, monthly. I'll set a price and your cut. But I can't set a price until I actually see more of the merchandise.'

'All right,' he said slowly, rising. 'I can show you. Come on.'

He led her down the hallway at the back of the living room to a small kitchen. Here he opened a door, reached in, and switched on a light. 'This way.'

It was a cellar, dark and dank. The stairs were of rough wood and creaked loudly under their feet. At the bottom they stepped on to a painted concrete floor. In the dim light of a single suspended bulb she saw dust-covered pipes, a hot water boiler, some stored luggage.

'Through here.' He opened a door on the left and switched on another dim light. She followed him into a small room and he closed the door. This room had been crudely Sheetrocked. A long aluminum conference table sat against the back wall.

'We'd better do this quickly in case your father comes home,' she said.

He smiled. 'Not a problem. He's in Boston on business today.' He turned to some makeshift shelves lined with large loose-leaf stamp albums. He ran his finger along them and selected one called *United States Liberty Stamp Album*, with a photograph of the Statue of Liberty on the spine. 'Stamps?' she said.

He chuckled, setting the album on the table and opening it to a random page. 'Here's some of my "product."'

She gazed down, forced herself to remain nonchalant though what she saw shocked her. Attached to the album sheet was a page from a pornographic magazine showing a man and a woman in a sexually explicit pose, except that the face of a little girl had been pasted on top of the woman's face.

'Can I see more?' she asked.

'Course.' He flipped to another page. Here were two women, their faces replaced by the faces of little girls. He pointed to one of the faces. 'That's Carlene, the one you've got. I use her a lot.'

'Mm,' she said with gusto. 'Love it.' She glanced over at the shelves. 'How many of these do you think you have?'

'Oh, hundreds. Maybe thousands. You really think you could do something with them? I've never sold them or anything before. I've just done them for me. But I guess other people would like them, too, right? They're different.'

'Absolutely.' She closed the album. 'I definitely get the idea. Very clever.'

'You bet it is. Those idiots at the church think I'm just taking pictures for the bulletin boards. They don't know what I do with the pictures of the girls. A few weeks ago I landed another gig, at this dorky youth camp in the Bronx called Bright Horizons. I teach photography, don't you love it? Lots of hot little girls there, too.'

'Perfect.' She frowned, puzzled about something. 'Why were you throwing out those pictures that Garry and Terrence found?'

'Oh, those were my rejects. It's really hard to do and they don't always come out right.'

'Do yourself a favor and don't throw them in the trash any more.'

'Ain't it the truth. I just bought this.' He stepped aside to reveal a small Fellowes paper shredder sitting on a lower shelf.

They went back upstairs. 'I think this is gonna work out really cool,' he said as they approached the front door.

'Me, too,' she said. 'I think we can pull in some real money. Now you're sure you've got time for this, right? You're not in college or anything.'

'Nah, college is a total waste of time. My dad wants me to go, but I know it's not right for me. The kinds of things I wanna do, they don't teach you at college.'

When Anna entered her building, Mrs Dovner was at her door, greeting Mr Herman, who handed her a large bouquet of flowers. The foyer smelled wonderfully of stuffed cabbage. Mrs Dovner was a great cook, Anna would give her that.

'You shouldn't have,' Mrs Dovner cooed as she took the flowers. 'Come in.' Over Mr Herman's shoulder she met Anna's gaze and her eyebrows rose. Her expression said, 'How do you like that?' Instantly she returned her attention to her dinner guest and firmly closed the door.

A little before ten o'clock that night, there was a knock on Anna's door. Anna was at the kitchen sink washing a plate. She dried her hands, went to the door, and looked out the peep hole into a distorted close-up of Mr Herman's smiling face. She opened the door.

'I hope I'm not interrupting anything,' he said, peeking around her. He was carrying a bouquet of pink carnations.

'What can I do for you, Mr Herman?'

'Please, call me Lionel. May I come in?'

'It is rather late and I have to get up early for work . . .'

'Which is why I won't keep you for more than a minute,' he said, strolling in.

With an inward groan she closed the door.

'These are for you,' he said, turning to her.

'Thank you, but you shouldn't have,' she said, puzzled, and took the flowers. 'Was there something you needed, Mr Herman?'

'Lionel.'

'Lionel.'

'No,' he said brightly. 'It's just that I realized we're neighbors and I've never properly introduced myself, told you about me, learned more about you.'

'I see,' Anna said, not even bothering to put the flowers in water. She set them on the kitchen counter and stepped back into the living room, where Mr Herman now sat in the middle of the sofa.

'You don't happen to have any coffee brewing?' he said.

'I'm afraid not. As I just said, I was getting ready for bed.' She remained standing.

'Right, right. You work in the Department of Sanitation, Iris tells me. You *would* need to get up early for that, wouldn't you?'

He glanced around the room. 'I enjoyed meeting your boyfriend. He's a police officer, Iris said.'

'That's right.'

'How very interesting. You both work for the city in your own
different ways.'

'Yes. Mr Her— Lionel, is there something . . .?'

'Me, I guess you could say I'm in finance. Or was, I should say.
I'm retired now.'

'I see. Where did you live before moving here, if you don't mind
my asking?' She figured if he wasn't leaving, she might as well
ask a few questions of her own.

'No, I don't mind at all. I lived in Norfolk, Massachusetts, south
of Boston. Have you ever been to Norfolk?'

'No, I'm afraid not. What brought you to New York?'

'It was always a dream I had, to live here. To be able to go out
any night of the week and attend a play, an opera, a ballet, the
symphony . . . It's just wonderful all that this city offers, don't you
think?'

'Mm.'

'At any rate, when my Winnie died last year, I realized I could
finally do it. She was very ill, and hated New York City anyway.'

'I see.'

'May I ask you something?' Mr Herman asked.

Now you need permission? 'Of course. I can't guarantee I'll
answer, though.'

He drew up the corners of his small mouth in a tiny smile. 'Why
do you dislike me so?'

She stared at him, nonplussed. 'I never said I disliked you.'

'You don't have to. It's in your body language, the way you
speak to me. You might as well be wearing a sandwich board: "I
hate Lionel Herman".'

Now she sat. 'All right. I don't trust you, Mr Herman. You say
you come from a finance background, you appear to be a refined,
affluent man, yet you move here, to this shabby brownstone. That
seems odd to me.'

He laughed lightly. 'It's not odd at all. The rent is extremely
reasonable, as you would know, and I'm retired. I need to watch
my pennies. I might ask you the same question. Why are you, the
daughter of a billionaire, living here?'

Touché. 'I also question your motives with respect to Mrs
Dovner.'

'Ah, you don't think they're honorable.'

'I don't know what to think.'

'Yes, you do. You so dislike Iris that you can't imagine anyone could like her.'

'Well . . . yes.'

'Let me assure you, you're wrong about her. She's a lovely woman, warm and caring.'

'*Mrs Dovner?*'

He nodded. 'You two seem to have gotten off on the wrong foot and never progressed beyond that point. But Iris and I . . . we're already good friends. She's lonely. At any rate,' he said, rising, 'that's all we have, a lovely friendship. You needn't be concerned that I have any ulterior motives.'

She followed him to the door.

'By the way,' he said, 'my condolences on the loss of that young man on your crew. And now this horrid Mews Murderer has claimed another victim, that pretty young woman. Do you know from your boyfriend if the police have any leads?'

'No, not as far as I know.'

He made a *tsk*ing sound. 'A terrible business. New York can be a frightening place, can't it, Anna?'

'Yes, it can.'

'Which is why we need friends. I hope you and I will become friends.'

She didn't respond, just closed the door and watched through the peephole as he started up the stairs.

Creep.

EIGHT

The 4,000-square-foot co-op apartment in Sutton Place that Anna's parents had owned for as long as she could remember had five bedrooms, five and a half bathrooms, and wrap-around balconies with views of the East River. In the current market it would have fetched more than eight million dollars.

Her parents almost never used it. Anna couldn't remember the last time she'd been there. Albert, the doorman, and William, the concierge, were delighted to see her.

'I thought your family had forgotten about us,' William said, tipping his cap with a white-gloved hand. 'Now we've got both you and your mother.'

Anna smiled. 'It's wonderful to see you both,' she said, and headed for the elevator. A few moments later its doors opened on to the apartment's vast white living room. Stepping out, she noticed that not a thing was out of place – not that there were many things. In her New York home Tildy favored a minimalist design approach.

The doors slid shut behind her. There was utter silence. 'Mother?'

No response. Anna went down the corridor to the bedrooms. 'Mother?'

'In here, darling!' came Tildy's voice from the master bedroom.

Entering the room, Anna saw several large suitcases lying open on the bed. Tildy stood between the bed and an armoire, taking clothes from one of the suitcases and carefully placing them on the shelves.

'Mother, what are you doing?'

'What does it look like I'm doing?' Tildy said, smiling brightly.

'It looks like you're moving in.'

'That's right, dear,' Tildy said calmly, neatening a shelf of sweaters. She faced her daughter. 'This is going to be home for me for a while. Maybe for ever.'

'Mother, what are you talking about?'

Tildy wrinkled her nose. 'Let's have lunch, dear, and I'll tell you.'

Tildy wanted to eat at Fred's, the restaurant on the ninth floor of Barneys at Madison Avenue and East Sixty-First Street. It was a beautiful day and they walked, Tildy barely speaking at all. Inside, Tildy admired several Balenciaga handbags as they made their way to the elevators on the left. 'Remind me to buy those after lunch.'

A few minutes later they were seated, glasses of white wine before them.

'All right, Mother, you can't put me off any longer. What's going on?'

'I've left your father.'

Anna nearly spilled her wine. 'What?'

'Mm-hm,' Tildy said matter-of-factly. 'You can't tell me you didn't see it coming.'

'Yes, I can. Why?'

Tildy took a sip of her wine. 'I told your father that if he didn't get some help for his drinking I would leave him. Well, he still hasn't, so I've left.'

At first Anna didn't know what to say. 'Well . . . are you sure you gave him enough time?'

'It wasn't a matter of time, dear. He told me flat out that I could wait as long as I wanted, said he had no intention of ever getting help because he didn't need any. He even made fun of me for going to my Al-Anon meetings.'

'So that's it? Almost forty years of marriage down the drain?'

Tildy gave a tiny shrug, looking sad for the first time. 'If that's how your father wants it. It's really up to him. I've told him that if he gets some help, I'll come back.'

The waiter arrived to take their orders. 'Are we ready, ladies?'

'Let's order,' Tildy said, pressing her hands warmly over Anna's. 'Then you can fill me in on this poor young man on your team who was murdered.'

The waiter's eyes grew wide.

'My daughter is a director at the Sanitation Department,' Tildy told him, as if that explained it all.

'I'm a section supervisor,' Anna told the waiter. 'He was a sanitation worker in my section.'

Now the waiter looked positively baffled. Then comprehension suddenly dawned. 'I know what you're talking about. That poor guy who went behind the building to grab some trash bags and disappeared.'

'No,' Tildy said, 'he was murdered.'

'Yes,' the waiter said, 'but he was gone for a while in between, right?' He looked to Anna for confirmation.

'That's right,' she said uncomfortably.

'Well, where was he?'

'Where was who?'

'The guy who got killed. You know, between the time he was snatched and the time he was found. Killer stabbed him through the eye, right?'

Two women at the next table were looking on in horror.

'I . . . I really don't want to talk about this,' Anna said.

The maître d' appeared at the table. 'Is everything all right?'

'Oh, yes, fine,' Tildy said breezily. 'We were just talking about a man in my daughter's section who got murdered.'

The maître d' looked at the waiter, who nodded. 'Have they ordered?' the maître d' asked.

The waiter shook his head.

'And what can we get you ladies for lunch today?' the maître d' asked, stepping between the tables to shield the women at the next table.

Tildy leaned forward. 'You know, dear,' she said in a conspiratorial whisper, 'when you think about it, you've got more urgent matters to deal with than your father and me.' She looked up at the waiter. 'The lobster club, please, but no garlic mayonnaise. Regular mayonnaise on the side.'

'Very good, madam.'

'He's always had the problem, you know,' Tildy said as they strolled along Madison Avenue after lunch. 'The drinking, I mean.'

Anna, a Barneys shopping bag in each hand, turned to look at her.

'Not that I completely blame him,' Tildy went on. 'You see, when your father and I were young, drinking was a much bigger part of life than it is now. At home we had wine with lunch and cocktails before dinner and liqueurs after dinner. And when your father went to business there was more drinking, mostly at lunch. Everyone drank at lunch.'

Tildy turned her head thoughtfully. 'But he had so much more in his life then. He was running a large company. He had you and your sisters and brother to help me raise. He had his tennis and his polo and his golf.

'But when he sold the company and retired, a big part of his life was gone. He kept up his sports but there was a big hole to fill. He did his best but I think he was bored a lot of the time. And when he was bored, he would drink. Some days he was already carrying a glass around at noon. And he just kept refilling it.

'Drinking more at home led to drinking more socially. I noticed that he would become nasty sometimes when we were out. He would say mean or sarcastic things to me. I told him it hurt my feelings, but he didn't stop. I don't think he could.

'The first time he screamed at me at a party, I was so shocked I ran out crying. When we got home he apologized, told me how much he loved me, promised it would never happen again. But it did. Finally I told him I thought he had a real problem he needed help with.'

'How did he react?'

'Exactly the way he's reacting now. He said *he* didn't have a problem with his drinking, *I* did. It wasn't until a few years later that I found out about Al-Anon. If I couldn't convince your father to get some help, I could go to these meetings where people understood what I was going through, where we could give each other support and learn the best ways to deal with the people in our lives who were addicted.'

Anna looked straight at her mother. 'Why didn't you leave him then?'

'I kept telling myself he would get help one day, that he would realize the extent of his problem. But it never happened. Meanwhile, the abuse got worse and worse. Soon it happened every time we went out.

'When he humiliated me at the Holtons' garden party, I realized I wasn't doing him any favors by letting the situation go on. I was an enabler – that's the word they use at Al-Anon. I'd been an enabler for years. So I told him, it's the booze or me, take your pick.'

'What did he say?'

'That I was being foolish, making something out of nothing, creating a problem. Now I knew I had to follow through on my promise, to leave if he wouldn't get help. So I left,' she said, her eyes welling with tears, 'and here I am, sixty-three years old and alone, and I'll most likely remain alone.' She looked at Anna. 'All I asked was that he go to one Alcoholics Anonymous meeting. One meeting! That's not as bad as checking into a rehab clinic. But you see, even one meeting meant admitting he had a problem, and his pride wouldn't let him do that.'

'Are you going to divorce him?'

'No, of course not. There's still a chance he'll get the help he needs, and if he does, I'll go back to him, just as I've promised. I love him.'

After she had dropped her mother off at the apartment in Sutton Place, Anna called Wendell Chandler, except that this time she didn't bother blocking her number.

He answered on the third ring. 'This is Wendell Chandler.'

'Hello, Mr Chandler, this is Anna Winthrop.'

'Who?'

'Anna Winthrop, from the Sanitation Department. I came to see you last Friday.'

'Oh. Yes. What is it?'

'I have those die-cut postcards for you.'

'That's all right, I don't want them. Thank you for calling.'

'Wait. Hold it a minute, Mr Chandler. I think you're going to want to speak to me.'

'Oh, really? And why is that?'

'Because while you were away I had a nice little visit with your son. I'm absolutely in awe of his artistic talents.'

There was a very long silence. 'Where?'

'Someplace public. How about Bryant Park?' she asked.

'When?'

'In half an hour. At the back of the park, near the Grill.'

He was sitting on one of the thin metal chairs that dotted the park, near the walkway to the Bryant Park Grill but far where from anyone else was sitting. He saw her approach but didn't react. She grabbed another chair and pulled it over, placing it a few feet from his.

'What do you want?' he said.

She gazed up at the back of the New York Public Library looming above the Grill. Then she focused her gaze on him. 'I want the truth.'

'You mean you don't want to distribute my son's "product"?' he asked mockingly. 'How dare you see him when I'm not there?'

'Uh, excuse me, Mr Chandler, but Danny is twenty-one years old. Not a minor. He can do whatever he pleases, and so can I. That's his home as well as yours. He invited me in.'

His expression was full of hatred. 'So what truth do you want? It appears you already know everything.'

'Not quite. I want to know exactly what happened between you and Garry and Terrence.'

He looked away, then back to her. 'All right. Danny made the idiotic mistake of throwing some of his pictures into the trash. His "rejects." We always put our trash bags with the ones from the apartment building on the other side of the mews. We pile them against the back of the building. One morning about a week before I found Garry's body, he came by for the trash, grabbed that bag, and it tore. Out poured all of Danny's pictures, along with some mail I'd thrown away, addressed to me. Garry called his partner over and they both had a nice look.

'I wasn't home when this happened, but Danny was. He happened to be going out and as he crossed the courtyard he saw Garry and Terrence pawing through the garbage bag. He knew what they were looking at. He went over to them.'

'Another smooth move,' Anna said sarcastically.

'It was, actually. He knew what to do. He came and got me and I gave them some money to keep quiet.'

'And that was that?'

'Of course not. They said they would be back for more, but they never came back.'

'So what did you do?'

'I went looking for them. I went to your garage, had to go a few times before I found Garry.'

'What did he say?'

Chandler shook his head in wonder. 'He'd decided he didn't want any more money. He said it wasn't right, and he was tired of not doing what was right. He was going to return the money I'd given him and Terrence. And he was going to report us to the police.'

'Did he?'

He looked at her as if she were an idiot. 'Obviously not, or I wouldn't be sitting here talking to you, would I?'

'No, I suppose not. Why do you think he didn't do it?'

Again the disdainful look. 'Because he's dead, remember? Apparently he didn't get around to doing it before he died.'

'You mean before you killed him.'

He blinked. 'Excuse me?'

'It's perfectly clear. You and/or Danny waited for Garry to come in again for the trash, and when he went behind the apartment building, you grabbed him and dragged him behind that shed, where you killed him. You left his body there until it was dark. Then you carried it out to the center of the mews, so that you could discover it the following morning, thus deflecting guilt from yourself.'

'You're out of your mind.'

'Am I? Where were you the morning of July twenty-first?'

He thought for a moment. 'I . . . took Danny to buy some clothes.'

'Where?'

'Bloomingdale's.'

'Bloomie's opens at ten. Garry was killed around seven thirty. So you still haven't accounted for where you were when Garry died.'

'I am perfectly aware of when Bloomingdale's opens. I took Danny to breakfast first.'

'Where?'

He heaved a great sigh. 'A coffee shop I like on Madison Avenue.'

'Which one?'

'It doesn't matter because they won't remember. But it's a place called Annie's, at Fifty-Fourth Street. It was chaotic, as it always is on a workday morning.'

'You're right, they won't remember you, not because it was chaotic, but because you weren't there. You were hiding behind the apartment building, waiting for Garry.'

'Think what you like.'

'How interesting that you and Danny can alibi each other, yet no one can alibi both of you. I don't suppose you used a credit card at the coffee shop.'

'No, I paid cash.'

'Of course you did. And I don't suppose you bought anything at Bloomingdale's.'

'No, there was nothing Danny liked.'

'Of course there wasn't.'

'Listen, Anna,' Chandler said, trying another tack. 'I know you don't believe me, but neither Danny nor I killed Garry, and this will come out in the investigation. In the meantime, I am begging you not to report my son.'

'Your son! Your son *and you*. You knew all about what he was doing, which makes you complicit in it.'

'And what exactly was he doing? Creating scrapbooks for his own enjoyment. They never left the house.'

'Nope, sorry. In the eyes of the law it's still creating child porn, a crime.'

'Please. I don't care about me – if you have to report this, put it all on me if you like. But leave Danny out of this. Nothing will be served by putting him in prison. He's . . . troubled.'

'Duh!'

He closed his mouth. 'My wife died when he was seven. You have no idea what it's been like trying to raise him, be a good father. This . . . isn't the first time something like this has happened. When he was fifteen he was caught with a little girl behind some bushes in Central Park. Nothing had happened, thank goodness. Fortunately, I have the resources to—'

'Buy people off?' She leaned toward him. 'Mr Chandler, Danny needs help.'

'Help! In our society, "help" is prison, followed by having to register as a sex offender for twenty years. By then his life will have been completely ruined.'

'It will be completely ruined if you *don't* get him some help. And you're wrong about prison. I'm no lawyer, but so far what Danny has been doing is a victimless crime, in the strictest sense. Take him to a counselor. Danny will get the help he needs.

That's what a good father would do. Besides, you won't be around forever to protect him.'

'If I'm telling the truth that Danny and I had nothing to do with Garry's murder, and I promise to get him some help, will you let this go, leave us alone?'

'I can't answer that right now, Mr Chandler. But you should get him some help no matter what. Start by taking him out of the Holy Legacy Baptist Church and Bright Horizons.'

She left him then, simply got up and walked away. Strolling down the south promenade under towering sycamore trees with bark like camouflage, past the little French carousel, she thought about Danny Chandler and the help he needed, the help she fervently hoped he would get.

Immediately after roll-call the next morning, Anna pointed to Terrence and tilted her head in the direction of her office. With a worried look, he followed her.

'I made a mistake,' she said, sitting at her desk.

'A mistake?' he asked from the love seat.

'I said you were a bad liar. I was wrong. You are actually a very clever liar. When I asked you about collecting money for the Teamsters, you said you had no idea what I was talking about, but you picked up on it quite easily, then admitted that you and Garry hadn't really been collecting for the union but for yourselves. But that was all a big lie to cover up what really happened. You found that kiddie porn in Wendell and Danny Chandler's trash and took some money to keep quiet.'

'We were going to give it back, I swear,' Terrence said. 'Garry said he didn't want to do it after all. He said we had to give back the money, that he wasn't going down that road.'

'But you didn't give the money back.'

'We were going to, but then Garry got killed.'

'You have legs. What's stopping you from returning it?'

'You didn't give me a chance to tell you. I *am* going to give it back.'

'How much money did Chandler give you?'

Terrence looked down and muttered something.

'What? I can't hear you.'

'Two thousand dollars, a thou for each of us.'

'And you're going to give it all back to him, isn't that right?'

'I don't have Garry's share!' he protested.

'Then you're going to make it up on your own.'

'Yes, Anna.' He looked up at her. 'What are you going to do?'

'There are several things I should do. Like reporting you to the police, for starters. Blackmail is a crime.'

'But I'm going to give the money back!'

She ignored him. 'I should also write you up so that I can get you out of here.'

He drew back as if she had hit him.

'I don't want people on my crew who do things like that. The Sanitation Department doesn't want employees who do things like that.' She gazed at him in disgust. 'Shame on you.'

He hung his head. 'When are you going to write me up?'

'I'm not. I said I should, but I'm not going to.'

He looked up in surprise. 'Why not?'

'It's not because I want to do you a favor. It's for Danny Chandler.'

'I don't get it.'

'It's very simple. If I report your attempted blackmail to the police, or write you up with a recommendation for termination, I'll have to explain what Danny has been doing. But I don't want to do that. I want him to have a chance. His father has promised to get him some help. So in a strange way, you've done some good.'

'You've lucked out this time,' she said, rising and opening her door. 'But I'm going to be watching you, Terrence, watching you very closely. Pull another stunt like that and there will be no more second chances. Now get out of here.'

He stood and hurried out without meeting her gaze.

She was still churned up from her meeting with Terrence when she left the garage at two o'clock. Not feeling like going home just yet, she walked east on Forty-Third Street to Fifth Avenue, then headed north.

She loved window shopping on Fifth Avenue – Tiffany, Mikimoto, Piaget, Prada, Harry Winston, DeBeers, Cartier, Van Cleef & Arpels . . . She rarely bought anything, though of course she could if she wanted to. Could buy lots. But she had few places to wear pearls and diamonds and couture. It was fun just to look.

She cut across Grand Army Plaza, with its brightly gilded bronze statue of Union General William Tecumseh Sherman, and at the corner of The Plaza Hotel she crossed Central Park South and entered the park.

She made her way up one of the wide walkways in the cool shadow of lush trees overhead. She breathed deeply, walked a little more, sat down to rest on a bench. She felt better now, calmer.

A hand touched her shoulder. She spun around.

It was Danny Chandler.

She jumped up, stared at him, swallowed.

'I'm sorry,' he said, putting up his hands. 'I didn't mean to scare you.'

'What is it? You've been following me.'

'I just want to talk to you. I couldn't go into the garage. I wanted to see you privately. So yes, I followed you into the park. We can talk privately here.'

'What do you want to talk about?'

'Can you sit down a minute?' he said, coming around the bench and placing himself at the end farthest from her.

She sat back down at the other end, waiting.

'My father told me what you said,' Danny began. 'About how you might not report me to the police.'

'You and your father have to do your part, did he tell you that?'

'Yes, sure. I have to get some help.' He leaned toward her, an earnest look in his eyes. 'I *want* help. I know I've got some problems. Years ago I tried to tell my father I didn't think I was right in the head, that I had . . . urges. There was an incident. Did he tell you about that?'

'Yes,' she admitted, 'he did.'

'It was after that. I told him I couldn't guarantee I could stop, because when I did those things, it was like someone else was controlling me. Do you know what I mean?'

'Yes, I do. So why didn't he get you help?'

'He said it was best to keep it quiet, that that was why he'd paid all that money to the parents of the little girl I . . . was with. He told me that when I got those feelings I had to just stop myself.'

She shook her head. 'It's not as simple as that. You need counseling, maybe medication.'

'I know that. And now that you've spoken to my father, he knows that, too. He's agreed to take me to a doctor. So when you think about it, in a weird way those two sanitation guys finding my pictures was the best thing that could have happened.'

She gave her head a little shake. 'So why did you follow me? What is it you want?'

He rose. 'I just wanted to thank you.' He put out his hand. She took it.

'I wish you the best,' she said, and waited for him to leave, but he remained there, looking down at her. 'Is there something else, Danny?'

He hesitated, inhaled deeply. 'Why did you do that for me, Anna?'

She frowned. 'Why?'

'Yeah. You don't know me. Why didn't you report me to the police for making child pornography?'

'I thought that was clear. Your father must not have explained it. I want you to have a chance. What you did with that little girl was wrong, but otherwise you haven't hurt anyone. You've kept your pictures to yourself. Your father doesn't want you branded as a sex offender, someone people don't want living in their neighborhood. He wants you to have a chance, and so do I.'

'But you still haven't answered my question. Why *me?* I think I know. I saw how my pictures turned you on, how you looked at me down in my basement. You dig me, isn't that right? You want me.'

She stared at him in amazement. 'So that's why you really followed me.'

He gave a tiny shrug of admission. 'Like I said, I wanted to see you alone, and this was the only way.'

Now she rose. 'Listen, Danny. You are a very disturbed young man. I want you to have a second chance because you're young and haven't really hurt anyone and you deserve it. We all deserve a second chance. That's all.'

He lowered his head in embarrassment. 'I feel like a jerk.'

'You're not a jerk, you're troubled. That's why you're going to get help. Why you're going to destroy all the pictures and quit your jobs at Holy Legacy and Bright Horizons.'

'I've already done that.'

'Good. When your father makes an appointment for you with a doctor, make sure you keep it. Do whatever he or she says. Give yourself that chance.'

'I will. I promise. Thanks.'

Head still lowered, he walked away. She watched him until the path turned a corner and he was gone.

hollering into his cell phone. I'd never seen him so angry. He said Zeus's name. He was yelling at him.' Evelyn gave one decisive nod. 'I'm sure of it. Zeus killed my Garry.'

'Do you have any idea where I might find this Zeus?' Anna asked, drawing a surprised look from Kelly.

'I don't know where he lives, if that's what you mean. But there's a bar where Garry used to hang out.' She reached to the coffee table for a pen and a small pad of yellow paper with a border of red roses. 'It's called Horatio's, on 128th Street,' she said, writing this down. 'Maybe you should start there.'

Anna pocketed the slip of paper but didn't stand yet. She'd had an idea. 'Mrs Thomason, there's something I'd like to ask you about.'

Evelyn waited.

'Did Garry send you e-mail from Iraq?'

'No. I don't have a computer.'

'What about letters? Did he write to you that way?'

'Sometimes. Why?'

'Did he talk about his friends there, any soldiers he was close to?'

Evelyn thought for a moment, then shook her head. 'I honestly don't remember.'

'Do you still have his letters?'

'Of course I do. I'll never throw them away.'

'Would you mind if I looked at them?'

'Why?'

How to explain this? 'I'll check out this Zeus, but it's also possible Garry's murder had something to do with his time in Iraq. Reading his letters may give us a clue.'

'Yes, I see. Just a minute,' Evelyn said, and stood and walked briskly out of the room. She returned a minute or so later carrying a cigar box, which she handed it to Anna. 'Please be careful with them. They're very dear to me.'

Sitting on Anna's couch, Kelly had opened the cigar box and begun removing Garry's letters and placing them on the coffee table. 'There aren't many,' she called to Anna, who was in the kitchen making coffee.

'I guess that makes our job easier,' Anna called back. 'Though fewer letters means it's less likely we'll find something.' She carried in two steaming mugs and sat down beside Kelly.

NINE

'How's our Rembrandt of refuse?' Allen asked Anna the next morning as she walked down the corridor to her office.

'That's cute,' she said good-naturedly. 'It must have taken you a while to come up with that.'

'A few days,' he admitted. 'See how he's doing, move him along. I want to get this whole thing over with.'

She checked her watch. It was a few minutes past six. 'I doubt he's in yet.'

But he was.

'Don't you ever sleep?' she joked.

He was using duct tape to better secure the rose-fertilizer bags. He stopped what he was doing and looked at her thoughtfully. 'Not much, no. Sleeping isn't something I look forward to.'

'I don't understand.'

He stood, wiped his hands on his pants. 'Shelters are no fun, Anna. For the most part the people who run them mean well, but we're treated like cattle. Sometimes there aren't enough beds and you have to try another shelter. Once you do get a bed, there's a fair chance someone else in the room will try to steal from you while you're sleeping.'

She didn't know what to say. It hadn't occurred to her that Clive might be homeless. She realized now that she really hadn't thought about it at all.

'Don't be embarrassed. I'm not.' He gestured around him. 'This is a big step for me, the first time I've ever been taken seriously as an artist. I can't tell you how grateful I am to everyone here. My life up to now . . . well, it's not something I like to talk about. Too painful.'

Tears had appeared in his eyes and Anna felt her own welling up. She smiled kindly. Telling him to hurry up was the last thing she intended to do. 'We're happy to have you,' she said, and left the courtyard.

No wonder her Google search for his name had brought up nothing, she thought as she crossed the garage. The workers were getting into their trucks, heading out. To her surprise, Damian and Ernesto stood together, talking and laughing. Damian headed for his truck, where Terrence was already behind the wheel. Anna turned quickly so as not to make eye contact with Damian.

In her office she worked on preparing payrolls. A little after nine, her cell phone rang.

'Miss Winthrop?'

She recognized the voice. 'Mrs Thomason, how are you?'

'Can you come see me?'

'Of course. Is everything all right?'

'I need to speak to you.'

'I'll bring Kelly,' Anna said. When Evelyn paused, Anna asked, 'Is that all right?'

'I suppose she'll hear it sooner or later. Just come soon.'

'I can come right after my shift ends at two.'

This time there were no coffee things on the table in the living room. Evelyn sat with her legs tightly together, a slip of paper in her hand. Opposite her, Anna and Kelly waited expectantly.

'I've been going through Garry's things,' Evelyn said. 'You know, cleaning out his room, gathering up the stuff I want to give to Goodwill. I was cleaning out his nightstand and found this.' She handed the slip of paper to Anna.

Anna held it so Kelly could see it, too. It looked as if it had been torn from the edge of a sheet of newspaper. Someone had written on it in pencil: *Z $1000*.

Kelly wrinkled her nose. 'What does it mean?'

Evelyn turned to Kelly. 'There are . . . things you don't know about Garry.'

Kelly frowned. 'Like what?'

'He . . . was never happy. He always wanted more than I could give him.'

'More of what?' Anna asked.

'Money,' Evelyn answered flatly. 'I've never had much. My husband, Bill, died even before Garry was born. He worked for the Postal Service. He was hit by a truck and killed. I receive his death benefit, but it's not very much, especially these days. It's been all I could do to keep this apartment. Like I told you, my daughter, Roberta – Garry's mother – she died when he was a baby. So now that I'm older, I've had no one to take care of me except Garry. I think I was part of the reason he did the things he did.'

'What things?' Anna asked.

Evelyn pursed her lips, paused, then said, 'Before Garry left for Iraq, he was selling drugs.'

'No!' Kelly burst out. Anna put a restraining hand on her knee.

Evelyn was nodding. 'It's true. He and I never actually talked about it, but I knew what was going on. Knew why he was doing it, too. Suddenly he had money, lots of it. He began to dress better. He gave me money for food and rent and to buy myself things.'

'I just don't believe it,' Kelly said.

'Believe what you like. It's true. You and Garry weren't dating before he enlisted in the army. You couldn't have known him very well. Garry wanted to better himself, and it didn't matter how.'

'Why did you want to tell us this?' Anna asked.

'Because of that note I just gave you. There was a man who used to come here looking for Garry. I could tell he needed drugs. He was jumpy, intense. I hated it when he came here – he was ugly, with a horrible scar down the side of his face. He terrified me.'

'Do you think he wrote this note?' Anna asked.

'No, Garry wrote the note. The man's name was Zeus. "Tell him Zeus needs him," he would always say. I think this man Zeus owed Garry money. Z means Zeus, *$1000* means the amount he owed.'

Anna shook her head. 'I still don't see where this is going.'

'I'll spell it out for you. I think once Garry got back from Iraq, he found Zeus and demanded his money.'

Anna said, 'And you think that instead of paying Garry back, Zeus killed him?'

Evelyn nodded.

'It doesn't make sense,' Kelly said. 'Why would this man Ze[us] wait for Garry behind New Amsterdam Mews, kill him there?'

'It makes perfect sense,' Evelyn said. 'Why would he kill h[im] up here where everyone knows him? He must have watched Ga[rry] found out where he went on his route, and then grabbed him.'

Anna shifted uncomfortably on the sofa. 'Forgive me – I k[now] this is painful for you – but the way Garry was killed suggests vindictiveness. What I mean is—'

'I know what *vindictiveness* means.'

'Why would this Zeus have wanted to kill Garry that[?] Wouldn't the situation between them have been just busine[ss?]'

'You haven't seen Zeus. I have. He's mean, you can tell [just] by looking at him. You don't know what kind of relation[ship he] and Garry had. A few days before Garry was killed, I h[ad]

'I wish Garry and I had started dating *before* he went to Iraq,' Kelly said. 'Then he might have sent *me* some letters we could look through.'

'We'll just have to make do with what we have.' Anna took a few letters from the table and read one aloud:

Dear Grandma,

Everything is fine. It's hard here but there are things that make it seem worthwhile. Like when we patrol the city and people run out of their houses waving and smiling and yelling, 'Thank you!' Sometimes children come up to us and smile and thank us also. One little boy said to me, 'Thanks, mister!' and he saluted. We give the kids candy.

I miss you and hope you're doing all right. Don't forget to take your blood pressure medicine. How is your bridge club? There's a new romantic comedy with that actor you like, I can't remember his name. I know you don't like to go to the movies but maybe you could catch it on Pay-Per-View.

I feel like I'm doing something good here and that's a new feeling for me. But I also think about coming home and I'm excited about that too because I see my life going in a good new direction.

Love from,
Garry

When Anna looked up from the letter, Kelly was gazing at the table with a forlorn expression. Then Kelly gave her head a little shake and began reading a letter to herself. 'Pretty much more of the same,' she said when she'd finished.

Anna read another one. 'More small talk.' She looked at Kelly. 'Are these in chronological order?'

Kelly leafed through some of the letters on the table. 'No, all mixed up.'

'Let's put them in order,' Anna said, and gathered them all up. After a few minutes she had them arranged. 'Hold on a sec,' she said, and went into her bedroom. She came back with the two newspaper clippings she'd found in Garry's locker.

'What are you doing?' Kelly asked.

'Just seeing something.' She held out the articles. 'The story about Travis Brown's murder is dated November twelfth, 2009. What's the last letter before that date?'

Kelly started flipping. 'Here we go. October thirty-first.' She quickly scanned it. 'More of the same, but with Halloween touches. The soldiers gave extra candy to the kids. Garry and some of his buddies wore goofy masks to the mess hall. Funny picture.'

Anna smiled. 'What's the date of the next letter?'

Kelly flipped some more. 'November thirteenth. Shall I?' Anna nodded. Kelly read:

Dear Grandma,

Sad news. One of my buddies, Travis, I don't know if I ever mentioned him to you, is dead.

War is complicated in ways people never think about. Dangerous, too. There's more than one enemy.

I don't think I've ever said this to you, Grandma, but if anything should happen to me, please know that I love you.

Your grandson,

Garry

Anna met Kelly's gaze. 'He tells her Travis is dead but he doesn't say how it happened. From his letter you would think Travis died in the line of duty, not that he was murdered.' She shook her head. 'He intentionally omitted the details. He also wants her to know he loves her, in case he should die. Why is death suddenly on his mind? He's a soldier – death is always somewhere around. Why does he mention it now?'

'Because he's afraid he might die the same way Travis did. It's just as Julie Carson said. *More than one enemy . . .*'

Anna looked sharply at Kelly. 'What did you say about the Halloween letter?'

Kelly frowned. 'That they put on masks?'

'You said "funny picture."'

'Yeah, there's a photo here.' Kelly lifted out a Polaroid snapshot.

'Let me see that.' Anna took the picture from Kelly. It was a close-up shot of four soldiers in green and sandy-brown camouflage uniforms. They had their arms around each other's shoulders and were leaning toward the camera.

Kelly slid over and they looked at it together. 'Someone's written something here at the bottom,' Kelly said, pointing to some writing in pencil at the photo's lower right-hand corner. 'A four and an *M*.'

NINE

'How's our Rembrandt of refuse?' Allen asked Anna the next morning as she walked down the corridor to her office.

'That's cute,' she said good-naturedly. 'It must have taken you a while to come up with that.'

'A few days,' he admitted. 'See how he's doing, move him along. I want to get this whole thing over with.'

She checked her watch. It was a few minutes past six. 'I doubt he's in yet.'

But he was.

'Don't you ever sleep?' she joked.

He was using duct tape to better secure the rose-fertilizer bags. He stopped what he was doing and looked at her thoughtfully. 'Not much, no. Sleeping isn't something I look forward to.'

'I don't understand.'

He stood, wiped his hands on his pants. 'Shelters are no fun, Anna. For the most part the people who run them mean well, but we're treated like cattle. Sometimes there aren't enough beds and you have to try another shelter. Once you do get a bed, there's a fair chance someone else in the room will try to steal from you while you're sleeping.'

She didn't know what to say. It hadn't occurred to her that Clive might be homeless. She realized now that she really hadn't thought about it at all.

'Don't be embarrassed. I'm not.' He gestured around him. 'This is a big step for me, the first time I've ever been taken seriously as an artist. I can't tell you how grateful I am to everyone here. My life up to now . . . well, it's not something I like to talk about. Too painful.'

Tears had appeared in his eyes and Anna felt her own welling up. She smiled kindly. Telling him to hurry up was the last thing she intended to do. 'We're happy to have you,' she said, and left the courtyard.

No wonder her Google search for his name had brought up nothing, she thought as she crossed the garage. The workers were

getting into their trucks, heading out. To her surprise, Damian and
Ernesto stood together, talking and laughing. Damian headed for
his truck, where Terrence was already behind the wheel. Anna turned
quickly so as not to make eye contact with Damian.

In her office she worked on preparing payrolls. A little after nine,
her cell phone rang.

'Miss Winthrop?'

She recognized the voice. 'Mrs Thomason, how are you?'

'Can you come see me?'

'Of course. Is everything all right?'

'I need to speak to you.'

'I'll bring Kelly,' Anna said. When Evelyn paused, Anna asked,
'Is that all right?'

'I suppose she'll hear it sooner or later. Just come soon.'

'I can come right after my shift ends at two.'

This time there were no coffee things on the table in the living
room. Evelyn sat with her legs tightly together, a slip of paper in
her hand. Opposite her, Anna and Kelly waited expectantly.

'I've been going through Garry's things,' Evelyn said. 'You know,
cleaning out his room, gathering up the stuff I want to give to
Goodwill. I was cleaning out his nightstand and found this.' She
handed the slip of paper to Anna.

Anna held it so Kelly could see it, too. It looked as if it had
been torn from the edge of a sheet of newspaper. Someone had
written on it in pencil: *Z $1000.*

Kelly wrinkled her nose. 'What does it mean?'

Evelyn turned to Kelly. 'There are . . . things you don't know
about Garry.'

Kelly frowned. 'Like what?'

'He . . . was never happy. He always wanted more than I could
give him.'

'More of what?' Anna asked.

'Money,' Evelyn answered flatly. 'I've never had much. My
husband, Bill, died even before Garry was born. He worked for the
Postal Service. He was hit by a truck and killed. I receive his death
benefit, but it's not very much, especially these days. It's been all
I could do to keep this apartment. Like I told you, my daughter,
Roberta – Garry's mother – she died when he was a baby. So now
that I'm older, I've had no one to take care of me except Garry. I
think I was part of the reason he did the things he did.'

'What things?' Anna asked.

Evelyn pursed her lips, paused, then said, 'Before Garry left for Iraq, he was selling drugs.'

'No!' Kelly burst out. Anna put a restraining hand on her knee.

Evelyn was nodding. 'It's true. He and I never actually talked about it, but I knew what was going on. Knew why he was doing it, too. Suddenly he had money, lots of it. He began to dress better. He gave me money for food and rent and to buy myself things.'

'I just don't believe it,' Kelly said.

'Believe what you like. It's true. You and Garry weren't dating before he enlisted in the army. You couldn't have known him very well. Garry wanted to better himself, and it didn't matter how.'

'Why did you want to tell us this?' Anna asked.

'Because of that note I just gave you. There was a man who used to come here looking for Garry. I could tell he needed drugs. He was jumpy, intense. I hated it when he came here – he was ugly, with a horrible scar down the side of his face. He terrified me.'

'Do you think he wrote this note?' Anna asked.

'No, Garry wrote the note. The man's name was Zeus. "Tell him Zeus needs him," he would always say. I think this man Zeus owed Garry money. Z means Zeus, *$1000* means the amount he owed.'

Anna shook her head. 'I still don't see where this is going.'

'I'll spell it out for you. I think once Garry got back from Iraq, he found Zeus and demanded his money.'

Anna said, 'And you think that instead of paying Garry back, Zeus killed him?'

Evelyn nodded.

'It doesn't make sense,' Kelly said. 'Why would this man Zeus wait for Garry behind New Amsterdam Mews, kill him there?'

'It makes perfect sense,' Evelyn said. 'Why would he kill him up here where everyone knows him? He must have watched Garry, found out where he went on his route, and then grabbed him.'

Anna shifted uncomfortably on the sofa. 'Forgive me – I know this is painful for you – but the way Garry was killed suggests a . . . vindictiveness. What I mean is—'

'I know what *vindictiveness* means.'

'Why would this Zeus have wanted to kill Garry that way? Wouldn't the situation between them have been just business?'

'You haven't seen Zeus. I have. He's mean, you can tell that just by looking at him. You don't know what kind of relationship he and Garry had. A few days before Garry was killed, I heard him hollering into his cell phone. I'd never seen him so angry. He said Zeus's name. He was yelling at him.' Evelyn gave one decisive nod. 'I'm sure of it. Zeus killed my Garry.'

'Do you have any idea where I might find this Zeus?' Anna asked, drawing a surprised look from Kelly.

'I don't know where he lives, if that's what you mean. But there's a bar where Garry used to hang out.' She reached to the coffee table for a pen and a small pad of yellow paper with a border of red roses. 'It's called Horatio's, on 128th Street,' she said, writing this down. 'Maybe you should start there.'

Anna pocketed the slip of paper but didn't stand yet. She'd had an idea. 'Mrs Thomason, there's something I'd like to ask you about.'

Evelyn waited.

'Did Garry send you e-mail from Iraq?'

'No. I don't have a computer.'

'What about letters? Did he write to you that way?'

'Sometimes. Why?'

'Did he talk about his friends there, any soldiers he was close to?'

Evelyn thought for a moment, then shook her head. 'I honestly don't remember.'

'Do you still have his letters?'

'Of course I do. I'll never throw them away.'

'Would you mind if I looked at them?'

'Why?'

How to explain this? 'I'll check out this Zeus, but it's also possible Garry's murder had something to do with his time in Iraq. Reading his letters may give us a clue.'

'Yes, I see. Just a minute,' Evelyn said, and stood and walked briskly out of the room. She returned a minute or so later carrying a cigar box, which she handed it to Anna. 'Please be careful with them. They're very dear to me.'

Sitting on Anna's couch, Kelly had opened the cigar box and begun removing Garry's letters and placing them on the coffee table. 'There aren't many,' she called to Anna, who was in the kitchen making coffee.

'I guess that makes our job easier,' Anna called back. 'Though fewer letters means it's less likely we'll find something.' She carried in two steaming mugs and sat down beside Kelly.

'I wish Garry and I had started dating *before* he went to Iraq,' Kelly said. 'Then he might have sent *me* some letters we could look through.'

'We'll just have to make do with what we have.' Anna took a few letters from the table and read one aloud:

Dear Grandma,

Everything is fine. It's hard here but there are things that make it seem worthwhile. Like when we patrol the city and people run out of their houses waving and smiling and yelling, 'Thank you!' Sometimes children come up to us and smile and thank us also. One little boy said to me, 'Thanks, mister!' and he saluted. We give the kids candy.

I miss you and hope you're doing all right. Don't forget to take your blood pressure medicine. How is your bridge club? There's a new romantic comedy with that actor you like, I can't remember his name. I know you don't like to go to the movies but maybe you could catch it on Pay-Per-View.

I feel like I'm doing something good here and that's a new feeling for me. But I also think about coming home and I'm excited about that too because I see my life going in a good new direction.

Love from,

Garry

When Anna looked up from the letter, Kelly was gazing at the table with a forlorn expression. Then Kelly gave her head a little shake and began reading a letter to herself. 'Pretty much more of the same,' she said when she'd finished.

Anna read another one. 'More small talk.' She looked at Kelly. 'Are these in chronological order?'

Kelly leafed through some of the letters on the table. 'No, all mixed up.'

'Let's put them in order,' Anna said, and gathered them all up. After a few minutes she had them arranged. 'Hold on a sec,' she said, and went into her bedroom. She came back with the two newspaper clippings she'd found in Garry's locker.

'What are you doing?' Kelly asked.

'Just seeing something.' She held out the articles. 'The story about Travis Brown's murder is dated November twelfth, 2009. What's the last letter before that date?'

Kelly started flipping. 'Here we go. October thirty-first.' She
quickly scanned it. 'More of the same, but with Halloween touches.
The soldiers gave extra candy to the kids. Garry and some of his
buddies wore goofy masks to the mess hall. Funny picture.'

Anna smiled. 'What's the date of the next letter?'

Kelly flipped some more. 'November thirteenth. Shall I?' Anna
nodded. Kelly read:

> Dear Grandma,
> Sad news. One of my buddies, Travis, I don't know if I ever
> mentioned him to you, is dead.
> War is complicated in ways people never think about.
> Dangerous, too. There's more than one enemy.
> I don't think I've ever said this to you, Grandma, but if
> anything should happen to me, please know that I love you.
> Your grandson,
> Garry

Anna met Kelly's gaze. 'He tells her Travis is dead but he doesn't
say how it happened. From his letter you would think Travis died
in the line of duty, not that he was murdered.' She shook her head.
'He intentionally omitted the details. He also wants her to know
he loves her, in case he should die. Why is death suddenly on his
mind? He's a soldier – death is always somewhere around. Why
does he mention it now?'

'Because he's afraid he might die the same way Travis did. It's
just as Julie Carson said. *More than one enemy . . .*'

Anna looked sharply at Kelly. 'What did you say about the
Halloween letter?'

Kelly frowned. 'That they put on masks?'

'You said "funny picture."'

'Yeah, there's a photo here.' Kelly lifted out a Polaroid
snapshot.

'Let me see that.' Anna took the picture from Kelly. It was a
close-up shot of four soldiers in green and sandy-brown camouflage uniforms. They had their arms around each other's shoulders
and were leaning toward the camera.

Kelly slid over and they looked at it together. 'Someone's
written something here at the bottom,' Kelly said, pointing to some
writing in pencil at the photo's lower right-hand corner. 'A four
and an *M*.'

Anna nodded. The first soldier on the left wore a Richard Nixon mask. 'This is Garry,' she said, pointing to his right chest-pocket flap, which bore the name THOMASON.

The next soldier was Freddy Krueger from *Nightmare on Elm Street*. Anna read his pocket flap: BROWN. 'That's Travis.'

The third soldier was Homer Simpson. CARSON, his flap read. 'That's Ron,' Kelly said.

The fourth soldier wore a Dick Cheney mask.

'Kelly, it's the fourth man,' Anna said, and pointed to the pencil jotting at the bottom of the photo. 'Four-M. The Four Musketeers.'

Kelly froze. Together they leaned closer to read the name on the fourth soldier's right pocket flap: ANDERS.

'Who's Anders?' Kelly asked, wrinkling her nose.

'That's what we need to find out. You take the letters before November thirteenth and give me the ones after. Look for the name Anders.'

They started reading. 'Here it is,' Kelly said after a few moments. 'His name is Mort Anders.'

'What does Garry say about him?'

'Just that Mort is one of his friends.'

'See if he's mentioned anywhere else.'

Kelly looked up after a few minutes more. 'Garry mentions him three other times, but that's all he does – mention him. Always along with Ron and Travis. These four definitely were musketeers. How about your batch? Does Garry mention him?'

Anna was finishing with her pile. 'Not once. I find that odd, don't you? Not only that, but the tone of the letters changes after that dark one you just read. The cheerfulness is gone. The letters are shorter, sometimes only a line or two, as if he just wanted his grandmother to know he was still alive.'

'He knows Anders killed Travis. Is that what you think?'

'Yes, I do. I also think Julie's right about Anders killing her husband.'

'Do you think he also killed Garry?'

'I think it's highly likely. These three men knew the truth about what happened to Neda Majeed. Ron told his wife what happened, but he never told her Anders's name. So now Anders's secret is safe.'

Kelly shifted on the sofa, tucked her legs under her. 'It doesn't make sense, though, Anna. Anders may have killed Garry, but why would he have killed Yvette Ronson?'

'That's easy. To make Garry's murder look like the work of a serial killer.'

Kelly thought about this. 'Clever. And dangerous.'

'Extremely. This man must be approached with extreme caution.'

Kelly's eyes bulged. 'What do you mean, *approached*? You're not going to try to find him, are you? You just said he's dangerous.'

Anna's gaze wandered with her thoughts. 'Aren't all murderers?'

'So what are you going to do? How are you going to find him?'

Anna got her laptop from the bedroom and googled the name Mort Anders in New York City. Nothing came up.

'How do we know he lives in New York?' Kelly asked.

'That's the problem – we don't. Julie Carson said only that the musketeers all lived in the New York City *area*.'

'So how are you going to find him?'

'I'm not,' Anna said, picking up the Polaroid snapshot from the coffee table and staring down at it. 'He's going to find me.'

A large sign over the nightclub, painted to look like embossed brushed metal, said Horatio's. Below the sign, a red awning that ran the width of the club bore the words COCKTAIL LOUNGE – HORATIO'S – LIVE JAZZ. Beneath the awning, to the right of the club's entrance, tables had been set up within a low green canvas partition that separated the dining area from the rest of the sidewalk.

Inside the club, a bar ran along the right side and tables filled the left. The bartender looked over, sized up Anna and Santos, and gave one nod of greeting.

They found a table at the back, a bit too close to the jazz trio for Anna's taste, but the place was full. A waitress appeared. 'What can I get you?'

Anna ordered a Diet Coke and was surprised when Santos ordered a beer.

'But you're not really drinking it, right?' she said to him when the waitress had gone. 'I need you alert.'

'Uh, right,' he said, not looking too happy about it.

In a surprisingly short time the waitress was back, setting down their drinks.

'Thanks so much,' Anna said.

The waitress didn't reply, didn't even glance at them.

'Tell me . . .' Anna said. 'Any idea where I might find a gentleman named Zeus?'

Santos looked at her in surprise.

The waitress's gaze shifted to her suspiciously. Anna realized the tables around them had suddenly grown quiet.

'Don't know anybody by that name,' the waitress said matter-of-factly, setting down two napkins, and sauntered away.

'Well, that was smooth,' Santos said sarcastically. 'You certainly didn't waste any time.'

'And what would you have suggested? If they know him, they know him, whether I ask right away or wait half an hour.'

'And she doesn't know him. So now what?'

'She *says* she doesn't know him. The night is young.'

They sat quietly for a few minutes. Then Anna excused herself to go to the ladies' room. On the way she stopped at the bar.

'Pardon me,' she said, leaning forward.

The man came over. 'What do you need?'

'I just want to ask you a question.' He waited. 'I'm looking for a man named Zeus. I understand he comes here a lot. Any idea where I might find him?'

'No idea who you're talking about,' the bartender said, already moving toward another customer.

Anna persisted. 'When does he come here, usually?'

He stiffened, came back, leaned toward her. 'Honey, I just told you I don't know who he is. If I don't know who he is, then I'm not going to know when he comes in here, am I?'

'Of course,' she said. 'My mistake.'

She knew he was lying. His eyes had said it all. Everyone here must think Santos and I are cops, she thought. They're protecting Zeus. The bartender would no doubt let him know a woman had been asking for him. Which was fine, because it might bring Zeus to her.

She continued to the ladies' room. On her way back she saw the bartender watching her.

'What were you saying to him?' Santos asked when she reached their table.

'What do you think? I asked him about Zeus.'

'Another smooth move.' He sipped his beer.

'I'm sorry I asked you to come with me. You're no help at all.'

He set down his bottle. 'Anna, I'm sorry, but I don't think you're going to accomplish anything this way. You've got to be more subtle about it.'

'Oh really? Is that how the NYPD does it?'

'Actually, it—'

A woman was standing at their table. In her mid-twenties, she was petite and shapely in a skintight, impossibly short, plum-colored dress. Her skin was a deep mocha color, her features pudgy but pretty. She was holding a set of keys. 'Excuse me,' she said. 'I think you dropped these.'

Anna frowned up at her in puzzlement. 'No, I—'

'Meet me outside,' the woman said in a barely audible voice through clenched teeth. Then, more loudly, 'No problem,' tossed her keys on to the table, and walked away.

Anna met Santos's gaze. He raised his bottle, and when it was nearly at his mouth he murmured, 'Give it a minute.'

She nodded, made an effort to look casual, bobbed her head a little to the music, tapped the table.

Finally Santos set down his bottle and stretched. 'Ready to roll?'

'Sure,' she said, and followed him out.

'Sh-h,' Santos warned as soon as they were on the sidewalk. She nodded. She looked around. The woman was nowhere in sight.

'Let's walk a little,' he said, taking her hand, and they started down Broadway. As they walked, Anna scanned the street. Finally, when they had walked nearly four blocks, she spotted the woman on the other side, a bit farther ahead, walking slowly.

'Let's cross,' Santos said.

The woman kept walking and they followed her, keeping their distance. Abruptly she walked between two buildings and was gone. When they reached the spot and looked down the alley, she was nowhere in sight. Then suddenly she appeared at the other end, beckoning them to follow.

They hurried through the dark, narrow space. Emerging at the other end, they jumped. The woman was standing only inches away, leaning against the back of one of the buildings.

'Sorry 'bout the wild goose chase,' she said, 'but if anybody in there knew I was talkin' to you about Zeus I'd end up dead.'

'Who are you?' Santos asked, handing back her keys.

'My name is Darteesha.'

'Darteesha what?' Anna asked.

'Darteesha's all you need to know. I'm gonna tell you where you can find Zeus. Isn't that what you want?'

'Sure,' Santos said, 'but why do you want to help us?'

'You're cops, right?'

'No,' Anna said. 'What makes you think that?'

'Why else would you be lookin' for Zeus? Unless you're lookin' to score, but somehow I don't think so.'

'We just need to speak to him,' Anna said. 'We can make it worth your while.'

'Oh, yeah? How worth my while?'

Anna had come prepared. 'Fifty dollars.'

Darteesha made a pouty moue with her lips. 'Don't think that's worth my while.'

'Then what is?' Anna asked.

'Couple hundred.'

'I'll give you a hundred, that's my limit.'

'Deal.' Darteesha waited. Anna fished the money out of her purse and handed it to her. 'OK. He's been pumpin', works out of St Nicholas Park. You know where that is?'

'Sure,' Santos said.

'Go in at the bottom, at 127th Street. Walk into the park a little ways and you'll see this statue of a man and a dog on the right. Stand on the other side of the statue and Zeus will come to you. That's where his customers know to wait for him.'

'When?' Santos asked.

'Any night after eleven.' Darteesha grabbed Santos's wrist and twisted her head around to look at his watch. It was a few minutes to eleven. 'By the time you get there, he'll be on duty.'

'Why are you telling us this?' Anna asked. 'How do we know you're telling the truth?'

'Because whatever you are, cops or no cops, I know you ain't after Zeus Holden 'cause you wanna tell him about an inheritance or somethin'. He's in trouble, I know that. And I want him nailed in the worst way.'

'Why? What is he to you?'

'What is he to me? Nothin' anymore. He *was* my boyfriend. Told me he loved me, that he wanted to marry me, have a baby with me. And I believed him . . . until I happened to meet another girl he told the same things to. And I hear there are others. Man's a dog.'

'Then we'll be sure not to mention your name,' Anna said facetiously.

But Darteesha wasn't laughing. 'Do, and *I'll* be the one comin' after *you.*'

Anna felt Santos tense at the threat, but he held himself back. 'Thanks,' was all he said.

'You already thanked me,' Darteesha said, holding up the money,

then stuffed it deep into her ample cleavage. 'Go back out that way.'
She walked off into the shadows. Anna and Santos went back through
the alley to the street.

'I never thought I'd see someone do that in real life,' Anna said.
'Do what?'
'Stuff money into her cleavage.'
Santos laughed.
'What's pumping?' Anna asked.
'Selling crack.'
She nodded. After they had walked a little while he put his hand
on her arm and stopped her. 'This is no game, Anna.'
'Who said it was a game?'
'These people are dangerous. You can't just walk into a park
alone and meet a dealer, have a chat.'
'I have no intention of walking into the park alone,' Anna said,
and smiled. 'You'll be with me. At least, you won't be far.'

TEN

Entering St Nicholas Park, Anna glanced around and immediately spotted the statue of the man with the dog, far to the
right in the deep night shadow of a huge oak tree. She cast
a surreptitious look back at Santos, who stood across the street at
a bus stop. He saw her and nodded reassuringly.

She left the path and made her way to the statue. As Darteesha
had instructed, she walked to the far side, and found herself in a
sort of enclosure formed by the statue, the oak tree, and two waist-
high hedges. She leaned against the tree and stood perfectly still,
listening. For what seemed like forever, but was in actuality only
minutes, she waited. She was about to give up and go back to the
street when she heard footsteps behind her. She watched for a figure
in the shadows, but instead from behind her came a deep, gravelly
voice.

'What do you want?'
'What do you think I want?' she replied softly, turning. 'Show
yourself.'

He stepped around the tree and was before her, a pale-skinned
man of medium height, with deeply shadowed, sunken eyes.

He wore sweatpants and a dark T-shirt with a vest over it that flapped as he moved.

'Turn around, spread your legs.'

She had expected this. She complied and felt his expert hands quickly search her for a concealed weapon.

'All right,' he said, 'turn around again.' He took a step closer, leaving the shadow. Now the scar on his cheek came into clear view, thick and deep, running from his neck to his temple. 'Who told you to come to me?'

She shrugged. 'Word on the street.'

'That ain't good enough. I need a name, and I need it fast.'

She broke into a cold sweat, felt her heartbeat quicken. 'I didn't get his name. Some guy I met at Horatio's.'

He considered this, chewing his bottom lip. 'All right,' he said at last. 'So how much you want?'

'Actually,' she said, 'all I want from you is information.'

He drew his head back. 'What kind of information? What is this? You a cop?'

'No, Zeus, I'm not a cop. But I am investigating a murder.'

'Whose?' he demanded.

'Garry Thomason.'

'Ah, I see. Word on the street. I think I know who that word came from. Who are you?'

'My name is Anna Winthrop. Garry was . . . a friend of mine.'

'So what do you want with me? You think *I* killed him?'

'I don't know what to think. I understand you owed him some money.'

'Yeah, that's right,' he said, challenge in his voice. 'Since when's that murder?'

'Murder can be a handy way of avoiding paying someone back.'

'How do you know about the money?'

'That doesn't matter.'

'Garry called me, said he needed his money back. We were gonna meet, but he never showed.'

'You were going to pay him back?'

'Yeah . . . somehow.'

'What's that supposed to mean?'

'I was gonna offer him some o' my product instead.'

'Garry didn't use.'

'Says who?'

'Are you saying he did?'

'I know he did, once in a while. Leastways he did before he went off to Iraq. I thought maybe he had that traumatic syndrome – you know, where you're all stressed out and all. Figured some o' my product would be just the ticket.'

'Where were you the morning of July twenty-first?'

'How do I know? Sleeping, most likely.'

'Where?'

'In my girlfriend's bed. Is that enough information for you?'

'Sure . . . if she confirms it.'

'Well, you're gonna have to take my word for it, 'cause she ain't gonna confirm it.'

'And why is that?'

'Because she's a married lady. Her old man was on some business trip, so I came over to keep her company. She'll never admit she even knows me.'

'Why should I believe you?'

He shrugged. 'Because it's the truth.' He moved closer, his body blotting out the night. 'You're barkin' up the wrong tree, Goldilocks.'

'What do you mean?'

'There's one person who would've wanted Garry dead more than anybody else. She's the one you need to talk to.'

'And who is that?'

'Tally Klaw.'

'Who's Tally Klaw?'

'I'll let you find that out for yourself. Tally wouldn't appreciate me shootin' my mouth off.'

She gazed up at him suspiciously. 'And where would I find this man?'

'Woman. Least that's what most people think.' He chuckled softly. 'Where would you find her? Try Bedford Hills. But don't tell her Zeus sent you,' he said, turning away, and called back over his shoulder, 'or you and me'll have some real business to attend to.'

'I did some research on Tally Klaw,' Santos said the next morning, slipping into a booth at Sammy's, their favorite coffee shop, at West Forty-Fifth Street and Tenth Avenue. 'That's some name, Klaw. Anyway, Zeus was telling the truth. She's at Bedford Hills. She must be one tough customer.'

'Why is that?'

'It's the only maximum-security women's prison in New York

State. The state's largest women's prison, too. It's had a lot of notorious "guests."'

'Like who?'

'Ever hear of Pamela Smart? Woman in New Hampshire who conspired with her under-age boyfriend and three of his friends to kill her twenty-four-year-old husband. She got life in prison without the possibility for parole. Have you ever seen a movie with Nicole Kidman called *To Die For*? It's based on Smart's story.'

'Who else?'

'Carolyn Warmus, an elementary school teacher who killed the wife of a man who also taught in her school because she wanted to get closer to him. She got twenty-five years to life. She'll be eligible for parole in 2017. Several movies were made about that case.

'Let's see, who else . . .? Amy Fisher, you remember her, right? "The Long Island Lolita"? She's out now. And Jean Harris. Remember, she killed Herman Tarnower, the diet doctor. She's out.

'Sante Kimes . . . she and her son, Kenny – who was also her lover – killed an eighty-two-year-old socialite whose body has never been found. Sante was also convicted of killing a guy who was a family friend. She's serving two life sentences. Also Remy Ma.'

'The rapper?'

He nodded. 'Got eight years for assault, illegal weapon possession, and attempted coercion. And I've got one more for you. Nixzaliz Santiago, got forty-three years for failing to stop her husband from torturing and beating to death her seven-year-old daughter Nixzmary over a cup of yogurt and a broken printer.'

'So what's Tally in for?'

'She's serving twenty years for running a major shoplifting ring here in Manhattan.'

Anna frowned. 'What has that got to do with Garry?'

'That's what we need to find out, isn't it? I've made some arrangements. I can take you out there day after tomorrow – Sunday. You free?'

'You bet.'

'I need your help,' Allen Schiff said to Anna the next morning, dropping on to the love seat in her office.

She looked up and smiled. 'You've got it. What do you need?'

'An idea. Clive says his sculpture will be finished soon. Remember I promised him that when he was done, we'd find a way to let the public in to see his masterpiece? How do I do that?'

'Good question,' she said thoughtfully, 'since the only way to the courtyard from the street is through the garage. You must have had something in mind when you made him the promise.'

'No,' he said easily. 'I just wanted him off the sidewalk.' He rose. 'Let me know when you've come up with something.'

She stared at her desk for a few moments, then shook her head and went out to the corridor. Damian was standing there, as if waiting for her.

'Hey, Anna. I couldn't help overhearing what Allen said. I'll be happy to help if I can.'

'Thanks, Damian,' she said – not too effusively, she hoped. 'I need all the help I can get. How are we going to get people safely from the street to the courtyard?'

'I've got some ideas,' he said. 'Let me think about it and get back to you.'

Nothing inappropriate about that, she thought as she watched him walk away. Maybe he would be all right after all.

From a back table in the Au Bon Pain café in the Port Authority Bus Terminal's South Wing, Anna watched for Thad McCormack. She hadn't seen him in six years and wondered if he'd changed. She hoped so, for his sake.

'Anna.' She turned. Thad had come in from the side. He hadn't changed a bit. Only an inch or two over five feet – that wouldn't have changed, of course – he was still oval in shape, very wide at the middle, small at the feet and head. He was perhaps even balder than the last time she'd seen him, with a patchy fringe of hair and a few wisps in front that blew about in the breeze. He squinted at her through impossibly thick, black-framed eyeglasses.

She rose, took his hand. 'Thad, it's good to see you.'

He pulled out a chair and fell on to it. He wore an open-collar short-sleeve shirt, dark with perspiration at the underarms. Heavy beads of sweat ran down his neck, though it was cool outside. 'Good to see you, too, Anna.' He took off his glasses, squinted again. 'You look wonderful.'

'Thanks, Thad, so do . . . you come here very often?'

'Yeah, it's convenient. The paper's offices are on Ninth at Thirty-Sixth, so I can just pop right in here.'

'How's the job going for you?' The last time she'd seen him, he was still with the *New York Post* and had just landed his present job with the *Daily World*.

'It's OK. Are you eating anything?'

'No, just got some coffee. Can I get you something?'

'Yeah, they have this butter crumb cake that I like. It's on the other side. And a coffee, please, lots of cream and sugar.'

'You got it,' she said with a smile, and hurried away. She returned a few minutes later and set a tray before him.

'What about you, Anna? How's the job going for you?'

'Great. I love it.'

'If you don't mind my asking, how did this happen? I mean, you getting into sanitation?'

She smiled. 'I don't mind your asking. People ask me all the time. You know – daughter of a billionaire working with garbage.'

'You have to admit that it's kind of unusual.'

'Yeah, I guess. As you know, I went to U Penn, studied finance. After I graduated I moved to New York to look for a job. I had a room-mate, this girl from Brooklyn, and she told me she was going to take the civil service exam. She wanted to be a sanitation worker. Just for kicks, I went along with her and took it, too. Well, guess what. I got offered a job as a sanitation worker. She didn't. I took the job.'

'How did your family react?'

'How do you think? They were horrified, thought I'd lost my mind. They were also embarrassed. To this day Gloria tries to find other, more respectable ways for me to make a living.'

'So you just started . . . collecting trash?'

She nodded. 'Had a partner, rode on a truck, grabbed those garbage bags, and threw them into the hopper.'

'Was it difficult? I mean, you're not exactly muscle-bound.'

'Sure, it was hard at first, but you get stronger over time. That's what they call sanitation workers, New York's Strongest.'

'You can't actually enjoy this work.'

'You know, I do. A lot. I find it fascinating. New York City is one of the largest garbage producers in the world. We throw out enough trash every day to fill the Empire State Building. And it's my job to help make it go away. I suppose at first taking the job was a rebellion thing. I was actually embarrassed that my parents were so rich. I also wasn't interested in the kinds of careers they felt were suitable for me.'

She leaned forward on the table, smiling. 'But I didn't ask you to meet me so we could talk about my career choice.'

He took a huge bite of butter crumb cake. 'You said you had something you thought I could use for a story.'

'That's right. Do you remember a case last year about a US soldier in Iraq named Travis Brown?'

'Of course. It was all over the place. He raped and murdered that beautiful Iraqi girl. Neda Majeed, right?'

'Right, and then he got murdered himself.'

'That's old news, Anna,' he said through another mouthful of cake.

'Of course it is,' she said pleasantly. 'But I've got something new on it for you. A development.'

'Yeah?'

She nodded. 'I've got it on good authority that Travis Brown didn't rape and murder that girl.'

'Then who did?'

'Another man. But let me start at the beginning. There were actually four men involved. One man stood at a nearby checkpoint as a lookout. His name was Garry Thomason.'

'Wait a minute, that name is familiar, too.'

'He was a sanitation worker, a member of my crew.'

'Right, he was the Mews Murderer's first victim.'

'We'll talk about that in a minute. Two men stood guard outside Neda's parents' farmhouse. One of them was Travis Brown. The other was a man named Ronald Carson, who has since returned to the States from Iraq . . . and disappeared.'

'Disappeared?'

She nodded. 'Lived on Staten Island. Last seen by his wife standing outside a shed in their backyard. His keys and cell phone were found on the ground.'

'He was snatched.'

'Right – and he's dead, I'm sure of it.'

Thad's eyes narrowed shrewdly behind his thick glasses. 'You said there were four men.'

'Yes. The fourth man is the one who raped and murdered Neda. The other three men had no idea he was going to do that. They thought he was simply going to scare her to get back at her for humiliating him somehow.'

'If this fourth man did it, then why was Travis arrested, and why haven't we heard anything about the other two men?'

'Garry, who was at the checkpoint, slipped away unnoticed. The fourth man, the rapist-murderer, escaped through a back door.

Ron Carson went in when he heard Neda scream, saw what the fourth man had done, and also fled by the back door. That left Travis standing out front when the authorities arrived. They thought he was just coming out, and arrested him.'

'All right. So who is this fourth man?'

'I don't know his name,' she lied.

Thad stopped chewing. 'Then how do you know he exists?'

'From Garry's letters home.' She wouldn't mention Julie Carson. 'It was this fourth man who slipped into the base jail where Travis was being held and shot him. It was this man who I believe killed Garry Thomason. And it was this man who snatched and murdered Ronald Carson.'

'Because they could all implicate him.'

'Exactly. Now his secret is safe.'

'Unless you find out his name,' Thad pointed out. He took a big gulp of coffee, set down the cup. 'This is a serious allegation, Anna. Even the *Daily World* has its ethical standards.'

'It does?'

'Yes,' he said peevishly, 'it does. Do you think I would go to work for a paper that didn't?'

She just stared at him.

'At any rate,' he went on, 'I can't tell this story without attributing it.'

'Who told you not to attribute it? I'm your attribution.'

'*You?* Why would you want your name associated with this?'

'Because I want to flush out this man. And because I want the investigation reopened. I want justice for this monster.'

'And if you're wrong? If none of it went down the way you said?'

'That's what the reopened investigation will ascertain, won't it?'

He gave this some thought, looked at her. 'You have no idea where this man is?'

'Only that he's in the New York City area.'

'Are you saying this man is the Mews Murderer, that he also killed Yvette Ronson?'

'I think that if I'm right about his killing Travis, Garry, and Ron, then yes, he also killed Yvette Ronson to cover up what he'd done . . . make it look as if Garry was the victim of a new serial killer.'

'All right,' Thad said slowly. 'I hope you know what you're doing. Let's have all the details.' He pulled a notepad and pen from his pocket.

Twenty minutes later, he closed the pad. 'Why are you giving me this story, Anna? Am I the only reporter you know?'

She smiled. 'Not simply the only reporter. You're the only reporter I know whom I've known since the second grade. But I also owe you.'

'You mean because of Gloria?'

She nodded. 'If you hadn't done me a favor and killed that story about her visit to the nudist colony, people would still be laughing at her.'

'True. But I offered you a way to pay me back at the time, if you recall. All I wanted was to take you to dinner. But I know,' he said, putting up a hand, 'I'm not your type.' He looked himself over, brushed off some cake crumbs. 'I know what I am. Fat guy from a poor family in Flushing. Reporter for the worst rag in New York. I know.'

'Oh, Thad, don't be so dramatic. Haven't you ever been turned down for a date before?'

He frowned. 'I can't honestly remember the last time I asked anyone. So,' he said, changing the subject, 'how is Gloria?'

'Fine. She got married, you know.'

'I know, to a handsome plastic surgeon.'

'Mm. Donald Stone.'

'Are they happy?'

'Not sure. For now, I suppose.'

Thad gave a wistful shrug and rose. Anna rose, too, and came around and took one of his hands in both of hers. 'Thanks, Thad.'

He winked at her. 'Don't forget to buy tomorrow's edition.'

ELEVEN

'This isn't how I expected to spend my Sunday,' Santos said good-naturedly as he drove north on the Saw Mill River Parkway in New York's Westchester County the following Sunday.

Anna turned to him. 'I appreciate your coming with me. It's always nice to have a cop around.'

'I thought you didn't want me to be a cop today.'

'Well, officially, no. You're just my boyfriend.'

'Just your boyfriend, eh?' He smiled. 'I'd better give you the background on Tally Klaw. I read up on her last night.'

'Before you do,' she said, taking up a copy of the *Daily World*, 'I want you to hear something.' She began to read the article at the top of page 3:

NEW EVIDENCE IN MURDER OF IRAQI TEEN
Exclusive to the Daily World
NEW YORK, NEW YORK – New evidence has come to light in connection with the rape and murder of a young Iraqi woman and the US soldier accused of the crime.

On November 5, 2009, a 17-year-old Iraqi woman named Neda Majeed was found raped and murdered in her family's farmhouse near Baghdad. A US soldier, Travis Brown, was caught fleeing the scene and arrested. Six days later, Brown himself was shot to death in the cell where he was being held. His killer has never been apprehended.

The *Daily World* has now learned that, in actuality, four men were involved in various ways in Majeed's rape and murder, and that Brown did not commit the crime.

Brown was one of three men who were friends of the actual perpetrator, whose name is not yet known. He told the three other men that he intended to merely scare Majeed to get back at her for embarrassing him publicly.

Brown and another soldier, Ronald Carson, stood guard outside the front door of the farmhouse while their friend went inside. Another soldier, Garry Thomason, stood at a nearby checkpoint as a lookout.

When Brown and Carson heard screams from inside the house, Carson ran inside while Brown remained at the front door. Carson found Majeed's body in the kitchen. Her murderer had fled out the back door. Carson also fled.

When the authorities arrived after a neighbor reported hearing screams, they found Brown at the door and, thinking he was leaving the house, arrested him and charged him with the crime.

The *Daily World* has obtained this new information from Anna Winthrop, a garage supervisor for the New York City Department of Sanitation, who obtained it from Garry Thomason, who worked as a sanitation worker in Winthrop's section after his return from Iraq. Thomason was found murdered in New Amsterdam Mews on July 21, 2010.

Ronald Carson went missing from his home in the West Brighton area of Staten Island on Sunday, July 24, 2010.

Based on the information received from Thomason, Winthrop believes it was the fourth, unnamed man who killed both Brown and Thomason, and who kidnapped and probably murdered Ronald Carson.

Anna looked at Santos. 'What do you think?'

He was staring ahead through the windshield, aghast. 'I think you're out of your mind. Why would you do such a thing?'

'Isn't it obvious? To flush out this fourth man.'

'Oh –' he chuckled grimly – 'you'll flush him out. And if you're right about him, you'll be next. Has that occurred to you?'

'Of course.'

'And you're not worried?'

'No, because I'm going to be careful.'

'Unbelievable.' He honked the horn at a car encroaching into his lane. 'Here's something I bet *hasn't* occurred to you. How is Rinaldi going to react when she sees this story?'

She looked at him. 'I've done nothing wrong.'

'Except play detective, which she's warned you about.'

'Santos,' she said angrily, '*you've* been helping me "play detective"!'

'I know that, but behind the scenes. Up to now what you've been doing is also behind the scenes, for the most part. But giving a story like that to a sleazy tabloid is definitely *not* behind the scenes.'

'Oh, well,' she said airily, gazing out of the window, 'it's done. Let the chips fall where they may.'

For a little while they rode in silence, as Anna gave Santos time to calm down. Then she said, 'So, you were going to tell me about Tally Klaw.'

'Right,' he said, taking a deep breath. 'Let me start by saying that as a police officer, I see my share of shoplifting. It's become a special interest of mine. In New York City it's big business. Let me give you the background on how it all works.

'Let's start with the shoplifters themselves – or boosters, as they're often called. The ones Tally used were heroin addicts who steal daily to support their habit. They usually work in groups. For instance, three people will go into a Duane Reade pharmacy.

Two of them will create a distraction while the other one fills a bag with merchandise. Some top products are pain relievers, baby formula, glucose test strips for diabetics. The booster bags are lined with foil so they won't set off the theft detectors.'

'Where do they take it all?'

'To fences. They're all over New York, and some are in small stores in Philadelphia. They're always open – a place a booster can always go to trade stolen merchandise for money to buy drugs.'

'What do the fences do with all the merchandise?'

'At least once a week, it's taken by the fence or collected by a middle man and taken to a "repacker" for "cleaning" – removal of all identification tags. That's what Tally was, a repacker, though she ran all aspects of the operation. She had a whole warehouse full of stuff in the Bushwick section of Brooklyn.'

'What did she do with it?'

'Resold it through flea markets, swap meets, pawn shops, Internet auction sites. She got caught when one of her customers turned out to be an undercover officer in a sting operation.'

Anna sat quietly looking out the window.

'You OK?' Santos said.

She turned to him. 'I was just wondering where Garry fit into all of this.'

He shifted his gaze back to the road, passing a slow-moving car. 'We know he was dealing drugs. Was he also taking them himself? Was he one of Tally's boosters?'

'That's what we're here to find out.'

Leaving the parkway, they drove through the quaint village of Bedford, with its charming shops and boutiques, then into the countryside. They passed estates with mansions on rolling lawns, some with fountains or brick walls with gates. Vast horse farms rolled by.

Checking a map he'd printed out from the Internet, Santos turned on to Babbitt Road, then guided the car on to the drive leading to the prison. They parked in the visitors' lot. Getting out, Anna took in the facility's many buildings, some modern, others of old red brick. Coils of silver razor wire on thick fences ringed the property. Anna checked her watch. It was 8:00 a.m.

Getting out, they followed a path from the parking lot through a gate in a chain-link fence and up to the prison itself, an old four-story building of red brick with steeply pitched roofs and gables. High razor-wire barriers ran around it.

Once inside, they were led to a locker room where they were

told to lock up everything except money (including a quarter for the locker) and photo IDs. In the small visitors' check-in room they presented these IDs and were instructed to fill out two visitors' forms and provide their Social Security numbers as well as the license plate number of Anna's car.

Anna told a guard in a starched white uniform that they were there to visit Tally Klaw.

'What is the purpose of your visit?' the guard asked.

What to say? Thinking fast, Anna said, 'We're here to tell her about the death of a mutual friend, Garry Thomason.'

'Does she know you're coming?'

'No.'

'Then she'll have to approve the visit,' the guard said, and left. Five minutes later he was back. 'She says she'll see you.' He stamped Anna's and Santos's hands with fluorescent ink for future clearances, then said, 'This way.'

He ushered them into a cage roughly eight feet square, surrounded by more razor wire. Once the door was secured behind them, they were buzzed through a door in front of them. The guard led them outside into an area surrounded by fences, and along a garden path to one of the prison buildings. Inside, they walked down a hallway and finally into the visitors' room. It reminded Anna of a school cafeteria, with its standard-issue tables and chairs. Brightly colored posters decorated the pale-blue walls.

Anna and Santos sat on one side of a rectangular table, facing the entrance. Two tables away, a female inmate played Scrabble with a teenage boy, stopping frequently to press her hand down on his.

After a few minutes, two guards appeared escorting a woman in gray sweats and running shoes. She was of medium height, heavy except for skinny bird legs. She had large, coarse features and steel-colored hair that had been roughly chopped short. She sized up Anna and Santos as if to see if she knew them, then frowned, but nodded to the guards. They stepped back and she came forward.

Anna and Santos rose.

'Ms Klaw,' Anna said, 'my name is Anna Winthrop. This is my boyfriend, Santos Reyes. We're here to talk to you about Garry Thomason.'

'Yeah, that's what I was told,' she said, sitting. She laughed, looked around her. 'You think *I* killed him?'

'We're trying to find out who did,' Santos said.

'Why?' Tally asked flatly.

'He worked for me,' Anna said. 'In the Sanitation Department. I was his supervisor. I liked him. I want to know what happened.'

'We get newspapers in here, TV. I know all about it. Somebody grabbed him and stuck a piece of mirror through his eye into his brain.'

Anna winced.

'It's this . . . Mews Murderer,' Tally went on. 'That's who you're gonna need to find. But what's the difference?' she asked, eyes narrowing. 'Garry's gone.'

'I . . . just want to know,' Anna said, suddenly resentful that she felt she needed to explain herself.

'The cops haven't been here,' Tally pointed out.

Santos smiled. 'Let's just say we're a few steps ahead of them.'

Tally shrugged, looking bored. 'So what, exactly, do you want from me?'

Anna said, 'We want you to tell us about your connection to Garry.'

Tally laughed, her ample bosom heaving. 'My connection? He worked for me, that was the connection.'

'You mean, he shoplifted for you.'

'Shoplifted for himself, I'd say. Got paid nicely – all my boosters did.'

'What do you think he did with the money? Don't most of the boosters buy heroin?'

Tally nodded. 'They're all addicted to it. That's why they boost. But not Garry. He was in it purely for the money. When he first started working for me, he told me he was sick of never having any money. He wanted to make some real cash, have all the things other people had.'

Santos leaned forward, his arms on the table. 'Word on the street is that you had Garry killed.'

Anna expected a violent reaction from Tally, but all she did was raise her shoulders once in a mild chuckle, as if having people killed wasn't an unusual thing. 'And why would I do that?'

'You tell us.'

'Hey, I'm not the one who told you that. Who did, by the way?'

'We can't say.'

'Probably one o' my competition. But –' she shook her head – 'nah, it wasn't me. Coulda been, but it wasn't.'

Anna frowned. 'Could have been?'

Tally folded her arms. 'A few months before Garry enlisted in the army, he came to me. He said he'd decided to get clean and he wanted out of my operation.'

'What did you say?'

'I laughed in his face.'

'Why?' Santos asked.

'I can't have people just *leaving*, shootin' their mouth off when they feel like it. Most of them die eventually. But this kid wasn't an addict and he wanted to quit workin' for me? I don't think so.'

'So what did you tell him?'

'What I just told you. That he couldn't quit.'

'Or else . . .'

Tally leveled a steely gaze. 'Or else.'

'What was his answer?' Santos asked.

'He never gave me one. One day somebody told me he'd enlisted. So I made myself a mental note to get his answer from him as soon as he got back. He came home two months ago.'

'I don't understand,' Anna said. 'You're in here. How could Garry have continued to work for you?'

Tally gave her that look again. '*I*'m in here. That don't mean I don't have people workin' for me on the outside. I sent one o' these people to talk to Garry, see what he'd decided. He said he needed a little more time. Weeks passed . . . no answer. So I told this person to go back and talk to him again. Then I hear he's dead. Guess he did get out after all. Shame.'

'What's a shame?'

'I hate to lose him. He was one of my best workers. With that handsome, honest face, no one ever suspected him.'

'How do we know you're telling the truth?' Anna said. 'How do we know Garry didn't give you his answer . . . and pay the consequences?'

The corners of Tally's mouth rose in a tiny smile. 'You don't.'

A guard approached the table. 'Time's up.'

Tally stood. 'Well, it's been a real treat, Anna, and . . .?'

'Santos.'

'Santos. Do come see me again.'

Her chest heaved in another chuckle as she was led away.

Anna had promised her father that she and Santos would swing by for a visit on her way home from the prison, since Greenwich was only half an hour from Bedford.

This time they found him at the back of the house, sitting in an Adirondack chair on the terrace overlooking the rolling lawn. 'They let you out!' he joked as they made their way toward him. 'How was the prison visit?'

'Interesting,' was all Anna wanted to say about it. She and Santos took chairs on either side of him. Anna noticed a glass of amber liquid and ice in her father's hand. 'Dad, what are you drinking?'

He looked up cheerfully. 'Oh, this? Whiskey and water. Would you like one?'

'No, we wouldn't like one.'

'Oh.'

Alma, a maid who had been with the Winthrops for years, came toward them from the house. 'Hello, Anna. Santos. Can I get you something?'

'A lemonade would be lovely, thank you, Alma,' Anna said.

'And you?' Alma asked Santos.

'The same, thanks.'

'Teetotalers,' Jeff remarked. 'Anna, why are you staring at me?'

'Because I can't believe you're for real.'

'I beg your pardon?'

'Daddy, either you're in complete denial or you just don't care. Mother has left you. Don't you miss her?'

'Of course I miss her. I wish she hadn't done this. I can't wait for her to come back.'

'She's not coming back unless you do something about your drinking.'

Jeff rolled his eyes heavenward. 'Not that again. *My* drinking. And what is it that I am supposed to do?'

'It's very simple. Get some help.'

'That won't be necessary. I am perfectly capable of stopping on my own.'

Anna gave him a pitying look. 'No, Daddy, you're not. That's the problem. Why don't you try a program and see how it goes?'

Alma brought Anna and Santos their lemonades. Jeff was silent until she was gone. Anna noticed that his eyes had welled with tears. 'That's just it, you see,' he said softly. 'I'm afraid that even if I get help, I still won't be able to stop.'

'Oh, Daddy,' Anna said, taking him in her arms. 'Of course you're afraid of that. But take it a step at a time. That's what they say at Alcoholics Anonymous meetings, isn't it? One day at a time. That's

all Mother is asking. That you try. Why don't you go to an AA
meeting?'

'I would be happy to come with you, sir,' Santos said solemnly.

Jeff smiled. 'You're a good man, Santos. But if I do this – and
I do mean *if* – I've got to do it alone.'

On Monday morning, Anna was crossing the garage toward
her office when Allen Schiff came up to her. 'Have you figured
out how we're going to get people into the courtyard to see the
masterpiece?'

She smiled. 'I wish you wouldn't call it that. He might hear you.'

'He's not here. He's out foraging. Well?'

'Actually, I have figured it out.' Damian had never come to her
with any ideas. 'I think we should make a walkway from the street
to the courtyard using retractable belt posts. I thought about using
street cones, but the belts will do a better job of preventing people
from straying from the walk. We could run the walk as close to the
outer walls of the garage as possible, for safety.'

His face lit up. 'Like at Disney World!'

'Exactly. Except that we won't be charging admission.'

'We won't have long lines, either,' he said dryly.

'Allen . . .'

'OK, OK. Brilliant idea. Now where are we going to get the
posts?'

'I've seen them used at Headquarters.'

'Of course. We'll borrow some of them. Let me get on that.' He
hurried away.

Anna went to her office. Someone had left a note on her desk
that Damian had called in sick.

She decided that while she was waiting for the belt posts, she
would map out the walkway's route. She found some chalk in the
storeroom and, starting at the street, began to draw lines as close
to the perimeter walls of the garage as possible.

As she neared the courtyard, her cell phone rang.

'Anna?' came a whisper.

She didn't recognize the voice at first. 'Evelyn?'

'Anna, I've seen him. On the street. There are things I haven't
told you. Please, can you come here?'

'Evelyn, *who* have you seen?'

Evelyn hung up.

Anna's heart was pounding. She dialed Santos. 'Evelyn Thomason needs help. I'll explain later. You've got to send someone up there.' She gave him the address. 'Hurry.'

'All right, I'll have a car sent up. I'll come by for you and we'll head up there, too.'

She hurried outside, not bothering to tell anyone she was leaving. In less than a minute Santos drove up in a patrol car and she jumped in. On the way uptown she called Evelyn's number. The phone just rang and rang.

There were already two police cars in front of Evelyn Thomason's building. Anna and Santos hurried through the lobby into the elevator. Upstairs, as they stepped out into the corridor, they saw that Evelyn's door was open. A uniformed officer stood nearby. Santos went up to him. Their eyes met. The officer slowly shook his head.

Santos looked at Anna. 'Stay here.'

'No.' She followed him in and immediately saw Evelyn's legs protruding from behind the sofa. A cop was standing over her. 'Don't touch anything. ME's on the way, and two detectives.'

Anna and Santos exchanged a look. 'Which detectives?' Santos asked.

'Roche and Rinaldi,' the officer said. Then, with a smirk, he added, 'I ought to say it the other way around, right? She's definitely in charge.'

As the cop wisecracked, Anna gazed down at poor Evelyn Thomason. She stared vacantly at the ceiling. Dark bruising encircled her neck.

'Why Rinaldi and Roche?' Santos asked.

'Because they're on the Garry Thomason case and this is his grandmother.'

Santos nodded. He looked up, glanced over at the apartment door. 'Guy broke in?'

The cop shook his head. 'She let him in.'

'Let's go,' Santos said to Anna. 'Nothing we can do here.'

'What's the rush?' she asked.

'I don't want to be here when Rinaldi and Roche get here.'

Remembering what he had said about Rinaldi's likely reaction to the story in *Daily World*, she nodded. As they started back down the hallway, something half under the door of Imogene Small's apartment caught Anna's eye. It was a small folded piece of paper, yellow with a border of red roses, and it looked familiar. Then Anna remembered. It was the same as the paper on which Evelyn had jotted down the address of Horatio's.

'Are you coming?' Santos asked, turning to look back at her.

Quickly she glanced up and down the corridor to make sure no one else was watching. Then she grabbed the note, tucked it into her pocket, and hurried after Santos.

His eyes were wide. 'What are you doing?'

'Come on,' was her only reply, and she and Santos hurried out to the car. As they rolled away from the curb, Rinaldi and Roche pulled up behind them.

As they drove along Amsterdam Avenue, Anna brought out the note.

'Why did you take that?' Santos asked.

'Because it's a note from Evelyn.' She fished around in her other pocket and found the slip of paper with the address of Horatio's. 'See,' she said, holding them both up. 'The same.'

'So?'

'So . . . I don't know. Maybe this will tell us something.'

Santos shook his head as Anna unfolded the note and read: *I. No more $. Do what you like. I don't care any more. E.*

'Sounds like blackmail to me,' Santos said.

'Turn around.'

TWELVE

A police officer still stood at Evelyn Thomason's door, but it was a different one from before. Rinaldi and Roche were inside Evelyn's apartment.

Anna knocked on Imogene Small's door. When she opened it, her eyes grew round and wide. She waited, saying nothing.

'May we speak to you for a few moments?' Anna asked.

'Sure, sure,' Imogene said in her raspy voice, and held the door open for them to come in.

Her apartment was as spare and minimalistic as Evelyn's was overfurnished and cluttered. On a low table of light wood sat a very new, very expensive plasma TV set. The sofa and chairs facing it were high-priced Italian modern in cream leather.

'Please,' she said, indicating the sofa, and Anna and Santos sat down. 'Coffee?'

They both smiled and shook their heads.

Imogene lowered herself on to one of the chairs. 'I can't believe what's happened to poor Evelyn,' she said, removing a small hand-kerchief from a pocket of her skirt and dabbing the inner corners of her eyes, though to Anna her eyes looked quite dry. 'Who would do such a thing?'

Santos opened his mouth to speak, but before he could, Anna said, 'We don't know yet, Ms Small.'

'Strangled, I understand.'

Anna gave her a small, professional-looking smile. 'I'm afraid we're not authorized to talk about that.'

'I understand.' Imogene knit her brows. 'Then why . . .?'

'Why do we need to speak to you?' Anna said. She brought out the cryptic note from Evelyn and held it up. 'We found this under your door a short time ago. We'd like you to tell us what it means.'

Frowning in puzzlement, Imogene took the note and read it. When she looked up her eyes were huge again. 'I have no idea,' she said, her voice low and full of wonder. 'Where did you say you found this?'

'Under your door.'

'This morning?'

'That's right.'

'You know,' Imogene said, turning her head a little to one side, 'I don't think that's right, you just taking something, a private note to me, from under my door.'

Santos said in an official-sounding monotone, 'This is a homi-cide investigation, Ms Small,' and Anna looked at him in surprise.

'That's right,' she said. 'Needless to say, a note Ms Thomason wrote shortly before she died is pertinent to our investigation.' She leaned forward, a searching look in her eyes. 'You're certain you don't know what the note means?'

Imogene held her plump chin in her thumb and forefinger and concentrated. 'You know,' she said after a few moments, 'I think I do know what it means. Evelyn told me she'd been having money problems lately. You see, our rent just went up. Evelyn lived on her late husband's death benefit and that was it. So things were tight for her. That's what she meant by "no money." She had no more for this month.'

'What about "do what you like"?' Santos asked.

'I was getting to that. Evelyn and I belong to a bridge club. We all take turns hosting. She and I always hosted together – either in her apartment or mine, but we always paid for the refreshments and prepared them together. This month it was our turn. So in her note Evelyn means she's out of money and that I should do what I like in terms of getting ready for the club meeting – I should choose the food, the dessert, and so on.'

'Why did she say "I don't care any more"?' Anna asked.

'Why do you think?' Imogene asked. 'She'd just lost her grandson. He'd been murdered. She was terribly depressed. She told me she didn't care about anything any more, that he had been all she lived for.' She folded her hands in her lap and smiled sadly. 'And now Evelyn has been murdered, too. Do you think she was killed by the same person who killed Garry?' Before either Anna or Santos could reply she said, 'Oh, that's right, you're not authorized to talk about it.'

'Exactly,' Anna said, and shifted on the sofa. 'While we're here, Ms Small, what can you tell us about Garry?'

Imogene tilted her head to one side. 'In what respect?'

'What kind of a young man was he?'

'I would say quiet. Secretive, really. He was always like that, ever since he was a little boy. Evelyn used to say "Garry plays it close to the vest."'

'You've known him for that long?' Santos asked.

'Oh, yes, since he was born.'

'Then you knew about the accident?' Anna said.

Imogene looked confused. 'What accident?'

'The car accident that killed his mother, Roberta. Evelyn's daughter.'

'Oh, yes, of course. That was horrible. But Evelyn did a wonderful job raising him. There was no sacrifice she wouldn't make for him.'

'How did Garry and Evelyn get along?' Santos asked.

'Oh, he was as devoted to her as she was to him. He would do anything for her. After all, she'd brought him up. She was the only family he had.'

Santos said, 'Mr Goldblum, who lives on the other side of Ms Thomason's apartment, told us he'd heard Garry and his grandmother arguing two nights before Garry was murdered. You must have heard it, too.'

She drew down the corners of her mouth, shook her head. 'Yes, of course I would have. When did you say it was?'

'The night of July nineteenth, a Monday.'

'Oh, I was out that night. Monday nights I go to my book group meeting.' She smiled pleasantly. 'Was there anything else you wanted to ask me?'

'No, not for the moment,' Anna said, rising. Santos followed suit. 'But if we think of anything else, you can rest assured we'll be in touch.'

Back outside, they were getting into the car when they heard a car horn honking loudly behind them.

'Oh, no,' Santos said, looking in the rear view mirror.

Anna spun around in her seat. Another patrol car had pulled up behind them and Rinaldi and Roche were getting out and walking quickly toward Anna's door.

'What if we just took off?' Anna said to Santos.

'Not funny,' he said, his expression grim. 'You'd better talk to her.'

'All right, but don't you dare leave my side.'

She got out as Rinaldi approached. Roche stood back a few yards, watching. Anna noticed he was holding a folded copy of the *Daily World*.

Rinaldi said, 'Well, if it isn't our star reporter.'

'Listen, Rinaldi, I've done nothing wrong. I'd appreciate it if you'd get out of my face.'

Rinaldi's jaw dropped. She shifted her gaze to Santos, who now stood next to Anna. Then she looked back at Anna. 'No, *you* listen, Winthrop. First of all, it's *Detective* Rinaldi. Second, I will get in your face and stay there as long as I please. I am a homicide detective and I am investigating not one but three murders. Now, what have you got to say for yourself?'

Santos took a step forward. 'What are you, her kindergarten teacher? Like she just told you, she's done nothing wrong. She had new information about the Travis Brown case and gave it to the press.'

'The press!' Rinaldi laughed. Behind her, Roche wheezed along with her. 'That's debatable. But it's not the point.' She turned to Anna. 'Along with your scoop about Brown was a whole new theory about Garry Thomason's murder. I've told you before and I'll tell you again, you are *not* a cop. You are not even a Sanitation cop. Why can't you get that through your thick head?'

Roche wheezed out another laugh. Suddenly Santos took a few fast steps toward him. 'You shut your mouth, Muttley, or I'll shut it for you.'

Roche jumped back in surprise.

'Whoa, whoa,' Rinaldi said, 'OK, calm down, everybody.' She turned back to Anna. 'Bottom line, you are not to feed to the press

any more of your theories relating to pending police investigations.
Is that understood?'

Anna stood her ground. 'I'll do anything I please. This is America.
As *I've* told *you* before, when the police aren't conducting an investigation properly, not following up on the obvious leads, I will. And
as long as I don't break any laws or interfere with your investigation, there's nothing you can do about it.'

Rinaldi smirked. 'Think you're real smart, don't you? Well, I got
a news flash for you, sweetheart. If your little theory is correct, and
this "fourth man" is guilty of everything you claim he is, then he's
coming after you next, and when he kills you, don't come running
to me.'

Anna, Santos, and Roche all frowned in puzzlement.

'You know what I mean!' Rinaldi blurted out. 'You'll have brought
it all on yourself.' She looked at Santos. 'Get her out of my sight.'

Anna and Santos got into his car. As they pulled away from the
curb, Anna saw Rinaldi and Roche walk back into Evelyn
Thomason's building.

That night, in St Nicholas Park, Anna waited in the darkness of the
oak tree, her gaze darting from the statue of the man with the dog
to the surrounding vegetation. The air was cool and very still. She
could smell earth and freshly cut grass.

There was a rustling in the bushes and Zeus stepped into view.

He scrunched up his face in disgust. 'Oh, man! You again?'

She emerged from the shadows, no longer afraid of him. 'Yeah,
me again.'

'What do you want?'

She stepped forward so that they were only a few feet apart, and
glared up at him. 'I want to know why you killed her.'

'Killed who?'

'You know who.'

He glanced impatiently about. 'Listen, lady, I'm workin' here.
State your business or get out of my office.'

'You strangled Evelyn Thomason because you found out she was
the one who sent me to you.'

'Oh, so it *was* her. But I didn't kill her. You know why? Because
I didn't kill Garry, so there wasn't anything Evelyn could say that
would hurt me. But you think what you like. Meantime, *I* got a
bone to pick with *you*.'

'And what is that?'

'Why'd you tell Tally Klaw I sent you to see her?'

Her eyes widened in surprise. 'I didn't!'

'Then who did?'

'I swear, I didn't say a word. She wanted to know, but I wouldn't tell her.'

Zeus stared at her as if trying to decide whether to believe her. His gaze shifted to the trees and shrubbery, deep in shadow. 'She's got people everywhere,' he whispered. 'One of them came to see me at Horatio's, said that if I sent her any more visitors I'd be out of business. You know what that means. If you're smart, you'll get out of this neighborhood and never come back, leave this whole thing alone.'

'I have no reason to be afraid of her or her people. You're the one with things to hide. Where were you this morning between seven thirty and eight thirty?'

'Is that when the old lady got killed?'

She nodded.

'Well, we're outta luck again, because I was with my lady friend, and she ain't talkin'. I'm gone.'

And in an instant, he was.

When Santos opened the door of his apartment to Anna, his smile turned into a frown of concern. 'What's wrong?'

'Nothing? Who said anything was wrong?'

'You don't need to say it. I can see it in your eyes. Where have you been?'

She fell on to the couch. 'Talking to Zeus Holden.'

'What?' He sat down beside her. 'Why?'

'Isn't it obvious? He killed Evelyn Thomason.'

'Did he admit that?'

'No, he didn't need to.'

'Then how do you figure it?'

'Evelyn told me and Kelly about Zeus owing Garry money. Zeus found out she told us. He had to shut Evelyn up, stop her from connecting him to Garry.'

'But this theory is based on the assumption that Zeus killed Garry.'

She frowned. 'I think he did.'

But Santos didn't look so sure. 'Does it really make sense? I mean, if Zeus had wanted to kill Garry, why would he have hidden behind New Amsterdam Mews and grabbed him there? He's not exactly someone who fades into the woodwork. Several hundred people live in that apartment building. No one would have forgotten seeing him there . . . and no one did see him, as far as we know.'

'Just because no one saw him there doesn't necessarily mean he wasn't there. And why wouldn't he kill Garry that way? It's a place he knew Garry would be. There's nothing private about a sanitation worker's route.'

'All right, let's suppose for a second that Zeus did kill Garry. Then why did Zeus kill him that way? Why did he feel the need to hide his body for hours until dark, so he could carry it out to the middle of the courtyard? And why would he have killed Yvette Ronson? Because that's the theory, right? That the same person – this "Mews Murderer" – killed both of them?'

Anna thought about this. 'All of that remains to be found out.'

He shook his head. 'Did you tell him we went to see Tally?'

'No, why would I tell him that? Besides, he already knew.'

'What?' She nodded. 'How?'

'This Tally apparently has very long "klaws."'

He took her in his arms. She nestled up against him. 'I don't like it when you do dangerous things,' he whispered, his face close to hers.

Their lips met, parted. As they kissed she ran her hands through his wonderfully thick black hair. Gently she pulled away. 'Well, I'm safe with you now,' she said in a low voice, and smiled. 'Protect me.'

At five o'clock the next morning her phone rang. 'Anna?'

'Daddy? Are you all right?'

'Yes, of course. Why?'

'It's kind of early.'

'I know you leave for work in a little while.'

'What's up?'

'Anna, when you were here on Sunday, Santos offered to take me to an AA meeting. It was extremely kind of him, but he's not family – not yet, anyway – and I don't know that I would feel comfortable.'

She smiled into the phone. 'Daddy, would you like me to take you?'

'I know I said I had to do it by myself, but . . . would you?'

'Of course. Just say when and I'll be there.'

'Actually, there's one at seven o'clock tonight at Christ Church here in Greenwich. I know it's short notice.'

'No, it isn't. I'll pick you up at six. And, Daddy?'

'Yes, dear?'

'I'm proud of you.'

After roll-call, Anna grabbed her chalk and finished mapping out the route for the walkway. Near the doorway to the courtyard she straightened up and saw Damian coming toward her wheeling a baby carriage. He was smiling. 'It's not what you think,' he said.

'I should hope not. What gives?'

'It's for Clive. Someone on my route threw it out. It'll look great on his sculpture, don't you think?'

She shrugged. 'You'll have to ask Clive.'

With a cheerful smile he rolled the carriage past her and out to the courtyard. A few minutes later, she was returning from the ladies' room when she saw Damian coming from the direction of the courtyard, still wheeling the carriage. His expression was glum.

'What happened?'

'He didn't want it.'

'Why not?'

'He said, "Thanks, but *I'll* decide what goes into my art."'

'Well,' she said, smiling at him, 'it was a good thought.'

She went out to see Clive. He was hunched over the sculpture and spun around when he heard her come in. 'Good morning,' he said.

'Good morning. I see you've been busy.' Next to the split mannequin he had added an old discarded computer. 'Wouldn't the baby carriage look nice next to the computer?'

'No,' he said, a stern look in his eyes, 'it would not. I'm sure Damian meant well, but as I told him—'

'I know, you'll decide what goes into your art.' She gazed down at it. She had decided it was the most monstrous-looking thing she'd ever seen. 'When will it be finished?' she asked brightly.

'I don't know yet. I'll let you know when it is.'

Clearly he didn't want company. She slipped out and returned to her office.

When Anna got home that afternoon, there was a message on her answering machine from her sister Gloria. 'Hey, could you give me a ring as soon as you get in? Thanks.'

Anna frowned. She had detected a definite tension in Gloria's voice. Anna called her sister's cell. 'Hi, what's up?' she said.

'Hold on, Anna, let me go somewhere quiet.' Gloria was a doctor at a large family medical practice on the Upper East Side. The sounds of many voices faded away and she came back on the line. 'That's better. Anna,' she said, a challenge in her voice, 'Daddy told me you're taking him to an Alcoholics Anonymous meeting tonight.'

Anna frowned, puzzled. 'Yes, that's right. What about it?'

'Why are you doing that?'

'What? Why wouldn't I do it? He asked me to. I'm delighted to go with him. Aren't you proud of him? I certainly am.'

There was a pause. Then Gloria said carefully, 'I'm proud of him for wanting to get help, but this is hardly appropriate. You must see that.'

Anna shook her head. 'See what?'

Gloria let out a grunt of frustration. 'This garbage business has really changed you, Anna. You're all . . . democratic now. Well, let me spell it out for you. If it gets out that Daddy is attending these meetings, we'll be the laughing stock of New York. I don't want to be an item in Cindy Adams.'

Anna couldn't believe what she was hearing. 'Gloria,' she said, her voice rising, 'you are actually more selfish and self-involved than I thought you were. First of all, it won't get out. These meetings are private, confidential – you must know that. Second, even if it *did* get out, since when is it embarrassing to admit you need help and get it? This is America, remember? Land of the second chance. Third, what Daddy does or doesn't do has nothing to do with you. If you're embarrassed by something he does, that's your problem. Don't be so . . . codependent!'

'No, I'm sorry, Anna,' Gloria said, her voice quiet now, 'it's you who has the problem. Doing this sanitation work has warped your sensibilities . . . stripped away your dignity. You really don't see what I'm saying.'

'No, I don't. Even if I did, what would you suggest? That Daddy just not go? That he drink himself to death? Lose Mother?'

'*Hello?* Haven't you ever heard of rehab? I've compiled a list of suitable places. I have it right here, in fact. There's the Betty Ford Clinic. Promises. The Meadows. Wonderland Center. Beau Monde—'

'I don't want to hear any more,' Anna said firmly. 'If Daddy says he wants to go to one of these clinics, I'll be the first person to volunteer to take him. But right now he wants to go to AA, and I'm not going to do or say anything to discourage him. What he needs right now is our unconditional support. I'm warning you, Gloria, if you start giving Daddy any of this nonsense, I'll . . .'

'You'll what?'

Anna opened her mouth but couldn't think of an answer. 'Goodbye, Gloria,' she said, and hung up.

That night at six she rang her father's doorbell. He opened the door himself.

She gave him a kiss on the cheek. 'Don't you look nice.' He wore Dockers and a crisply pressed navy-blue polo shirt, and smelled of his long-time favorite cologne, 4711.

'I wasn't quite sure what to wear to one of these things.'

'I don't think it matters. But you look terrific. Ready to go?'

He nodded. 'I told the staff I was taking you to dinner,' he said in a low voice.

She refrained from saying he hadn't really needed to tell the staff anything.

'Would you believe I'm nervous?' he said as she guided the car off the front drive and pulled on to the road. 'I've run a multimillion-dollar corporation and I'm nervous.' He shook his head, laughing.

She gave him an affectionate smile. 'It's normal, Daddy. I'm sure the meeting will go wonderfully.' A thought occurred to her. 'You're sure I'm allowed to go to this meeting with you?'

'Oh, yes, absolutely. I checked. It's an open meeting. That means anyone interested can attend.'

'I'm interested.'

They rode in silence for a few minutes. Then her father turned to her. 'Did Gloria call you?'

'About what?' she said lightly, eyes on the road.

'About my going to AA instead of one of these fancy celebrity rehab places?'

'Did she call *you*? I told her not to. When was this?'

'This afternoon. She said she tried to talk some sense into you, but that you've become hopelessly egalitarian.'

'I'm so sorry, Daddy. You need our support and Gloria's worried about being embarrassed in the gossip columns.'

He waved the idea away. 'You don't think I took what she said seriously, do you? That's just Gloria, always worried

about what people will think. It's why she married a promi-
nent plastic surgeon who's good-looking but has no personality,
why she had him do all that unnecessary work on her face,
why she's embarrassed by what you do for a living.' He laughed.
'She's always been that way, always will be. I know I'm doing
the right thing.'

A few minutes later they pulled up in front of the church. The
meeting was in an all-purpose room in the basement. Chairs had
been arranged in a large circle. Most of the seats were already
occupied. Anna estimated there were about twenty people in all.
There were young people with spiky hair, mature seniors with
silver hair, and seemingly everything in between. As Anna and
her father took their seats they were met with warm, welcoming
smiles.

At precisely seven o'clock a middle-aged man with a light-
brown beard stood and welcomed everyone. 'Good evening. My
name is Barry, and I'll be leading the meeting tonight.' A number
of people called out greetings to Barry. When the chatter had died
down, he said, 'Our meeting tonight will last one hour. I'd like
to begin by reading the AA Preamble.' He opened a book and
read: '"Alcoholics Anonymous is a fellowship of men and women
who share their experience, strength and hope with each other
that they may solve their common problem and help others to
recover from alcoholism. The only requirement for membership
is a desire to stop drinking."'

Anna sneaked a look at her dad. He was listening intently.

Barry continued, '"There are no dues or fees for AA membership. We are self-supporting through our own contributions. AA
is not allied with any sect, denomination, politics, organization
or institution; does not wish to engage in any controversy; neither
endorses nor opposes any causes. Our primary purpose is to stay
sober and help other alcoholics to achieve sobriety."' He smiled,
looking around the room. 'And now a moment of silence.'

Jeff looked uneasy as the people around him and Anna simply
sat in quiet contemplation.

'I would like to welcome you all to Alcoholics Anonymous,'
Barry said. 'This is an open AA meeting, meaning that any member
of the community, alcoholic or non-alcoholic, may attend. We ask
only that all who share limit their discussion to problems and solu-
tions related to alcoholism, and that you do not disclose the names
of AA members outside the meeting.

'Now,' he said, looking around the room, 'is there anyone here for their first AA meeting?'

A young woman across the circle raised her hand. 'I'm Jessie.'

'Hi, Jessie!' everyone said in unison.

Anna met her father's gaze. She gave him an encouraging smile. He hesitated, then tentatively raised his hand. All heads turned to him.

'Hello. I'm Jeff.'

'Hi, Jeff!'

Anna put her arm around him and squeezed. He was looking down, embarrassed.

'Now let's *all* introduce ourselves,' Barry said, and everyone took turns around the circle.

'We have a speaker tonight,' Barry said brightly. 'His name is Jonathan and he's going to tell us about his experiences with alcohol and how they affected his business career.'

A man a few seats away whom Anna hadn't noticed before raised his hand and smiled. 'Hi. My name is Jonathan and I'm an alcoholic. My sobriety date is the tenth of April, 2000.'

'Hi, Jonathan!' everyone said.

Anna guessed him to be in his early seventies – her father's age. He had short-cropped gray hair and a handsome face. Calmly and easily, as if he were speaking to a group of old friends, he talked about years of hiding his drinking at work . . . and about how it became increasingly difficult to hide. He talked about a mortifying experience at an important trade show, and about how when he got home he drank even more and nearly killed his wife and son in a car accident. He talked about finally "giving in" and joining AA, and how the recovery process went for him. Finally, he talked about what sobriety had meant to him personally.

Jeff Winthrop sat as if transfixed.

'Thank you,' Barry said when Jonathan was finished, and others chimed in with their thanks. Anna looked at her father. He was still looking at Jonathan, brows lowered in thought.

A basket was passed into which each person dropped a dollar or two. Anna reached for her purse as her father reached for his wallet.

'First-timers usually don't contribute,' the woman on Anna's left said softly, and she and her father put their money away.

Barry said, 'Now let's stand and join hands for the Serenity Prayer.'

The man to Anna's left gently took her hand. Anna saw the woman to her father's right take his hand.

Together the group recited: 'God, grant me the serenity to accept, the things I cannot change, courage to change the things I can, and wisdom to know the difference.'

'What's the most important thing we can do for ourselves in achieving sobriety?' Barry asked.

Everyone answered together: 'Keep coming back!'

The meeting over, Barry invited everyone to stay for refreshments. Anna saw that a table at the back of the room had been set up with coffee, tea, soft drinks, and cookies.

Assuming her father would want to leave right away, she stood and started for the entrance. She felt his hand on her shoulder and turned.

'Let's stay a few minutes,' he said.

She gave an enthusiastic nod and watched him approach the speaker, Jonathan. Jeff's voice was low but Anna heard what he said: 'I want you to know your story meant a lot to me. I also come from a business background. I see now that my experiences haven't really been very different from yours.'

Jonathan beamed. 'We're all in this together, aren't we?' He put out his hand. 'Jonathan.'

'Jeff.'

Anna chatted with a young married couple who had come to the meeting together, while her father spoke further with Jonathan. After a few minutes the two men shook hands again and her father came over to her. 'Ready to go?'

The night was cool and fresh, a breeze stirring the trees. Anna inhaled deeply. 'Beautiful night.'

'A very beautiful night,' her father agreed as he got into the car.

'So what do you think?' she asked him after they had been on the road for a few minutes. 'Do you think you might go back?'

'Well, it seems apparent that you've got to keep coming back, as they said, to make this program work. Jonathan said I should shoot for attending a meeting every day for ninety days.'

'Really? Ninety days? That's a tall order.'

'No, it isn't. What else have I got to do? And what could be more important? This could bring your mother back to me.'

He had turned to look out the window, but Anna could see the tears welling in his eyes.

THIRTEEN

'Darling,' Tildy said when Anna picked up the phone the next morning, 'this killer is gaining speed. I want you to be extra careful. Maybe you should come live here at the apartment with me.'

'Mother,' Anna said, sitting up and rubbing her eyes. She checked her bedside table. It was a few minutes before five. 'What are you talking about?'

'This Courtyard Killer – no, Mews Murderer, that's what they're calling him. Now that he's struck a third time, we definitely know this is his pattern, killing people in courtyards and such. I know you go to a lot of these kinds of places in your work – you know, when you're collecting the rubbish – so I wanted to warn you to be careful.'

'I don't collect trash any more, Mother, not for years. I'm a supervisor.' She yawned, stretched. 'What third time?'

'Oh, really, dear, you are very dense this morning. Turn on your TV.'

She grabbed the remote from her nightstand and switched on the set on her dresser. A pretty newscaster was speaking into the camera.

'. . . called the Mews Murderer appears to have struck again. Early this morning the body of Horace Beaumont, a fifty-six-year-old professor at New York University School of Medicine, was found in Washington Mews, a courtyard north of Washington Square Park that connects Fifth Avenue and University Place. The mews is open to pedestrian traffic from seven a.m. to eleven p.m. The body was found by a resident walking her dog.'

Now a middle-aged woman with flyaway brown hair was on the screen, a microphone in front of her face. 'Well, I was walking my dog and she suddenly got all crazy. She dragged me over to a window well in front of my building, and there he was. It was horrible. Who's next? This city isn't safe . . .'

'Anna, are you there?'

'Yes, sorry, Mother.'

'Did you see it?'

'Yes. I need to go.'

'Wait, I want to ask you something. I understand you visited

your father on Sunday.' Anna hadn't told her about the AA meeting
and had no intention of doing so. It wasn't her place to tell.

'That's right. How did you know?'

'Your father told me.'

Anna smiled. 'So you're speaking.'

'To a certain degree. I called to remind him to take his glau-
coma medication. How did he seem?'

'With respect to what?'

'I don't know – in general.'

'He misses you terribly.'

'And I miss him. But this is for his own good.' Tildy sniffed. 'I
know he's afraid of facing this problem. I think he's afraid it may
not help him.'

'Did he tell you that?'

'No, but I know him. Better than he knows himself.' Tildy began
to cry. 'But he's got to go anyway. He's got to make a start.' She
quickly said goodbye and rang off.

Anna immediately dialed Santos. 'I just heard.'

'I was about to call you.'

'How was he killed?'

'You really want to know?'

'Of course I do.'

'An ice pick driven into the back of his head into his brain.'

She drew in her breath. 'He was a professor?'

'Mm. At NYU Medical School. That's all we know as of yet.
I'll come by for you at the garage at noon and we can have a look.'

Washington Mews was a block-long alley with charming two-story
buildings of brick and stucco on either side. Anna and Santos entered
through the gate at the University Place end. A cop whom Santos
knew shook his hand and let him and Anna through.

Just ahead on the left was the red-brick and wrought-iron facade
of La Maison Française, NYU's French studies department. A few
doors beyond that was a window well with a black, waist-high
wrought-iron railing encircled with yellow crime-scene tape. Anna
peered down and saw the large gated windows of the basement
apartment. A large aluminum pipe ran the length of the well, just
above its dirty concrete bottom.

'The body would have had to be thrown over this railing,' Anna
said.

'Once again, no sign of it being dragged,' Santos said. 'This place is open from seven to eleven. Whoever did this must have come in with the body between nightfall and eleven. No one saw anything suspicious. All kinds of people walk through here all day – faculty and other university personnel, students, people who work in the area, tourists.'

'I heard on the radio that New York University own this mews,' Anna said.

'That's right.'

'And the victim was a professor at NYU Medical School. That's got to be significant.'

Two figures were walking toward them from the Fifth Avenue end of the mews. 'Oh no,' Santos said under his breath. It was Rinaldi and Roche. Under her blue blazer, Rinaldi was wearing a V-cut blouse that actually showed some cleavage.

'Well, look who's here,' she said. 'The detective wannabes.'

Roche laughed silently.

'Yeah,' Santos said. 'We wannabe, 'cause you're not.'

Roche stopped laughing. Rinaldi's face grew red. 'What do you mean, we're not?'

'It was Anna who started pursuing the pattern – long before you guys were willing to even entertain the idea.'

'That's not true. I just said that two cases don't make a pattern. Three do. So now it's a pattern.'

'Very good. Maybe you'll catch up to us some day.'

'Catch up?'

'We're way ahead of you.'

Anna shot him a warning look.

Rinaldi caught it. 'Just what have you two been up to?' She turned to Anna. 'You playing detective again? We've spoken to you about that.'

Anna shrugged. 'As I told you, I'm not breaking any laws. That's all you need to know.' She cocked her head in the direction of University Place and she and Santos started to walk away.

'I'm warning you two,' Rinaldi called after them. 'Get in my way and you'll be sorry you ever started this game.'

They didn't stop walking, didn't even look back.

They bought sandwiches and ate them in Washington Square Park on a bench near the Tisch Fountain, recently moved to align with Washington Arch.

'What could Garry, Yvette, and this Horace have in common?' Anna wondered aloud.

'As far as we've been able to tell, there's nothing connecting Garry and Yvette. The only way to know whether there's any link between Yvette and Horace, or between Garry and Horace, is to find out more about Horace. I'm sure even Rinaldi and Roche will know to do that.'

'Maybe,' Anna said. 'But I'm convinced they rarely ask the right questions.'

The office of Nolan Stewart, New York University's associate dean for graduate medical education, was on the first floor of the Langone Medical Center, at East Thirty-Third Street at First Avenue. Stewart, a tall, lanky man in his fifties with a boyish smile and a shaved head, sat down behind his desk after Anna had taken the guest chair.

'I appreciate your seeing me,' Anna said.

'Not at all,' Stewart replied. 'My reasons are largely selfish.'

'I don't follow you.'

He leaned forward, resting his hands on the desk and intertwining his fingers. 'I don't know if you're aware that NYU owns Washington Mews.'

She nodded.

'For some time there's been a debate over whether it should remain open to the public. Some of our faculty and their families live there, and they have professed to feeling unsafe.'

'But the mews *is* closed at night,' Anna pointed out.

'Yes, but from eleven p.m. to seven a.m. A lot can happen between nightfall and eleven . . . as we've now seen. I need to be armed with as much information about what happened as possible. From what you said on the telephone, it sounds as if you may be able to help me.'

Anna smiled. 'We may be able to help each other. If you don't mind my asking, what information did the police share with you?'

He let out a dismissive laugh. 'None. The detective on the case is an insufferable woman, incredibly rude.'

'Detective Rinaldi.'

He nodded. 'You know her?'

'Our paths have crossed a number of times, most recently because of the murder of my crew member, Garry Thomason.'

'Yes, of course. At any rate, she was willing to tell me nothing at all, said she would ask all the questions.'

'So what did you tell her?'

'Horace Beaumont was a professor in our medical school. I had met him, of course, but didn't know him well. I've spoken to his colleagues and apparently no one knew him well. He was a widower, a loner. He did not live in Washington Mews, as some of the news reports are incorrectly reporting.'

'If none of his colleagues knew him well, then I assume no one knew of anyone who might have wanted to hurt him.'

'No.'

'Does the name Yvette Ronson mean anything to you?'

He shook his head. 'Should it?'

'No, not necessarily. She was the Mews Murderer's second victim.'

'Yes, that's right, the woman found in Amster Yard. As far as I know, she had no connection to our school. As to a possible connection to Professor Beaumont, I have no idea.'

Anna nodded thoughtfully. 'Have you ever heard the name Jared Roberts?'

Stewart searched his memory, finally shook his head. 'I don't believe so. Who is he?'

'Off the record?'

'If you wish.'

'Someone tipped the police that he's the Mews Murderer, and even gave his address in Princeton. But when the police got there, he'd cleared out without leaving a trace. He's also lived a trace-free life, which in itself is interesting.'

'So the police haven't found this man?'

'No.'

'But you're saying it's this man who may have killed Professor Beaumont and also Miss Ronson and Mr Thomason.'

'That's right.' Suddenly an idea occurred to her. 'NYU owns the mews.'

'Yes, that's why you're here, remember?'

'No, what I mean is, doesn't the university have surveillance cameras everywhere? Most universities do these days.'

Now it was Stewart who sat up. 'Of course. What a fool I've been not to think of it. The police didn't think of it, either. We have over five hundred surveillance cameras on university-owned property, which of course would include Washington Mews.'

'You think there's a camera there?'

'Oh, absolutely. The German, Irish, and French studies departments are all there. Plus we have faculty housing. As I mentioned, we've had complaints over the years from residents who don't feel safe because the mews is open to the public. So we have cameras there as a way of making it safer without locking it up full-time.'

'How can we have a look?'

Stewart was already on his feet. 'Come with me.'

He led her out of his office and down the corridor to the elevator, which they took to the building's top floor. Here they followed a narrow hallway to a door on the end marked SECURITY. Stewart knocked on the door, then opened it and preceded Anna into a small office containing a desk and a wall of live video feeds. At the desk sat a petite woman in her forties with a long brown braid trailing down her back. She wore a blue uniform and cap.

'Dr Stewart,' she greeted him.

'Molly, this is Anna Winthrop. She's here about the murder in Washington Mews.'

Molly's face darkened. 'Horrible thing.'

'We have a camera in the mews, yes?' he asked.

'Absolutely. It's mounted at the top of the Fifth Avenue gate, way to the side where it's hard to see. But it gets a clear view all the way down the mews to University Place.'

'Excellent. Can we look at some recordings?'

She gave him a pitying look. 'You don't think I've already done that, sir? I did it myself, and then I did it again for the police. Came up blank. Guy's a magician.'

'So the police did think of it,' Stewart said to Anna. Then he turned back to Molly. 'Humor us.'

'No problem. You want the camera I just told you about, right? What time period?'

Anna said, 'My bet is that he dumped the body after dark. This time of year, that's around nine. Can we see footage from then until eleven when the mews closes?'

'You got it,' Molly said, and deftly worked the controls on her desk console. 'OK,' she said after a few moments, 'I'm going to run it on the first screen, second row up. Starting at nine p.m. on Tuesday, August tenth.'

As Anna watched, the screen went dark, then came to life with a full but dim and slightly distorted view of the mews from the Fifth Avenue end. Molly had it running at regular speed. A couple with a stroller came into view and headed down the center of the paved roadway. Far down, at the University Place gate, a woman in a suit entered and walked briskly along the south sidewalk until she was out of range again. Others came and went – tourists, people clearly with destinations in mind, people entering the various buildings.

'Can you speed it up a bit?' Stewart asked Molly.

'Sure.' She turned a knob and people started walking faster. Meanwhile, the screen grew darker and darker.

A woman appeared from the dimness at the far end and moved especially fast toward the camera. 'Jogger,' Anna said.

Fewer people appeared as the time grew later. Two young men with backpacks. An elderly man walking a tiny dog. A woman eating what looked like a slice of pizza as she walked. A man in a wide-brimmed hat and trench coat pulling a large black suitcase on wheels.

'Stop,' Anna said. Stewart turned to her. She pointed. 'Interesting.'

'What?' Stewart and Molly asked in unison.

'That this man would choose to take his wheeled suitcase through the mews, with its uneven surface of Belgian blocks.'

'Maybe he's never been through there before,' Molly said. 'So he wouldn't have known about the rough pavement.'

'And there is a sidewalk on each side,' Stewart pointed out. 'Maybe he's going to use one of them.'

Anna nibbled her lower lip, thinking as she studied the screen. 'That was a hot night. No rain in sight. Yet he's wearing a hat and a long trench coat. Don't you find that odd?'

They both shrugged.

'Can you please start it up again, but at regular speed?' Anna asked Molly. The image came back to life. The man continued with his suitcase down the very center of the roadway. 'If he's never been through there before and didn't know about the rough road, he doesn't seem to mind it, even though he's certainly having a hard time.'

It was true. At times the man tugged on the suitcase to get it over a particularly rough spot on the paving blocks.

'The suitcase is heavy, can you see that?' Anna said. 'If it were light it would bounce up sometimes on the rough surface.'

'And he's not using either sidewalk,' Stewart observed. 'But why?'

Anna said, 'Maybe because there are dozens of windows along those sidewalks and he doesn't want to be seen up close.'

They continued to watch. Far down the mews, as the man approached the window well on the right, he slowed.

'He's going over to the railing,' Stewart said, and they all moved closer to the screen.

As they watched, the man veered over to the window well and stopped. Though he was far from the camera now, they could see him looking up and down the length of the mews.

'There's no one else on the street,' Stewart said.

'Perfect,' Anna said.

What the man did next was not clear at such a distance and in the near-dark. He appeared to open his coat so that it obscured the suitcase. Then he busied himself at the railing of the window well.

Whatever he was doing, it was over in less than fifteen seconds. He buttoned his coat and pulled his suitcase the rest of the way along the mews, exiting at the University Place gate.

'That's him, isn't it?' Stewart said in an ominous tone. Molly's eyes were wide, fixed on Anna.

She nodded. 'Has to be. That's how he's doing it. He puts the bodies in that huge suitcase and just wheels it to where he wants to dump them.'

'Do you want me to try to get a closer look at him?' Molly asked.

'Thanks, but it won't make any difference. The hat completely obscures his face from the camera and he knows it. The coat not only hides his body but serves as a screen when he's ready to dump the corpse.'

'I'll need to get the police in to see this,' Stewart said.

'Absolutely,' Anna agreed, 'but can you do me a favor?' Stewart waited. 'Don't tell them I was here.'

The sun had nearly gone down when Anna came up out of the subway at West Fourth Street and Sixth Avenue. She walked east on Fourth, then cut north through Washington Square Park. On the north side of the park was the start of Fifth Avenue, and half a block north of that, on the right side, was the western entrance to Washington Mews. Euphemia Black stood near the open black six-foot wrought-iron gate, casting a long, very thin shadow. She saw Anna and came up to meet her.

'Thanks for coming,' Anna said as they shook hands. 'I appreciate your taking the time.'

Euphemia waved it away, an excited gleam in her eye. 'Don't be silly. I can't remember the last time I've been able to use my knowledge in such an interesting way. It's right up my alley, you might say.' She started to laugh but stopped herself. 'Listen to me. People are getting killed and I'm talking like it's a game.' She grew serious. 'Now what would you like to know?'

Anna led the way through the gate. 'We've had two "fake" mews so far. Is this one a fake, too?'

'Actually, part of it is.'

Anna looked at her with interest.

'Let me give you a brief history,' Euphemia said, strolling beside Anna down the center of the paved alley. 'This land was once part of a large farm belonging to a Captain Richard Randall. When he died in 1801, he left the land, along with a large amount of money, to an institution called Sailors' Snug Harbor. His wish was that a home be built here for elderly and disabled sailors.

'But Sailors' Snug Harbor didn't follow Randall's plan. They decided it would make better financial sense to lease the land for people to build houses, and use the proceeds to build and maintain an old sailors' home elsewhere. So a home was built on Staten Island. Row houses were built along Washington Square North, south of us, and along Eighth Street, north of us. This narrow road was the back alley that ran between the two rows of houses. The stables were here, as well as housing for groomsmen.'

Euphemia glanced at the gates at either end of the mews. 'The alley was open to the public until it was gated off in 1881 to separate it from the public streets. By the early 1910s, cars were phasing out the horse and carriage, so in 1916 Sailors' Snug Harbor converted a dozen of the stables into artists' studios and housing. At this time the mews was opened again to pedestrians.

'Like Amster Yard, this place had its share of celebrity residents. Gertrude Vanderbilt Whitney, the sculptor, was one of the first artists to move in. Another sculptor, Paul Manship, lived at number 44, and next door in 46 he set up a studio.' She pointed to a building marked DEUTCHES HAUS AT NYU.

'Around 1950, New York University leased the entire property from Sailors' Snug Harbor. The buildings were gradually taken over for offices, faculty housing, and other facilities for the university, though the most famous artist who lived here, Edward Hopper, remained until he died in 1966. Since then, the property has mostly been occupied by NYU. The headquarters for the university's German, Irish, and French Studies departments are all here – Deutsches Haus, Glucksman Ireland House, and La Maison Française.

'Over the years, residents have complained of feeling unsafe. So in the 1980s the university built the six-foot-high gate for the Fifth Avenue end and began locking both gates at night.'

Anna looked at her. 'You said a little while ago that part of the mews is fake. What did you mean?'

'It's these ten two-story houses on the south side of the alley. They were built in 1939 and made to *look* like the converted carriage houses across from them. Now,' Euphemia said, turning to Anna. 'Show me where the body was found.'

Anna led the way down the alley to the window well on the right. They peered over the wrought-iron railing. Shaking her head, Euphemia straightened and turned away.

'Horrible. But I've got to give this person credit – he knows his stuff. This is the only private alley left in New York City that's open to the public. Now what's he going to do?'

'Maybe not kill any more?'

'Perhaps,' Euphemia said, but the look in her eyes made it clear she had her doubts.

So did Anna.

FOURTEEN

In the dark theater, the credits began to roll and the lights came up. Anna turned in her chair. Tears ran down Kelly's cheeks.

'What's wrong?' Anna asked her.

Kelly stood and brushed popcorn bits from her jeans. 'I was thinking about poor Garry.' She laughed through her tears. 'What else?'

'And I thought a comedy would take your mind off . . . all that.'

Kelly smiled. 'You're a good friend, Anna. I did enjoy the movie.'

They started up the aisle. Anna knew Allen Schiff frowned upon her being friendly with members of her crew, but she didn't care. Kelly was her friend, and she was in serious need of distraction.

They emerged into a crisp, unseasonably cool night. A trickle of cars moved up Third Avenue.

'Come on,' Anna said. 'There's a wonderful café a block up.'

Chocolat had tiny bistro tables pushed too close together, soft lighting, and an exposed-brick wall covered with blown-up photographs of sumptuous chocolate desserts. They both ordered hot chocolate made with chocolate ganache, with mini mint marshmallows.

Kelly took a sip from her steaming mug. 'I can't stop thinking about it,' she said, her gaze wandering. 'First Garry, then Yvette, then Garry's grandmother, and now this professor.' She looked at Anna. 'What is going on?'

'I'm afraid I don't know,' Anna replied with a helpless shrug. 'At least not all of it. I think this Zeus character I told you about may well have killed Garry to avoid paying him the money he owed him. Why Zeus would do it that way – ambushing him behind the mews, and later dumping his body in the middle – I still have no idea.

'Let's say Zeus did kill Garry. Then he would have had good reason to kill Evelyn. He had to wipe out any connection between him and Garry. He knew Evelyn had told me about him and was worried about who else she might tell. Evelyn told me she was terrified of this man. That's how she sounded when she called me – terrified. She'd seen him down on the street. Then he somehow got buzzed in, or followed someone in, and went upstairs. But why would she have let him in? It doesn't make sense.'

'It doesn't make sense that he would kill Yvette Ronson and Horace Beaumont, either,' Kelly said. 'Because we are assuming the same person killed all three, right?'

'I think so. Same MO.'

'You mean the mews, courtyards, alleys.'

'All private places, worlds within worlds.'

'But why?' Kelly wondered aloud.

'I'm looking for connections. It's interesting that Amster Yard is owned by the Cervantes Institute, a major Spanish cultural center, and Washington Mews is home to not one but three cultural centers – Deutsches Haus, Glucksman Ireland House, and La Maison Française.'

'So he hates foreign countries?' Kelly said, wrinkling her nose.

'Then there's the fact that all three mews, to one degree or another, are not real. New Amsterdam Mews is completely phony. Amster Yard is basically a perfect replica of the original. And one side of Washington Mews was built only about seventy years ago to *look* like the real mews on the other side.'

'So this guy's an architectural purist?'

They looked at each other, baffled.

Kelly said, 'Maybe the killer's identity will become clear once we figure out the connection between Garry and Yvette and Horace.'

'Don't forget Jared Roberts.' Anna had told her about the

anonymous tip and the mews apartment in Princeton. 'Who is he? Someone saw Garry there. What was he doing there? What was his connection to Roberts?'

Anna's cell phone rang. It was Santos. 'Just checking in. How was the movie?'

'OK. Any news?'

'Horace Beaumont was grabbed from the steps of his brownstone on West Fifteenth Street, dragged into the dark stairwell beside them, and killed. Pretty much the same as Yvette. His apartment has been searched but nothing helpful was found. His photo has been shown to everyone who lives in New Amsterdam Mews and in the apartment building next door, everyone who works at the Cervantes Institute, and of course everyone who lives or works in Washington Mews. A few professors in Washington Mews knew him slightly, but no one knew him well. No one has ever heard the name Jared Roberts. No one in Washington Mews has ever seen Garry or Yvette before, or knew their names. No one in Washington Mews saw anything suspicious. In other words, one big nothing.'

When Anna and Kelly left Chocolat, thunder had begun to rumble in the sky. Fat drops of rain began to dot the sidewalk. Kelly, who lived in Brooklyn, said goodnight and ran down a nearby stairway to the subway. Anna opened the mini-umbrella she kept in her purse and started south on Third Avenue as the rain began in earnest. She passed a news-stand. The headline of the *Post* screamed out at her: NYU PROF LATEST COURTYARD KILL. She turned away, quickening her pace.

When she had gone two blocks, the sky really opened up. The rain beat down on the pavement, hitting so hard it bounced. Around her, people squealed and ran for cover. She brought her umbrella down closer to her head and found that while her head was now staying dry, the rest of her was becoming soaked. She decided the better part of valor was to take a taxi home.

New York taxis disappear when it rains. It's a proven fact. She looked down Third Avenue and saw not a single one. Then, as if on cue, a whole slew of them appeared, but none was available. She walked farther south and as she did she saw a taxi a block down pull to the curb and let a woman out. The 'available' light went on and Anna waved her hand wildly. The driver saw her, flashed his lights to let her know, and zoomed to the curb just as a young man darted in front of her and grabbed the door handle.

'Hey! That's *my* cab,' Anna said. 'I flagged him down. He *saw* me.'

Completely ignoring her, the man got in and slammed the door. As the cab pulled away from the curb its rear tire splashed her with muddy water. With a sigh of resignation, she decided to take the subway. Huddling under the inadequate umbrella, she turned around and pressed on toward the station. A sudden gust of wind turned the umbrella inside out, the cheap metal bending. She tried to pull it closed but only succeeded in snapping off several of the sharp metal spokes.

'Taxi, lady?'

She stopped, looked to her left. A cab had pulled up to the curb and its driver, a man in his late twenties, had rolled down the passenger window and was leaning forward to speak to her. 'I saw what just happened.'

'Bless you.'

As she reached for the door, an older woman with a heavily made-up face rushed up to her. 'This is my cab. How dare you?'

'No, it isn't, lady,' the driver yelled out the window. 'Go find your own.'

Anna jumped in, slammed the door, and laughed as he pulled into traffic. 'Thank you.'

He shrugged, smiled at her through the wraparound Plexiglass divider. 'Right is right, you know? Where to?'

'Forty-Third between Ninth and Tenth, please.'

'Comin' right up,' he said, smiling, and signaled to turn left. He was nice-looking, with straight, even features, sexy green eyes, and a full head of wavy dark hair that just touched his collar. A student, maybe, or an artist, making some extra money, she guessed.

'So, you out shopping on a night like this?' he asked, making conversation.

'No,' she said, struggling to close the umbrella. 'I caught a movie with a friend.'

'And grabbed a bite. That chocolate place any good?'

She looked at him. 'Excuse me?'

He laughed. 'Don't worry, I wasn't spying on you. I was parked across the street waiting for a fare that never showed. I happened to see you and another woman come out of there.'

She smiled. 'Yes, it's a wonderful place. But too many calories.'

He gave a little nod but said nothing. They crossed Broadway, then Eighth Avenue. At Ninth Avenue he stopped at a red light.

She expected him to turn left in order to go downtown, but when the light changed he drove straight across.

'You should have gone down Ninth. I told you I'm between Ninth and Tenth.'

'Huge accident on Ninth. Better to take Tenth.'

'Oh. All right.'

But he didn't go down Tenth either, instead zooming straight across that as well.

'What are you doing?'

He didn't answer.

She felt a weightless tickle of fear in her stomach. 'On second thoughts, I'll get out here.'

He kept going west, didn't answer.

She knocked on the thick divider. 'Hello! I said I want to get out here. Stop the car.'

Still he ignored her. Quickly she looked around. They were approaching Twelfth Avenue now and he was slowing for a red light. When he stopped she would jump out. The light stayed red and he cruised slowly to the white line.

With a sudden movement she wrenched on the door handle. Nothing happened. The door was locked. She looked for a lock button but found none. She leaned over and tried the other door. Locked.

She would scream for help. She pressed the button to roll down her window. Nothing happened. He had them switched off. She beat on the divider but it was rock solid, the only opening the little money tray. He slowed the car to get around a parked truck. As he did, he came up beside a woman waiting to cross the street who peered straight into Anna's window. Anna beat on the glass, mouthed the word 'help,' but the woman just stared at her and then looked away, uninterested.

'Why are you doing this?' she demanded.

His shoulders rose in a single laugh. 'Why am I doing this? Honey, you're the one who placed the ad.'

'The *ad*? What are you talking ab—?'

Suddenly she knew. The story in *Daily World*. Mort Anders. She remembered Rinaldi's warning.

'Where are you taking me?'

'Someplace where you can't do any more thinking.'

Now he was heading downtown. In the thirties he got on the approach to the Lincoln Tunnel. New Jersey.

Ever so slowly she removed her cell phone from her purse and dialed Santos's number. He answered on the first ring. 'Anna?'

Suddenly the car swerved sharply to the side of the street and screeched to a stop. Anders jumped out of the car and yanked open her door. She could see now that he wasn't as slim as his face had led her to believe. Instead he was solidly built, his chest muscles showing through a dark T-shirt. He leaned far into the car, grabbing for her cell phone. She pulled it back so that he missed, but he grabbed at it again and this time he got it. She held on and they struggled for a few moments, until Anders ended it by slapping her hard across the face with his other hand. Momentarily stunned, she loosened her grip on the phone and he snatched it. Then in an instant he had slammed her door, jumped back behind the wheel and relocked all the doors. He pulled back into traffic, entering the tunnel.

Her face burned where he had hit her. Her hand to her cheek, she watched helplessly as the car emerged from the tunnel and started around the ramp.

Anna knew Jersey. From 495 he got on to Route 3 and then 17 South. But from there he took a tangle of small roads she'd never seen before. Soon there were no other cars around. They crossed a set of railroad tracks. Ahead lay a large marsh whose water glimmered faintly. Tall grasses grew at the edge. Anders stopped the car at the shore and killed the engine.

He got out and opened her door. Before she could scoot to the other side of the car he grabbed her roughly by the upper arm and yanked her out. His grip was like a vice.

'Let's get this over with,' he said. 'I don't like it any more than you do.'

The rain had stopped. He dragged her toward the shore beside some of the tall grasses, his shoes splashing a little in the dark water. He spun her around to face him.

'You knew my name, didn't you?' he said.

'What do you mean?' Her voice was shaking.

'When you gave that story to the paper and said I was the fourth, unnamed man. That was nonsense, right? You knew my name. But you didn't want the police going after me. You wanted to flush me out yourself. Why?'

'It was far-fetched. I didn't think the police would take it seriously.' She looked up into his face. 'And I wanted to see what evil looks like.'

'Ooh, so dramatic. But it's not far-fetched at all. That's the problem.'

'Then you did kill Travis Brown in his cell?'

'Mm-hm,' he said matter-of-factly. 'One down.'

'And Ronald Carson?'

'Right again, pretty lady. In fact, if you were to dredge this marsh, you'd find him. Pretty soon he'll have some company.'

'And Garry Thomason?'

He tilted his head thoughtfully. 'Now there I'm afraid you had it wrong.'

'What do you mean?'

'That one wasn't me.' He laughed ironically. 'I'm a murderer, all right. Just not the one you were looking for. I've got no clue who offed Garry, but whoever it was did me a favor. As for Yvette Ronson and Horace Beaumont –' he shook his head – 'not me, either.'

'I don't believe you.'

'Believe what you like. Doesn't really matter. What matters is you need to disappear. What I don't know, and I don't expect you'll tell me, is who else knows that fourth guy is me. So, once I've dealt with you, I've got to disappear, become someone else. And I don't appreciate that, I can tell you.'

He reached under his belt and brought out a sawed-off shotgun. It glowed darkly. For an instant he took his gaze from her to release the safety catch, and in that instant with one deft motion Anna slid out the broken umbrella spoke she'd hidden in her pants. Forcing herself not to hesitate, holding it in her right fist with her left hand tight around it, she drove it with all her might upward into the middle of his chest.

He gasped, his eyes protruding in amazement. 'What did you—?' he croaked before dropping to his knees and falling over.

She realized she was crying. Fearfully she prodded him with her foot. He didn't move. She looked at his face. His eyes were open, staring up at her accusingly.

She made her way back to the taxi and got in. He'd left the keys in the ignition. She started the car, turned it around, and drove back along the narrow road until she saw a sign that said NEW JERSEY MEADOWLANDS COMMISSION. She turned down the drive and a long white structure with a roof consisting of three slopes came into view. It would be closed now, she thought, then saw a single car parked against the building.

Exhausted, sobbing against the wheel, she leaned on the horn.

* * *

It was nearly three in the morning when Anna and Santos entered her building. She'd spoken to the Kearny, New Jersey, police, who had assured her they would send divers into Kearny Marsh to look for the body of Ronald Carson.

In her apartment, Santos made them some tea. Anna was deeply tired but knew she wouldn't be able to sleep. They sat together on the sofa and quietly sipped.

'What do you think will happen?' she asked.

He thought for a moment. 'They'll look for Carson's body, like they said. They'll speak to the Staten Island police and Carson's wife. They'll get in touch with the Iraqi police about Neda Majeed, and also the military police, of course. Anna, what is it?' She was crying. He put his arm around her.

She looked at him. 'Santos, I just *killed* someone. He's gone . . . because of *me*.'

'True,' he said philosophically. 'But if you hadn't killed him, more people would probably have died, you know that. So you've actually saved lives.'

She had to laugh through her tears. 'You always know how to spin things. You should be in public relations.'

'I am!' he said with a laugh. 'I'm a cop, remember?'

But she was lost in her thoughts again. 'What do you think happened to the real driver of that cab?'

He shifted uneasily. 'The last time he checked in with his dispatcher, he was on Twelfth Avenue in the forties. It figures Anders would steal the cab there. It's quiet, not many people around. What he did with the driver remains to be seen.'

'I can't believe I did such a stupid thing. I must have a death wish.'

He gave her an arch look. 'Sometimes I wonder . . .'

'And we're no closer to finding out who killed Garry.'

'Yes, we are. We now know Anders didn't do it.'

'*If* he was telling the truth.'

'I don't see why he would have lied to you. He thought you would be dead within the next five minutes.'

'Poor Garry. He enlisted in the army to make a new start, only to get involved with this crazy guy who involved him in a murder. So he came home with this dark secret to carry around on top of all the others waiting for him here.'

'But he didn't intend to keep the secret,' Santos pointed out. 'He and Ronald were planning to go to the police.'

'True. But they never did. So Garry died with all that inside him. He never really had a chance to make that new start.'

She was crying again. Santos pulled her gently against his chest. 'I can't contradict you there. But you're getting all those secrets out for him, Anna. That's a gift you're giving him.'

She looked at him, nodded. Then she checked her watch. 'We'd better get some sleep or we won't be good for anything.'

But she doubted sleep would come.

When she arrived at the garage the following morning, her whole body felt tired, as if she'd run a marathon. Her eyes were hot and red. Sleep had come, but not much of it.

The first thing she did was tell Kelly what had happened. It would all be in the newspapers, she was sure of that, but she wanted Kelly to hear it from her.

'And here I figured you just got in a cab and went home,' Kelly said.

'I did get in a cab, but I didn't go home.'

In the corridor Allen ran up to her. 'Anna, what the blazes have you been up to? Are you all right?'

'I'm fine, Allen.'

'Is it true what I heard? That you actually killed a man?'

She took a deep breath, realizing this was a question she would be answering for a long time. 'I really don't want to discuss it, but yes, I had to kill him in self-defense. How do you know about this, by the way?'

He looked at her as if she were crazy. 'Anna, this is the DSNY. We hear everything.'

With a shrug she went into her office and tried to concentrate on her work, but she was exhausted and still on the edge of tears and it was nearly impossible.

Around eight thirty, Santos called. 'Anders was telling the truth – they've found Carson's body in Kearny Marsh. I feel so sorry for his wife and kids.'

'What about the cab driver?'

'I was going to tell you that next. He was found this morning, dead in an alley off Twelfth Avenue. Shot in the head. Remember what I said, Anna. What you did saved lives. This man Anders was a monster.'

She had no sooner hung up from Santos than a call came in on her department phone.

'Anna, it's Thad. Are you all right?'

'Yes, I'm fine, Thad, thanks. How did you hear?'

'It's all over the place.' He let out a mirthless laugh. 'I guess your ploy worked.'

'Definitely.'

'Can I ask a favor now, Anna?'

'Sure.'

'Give me an exclusive on what happened to you last night. We'll do it in your own words, an "as told to." I WAS KIDNAPPED BY A COLD-BLOODED KILLER, by Anna Winthrop as told to Thad McCormack. Will you do that for me?'

'I don't know, Thad . . .'

'Oh, come on, Anna. It's all going to get out anyway.'

'All right, but only after all this is resolved.'

'What's "all this"?'

'Garry Thomason's murder.'

'Oh,' he said, sounding disappointed. 'It'll have much more impact now, while it's fresh.'

'Sorry, Thad. Take it or leave it.'

'I'll take it. Good luck with it, Anna. I'll be in touch once you've figured this all out.'

She laughed. 'You seem to have a lot of faith in me.'

'Sure I do. I've been watching you. You've solved murders before – two of them, if I'm not mistaken. You can do it again. Just be careful.'

She promised him she would and rang off, then went out to the garage.

Damian had been missing at roll-call. Now Allen approached her and said Damian had called in sick again.

The retractable belt posts had arrived from headquarters. Enlisting the help of Gerry Licari, Anna set up the walkway, following the chalk lines she'd made on the floor. When they reached the entrance to the courtyard, Anna thanked Gerry and went out to see Clive.

'We're all set,' she announced.

He looked up brightly. 'Fantastic. I'm almost done. Have a look.'

To Anna the sculpture looked about the same, except that Clive had added two strands of heavy electrical cable to the base. The strands were twisted together and coming apart at the ends.

'What do you think?'

'Interesting.'

'I know you hate it.'

She looked at him, at a loss for words. Then they both burst out laughing.

'It doesn't hurt my feelings, Anna. When you're an artist, you put yourself out there. You don't expect everyone to love your work. That's the whole point of art.'

She smiled. 'Let's just say this isn't my favorite kind of art. I guess I'm more . . . conventional.'

'Fair enough. I really have to thank you, Anna.'

'For what?'

'For supporting me, for helping make all this happen.' He gestured toward the courtyard entrance, where the end of the walkway could just be seen.

'It's my pleasure, really,' she said, remembering what he'd told her about being homeless. Was he still? Why wouldn't he be? Where did he sleep? Where did he eat? 'I'm happy to do anything I can for you.'

It didn't take long for word of Anna's ordeal the previous night to get out. By noon she had received telephone calls from both her parents, her two sisters, her brother, and several friends from the Department. Interestingly, she had not heard from Detective Rinaldi.

At lunchtime she decided to take a walk to Mr Carlucci's to buy something to eat. After the previous night's storm the air was fresh and clean, the sky a high cloudless blue. As she turned on to Ninth Avenue a dark-blue van marked *CityWide News* screeched to the curb. A camera crew hopped out of the back, while a woman in heavy make-up and a stylish white pant suit got out of the front. Anna recognized the reporter, a petite blonde with a turned-up nose, though she couldn't remember her name.

The woman approached and put out her hand. 'I'm Arlene Volchok. You're Anna Winthrop, right?'

'That's right,' Anna replied hesitantly.

'It's her,' Arlene yelled to her crew. They all scurried over. 'I'd like to interview you about what happened last night. We're doing a segment for tonight's six o'clock news. How it wasn't Travis Brown but Mort Anders who raped and murdered Neda Majeed, how Anders also killed Ronald Carson and Garry Thomason to keep them quiet as well. Start the tape,' she told her cameraman.

Information did travel fast. Anna put up a hand. 'Wait a minute. Who said Mort Anders killed Garry Thomason?'

Arlene frowned. 'Well, it makes sense, doesn't it? Garry was involved in the Neda thing. He waited at the checkpoint while the other three went to the farmhouse. Right?'

'Right, but Anders told me he didn't kill Garry.'

Arlene looked at her crew. They all started laughing. 'Forgive me, Anna, but do you really think we should believe anything he said?'

Anna started to answer, then thought better of it. She wasn't going to get into this. Besides, she'd promised Thad an exclusive. 'I have nothing to say,' she told Arlene, and turned and walked on.

'Nothing to say!' Arlene cried, walking quickly after her, her crew scurrying in her wake. 'Anna, don't do this to me. This is a big story. OK, so you don't think Anders killed Garry. You can tell me that in the interview.'

As Anna turned to tell Arlene no again, a police cruiser slid to the curb and Santos got out. 'Problem?' he asked Arlene.

'No, not at all,' she said with a nervous laugh. 'I was just trying to get a few words on camera with Ms Winthrop for the six o'clock news. She killed Mort Anders, the guy who really murdered Neda Majeed in Iraq.'

'I'm aware of that,' Santos said, and turned to Anna. 'Are you OK with doing the interview?'

'No, actually I'm not,' she told him.

'You heard her,' Santos told Arlene. 'She doesn't want to talk to you. So beat it.'

Arlene snarled. 'I know about you two. Don't you think there's a conflict of interest here, Officer Reyes?'

He didn't back down. He continued to stare at her. 'I said beat it.'

Arlene gave a quick hand signal to her crew and they all scuttled away like cockroaches. Anna and Santos watched the van disappear into traffic.

'Thanks,' she said.

'Any time. Good thing I happened to be passing. Where are you going?'

'Mr Carlucci's. Want to come along?'

'Thanks, but I can't. You be sure to call me, though, if she or any other reporters give you any trouble. You don't have to talk about any of it if you don't want to. You've given all the information to the police.'

She smiled and started to give him a kiss, but he looked quickly around and shook his head. 'Better not.' He smirked. 'Conflict of interest, and all that.'

'No conflict.' She raised her brows suggestively. 'Lots of interest.'

Laughing, he got back into the cruiser and took off.

She would have to be more vigilant, she thought as she walked. Suddenly she wondered if she had made a mistake. If she had agreed to do the interview and said Mort Anders had told her he killed Garry Thomason, then Garry's actual killer might relax, let down his guard.

She'd arrived at Mr Carlucci's. She stepped inside and stopped. Mr Carlucci was at the register, chatting with Mrs Dovner and Mr Herman.

'Ah, Anna!' he called out before she could duck out.

Mrs Dovner and Mr Herman turned. Mrs Dovner had a superior smirk on her face. Mr Herman had a cold, calculating look.

She forced her smile back on. 'Hello,' she said, approaching them. 'How is everyone today?'

'Just fine, Anna,' Mr Carlucci said, 'on this glorious day.'

'Fine,' Mrs Dovner said.

Mr Herman said nothing, just watched her.

'Here you go,' Mr Carlucci said as he handed Mrs Dovner her change and a receipt. 'Enjoy.'

Without another word Mrs Dovner and Mr Herman turned and walked out.

Mr Carlucci watched them go. His gaze lingered on the store entrance. 'I don't know . . .' he said.

Anna gave him an inquiring look.

'I don't like that man,' Mr Carlucci said. 'Don't like him at all.'

'Neither do I,' Anna confided in a low voice. 'But I haven't quite been able to figure out why.'

'You don't need to figure out why.' He tapped his head, then patted his chest. 'We just know. He is not a nice man and I worry for Mrs Dovner. She's clearly very fond of him. In all the years she's been coming here I've never seen her like this.'

'As you know,' Anna said, 'I'm not a big fan of Mrs Dovner – we just can't seem to get along. But I don't wish her any harm. In fact, I'm happy for her. I think she's lonely.'

'Of course she's lonely. She adored Sam.'

'Who's Sam?'

'Her husband.'

'Mrs Dovner was married?'

'Of course. For a very long time. Sam worked in the garment district. I'm not exactly sure what he did. He was a lovely man.'

'Really?' Anna said, having difficulty imagining Mrs Dovner married, let alone to a lovely man. 'Any children?'

'Yes, a daughter, Julie. Nice girl. She lives in Texas. Her husband is an engineer with a firm in Austin. I don't think she comes to New York much.'

'Do they have children?'

'No, though Mrs Dovner has said she would love to have grand-children to spoil.'

'Gianni!' Mrs Carlucci stood next to a shelf of bananas with her hands on her wide hips. 'Are you gonna help me or gossip all day?' She shot Anna a cold look.

'Yes, of course, dear,' Mr Carlucci said, only now realizing there were three customers waiting at the register. He hurried over, full of apologies.

Anna began perusing the fruits and vegetables, reflecting on what she had just learned about her impossible downstairs neighbor. Life was full of surprises.

FIFTEEN

Somewhere a phone was ringing. It grew louder and louder, more and more insistent. Finally Anna woke from a deep sleep and realized it was the phone beside her bed. The digital clock beside it said 4:11 a.m. A feeling of dread – the kind you get when the phone rings when it shouldn't – came over her as she reached for the receiver.

'I'm sorry to wake you,' Santos said.

'What's wrong?'

'Nothing. Not with me, anyway. But I knew you'd want to know. Another body has been found.'

'Oh, no. Where?'

'Freeman Alley. Ever hear of it?'

'No.'

'I'm near there now.'

'Who . . .?'

'Got killed? A young man, that's all I know so far. You wanna come down?'

'Yes. Tell me how to get there.'

The taxi sped down a nearly deserted Broadway. At Houston Street the driver went east about five blocks, then went south again on the Bowery. Pulling to a stop in front of a Chinese kitchen supply store with a bright red awning, he pointed across the street. 'That's the beginning of Rivington Street. Go in there and your alley's on the left. Rivington's one-way so I can't go in there.'

'You mean you're too lazy to go around the block,' Anna corrected him, paying and getting out. Without responding he zoomed away, switching on the 'available' sign.

Anna crossed the two lanes of the Bowery and started along Rivington Street. Almost immediately she saw flashing lights coming from up ahead on the left.

'Anna.'

She turned. It was Santos, in jeans, T-shirt, and a light nylon jacket. He came up to her and gave her a kiss.

'So what happened?' she asked.

'This Freeman Alley has a little restaurant at the end called – guess what? – Freemans. They close at eleven thirty, but three guys were still in the kitchen, cleaning up. Two of them left around one. The third one closed up a little after two and found the body right in front of the entrance.'

'So it was dumped between one and two.'

'Looks like, yeah.'

'He's getting more and more brazen.'

'Absolutely,' Santos said, walking ahead. 'Have a look. Ahead on the left.'

They reached the alley and she peered in. The space between the buildings was narrow, not much more than the width of the patrol car that sat in a puddle in the middle with its lights flashing. Bold graffiti adorned the brick and stucco alley walls. Overhead lay a tangle of wires and fire escapes. Santos headed in and Anna followed.

As Anna squeezed past the police car she realized there were two large glass doors in the alley's left wall. She peered inside and saw that it was an art gallery.

Freemans stood at the end of the alley. A Provence-style doorway and large mullioned window sat beneath an awning, all painted white.

Santos pointed. 'Up at the end on the right, perpendicular to Freemans, is the back of a dinner theater on Chrystie Street called the Box.'

'So the body could have been dumped by someone who came out that door.'

'Possibly.'

Anna peered down the alley. 'Are *they* here?'

He nodded, knowing who she meant. She looked again and this time saw Rinaldi, hands on hips, speaking to Heller, the ME, who was crouched over the body. Roche stood off to one side, observing.

They continued through. Rinaldi happened to look over and did a double take. She walked over to them. 'This is a crime scene.'

'And I'm a cop,' Santos said.

'Haven't we had this conversation before?' Rinaldi said. 'You're an *off-duty* beat cop. And she's *no* kind of cop, if I'm not mistaken.'

'And like I told you before, she's with me.' Santos strode past Rinaldi, Anna behind him. Heller, totally apolitical, looked up and nodded a greeting to them.

'Who is he?' Santos asked, indicating the body.

Heller shook his head sadly. 'Young guy – twenty-seven, from his driver's license. Name Quillan Frank. Nothing appears to have been taken . . . just like the others.'

Rinaldi elbowed her way past Santos to stand next to Heller, who now spoke to all of them. 'Has an NYU ID card in his wallet. Student, maybe.'

Anna forced herself to look at the man's face for the first time and saw blood at the corners of his mouth. 'What's that?'

'Uh, excuse me,' Rinaldi said, 'but if you're gonna be here you gotta keep quiet.'

So Santos pointed to the young man's mouth. 'What's that?'

'Darnest thing,' Heller said. 'Creep cut the corners of his mouth way up to make this weird smile.'

Anna looked closer. Quillan Frank did, indeed, wear an obscene bloody grin.

'How was he killed?' Santos asked.

With his latex-gloved hand, Heller touched the upper right side of Quillan's head. 'I'll know for sure later, but it looks to me like he was killed by blunt trauma from some kind of heavy, disk-shaped object.'

Santos knit his brows. 'Like what?'

Heller shrugged. 'No idea. I'll need to look closer, like I said.'

Rinaldi had turned to Roche, who stood at attention with a pad and pen. 'We'll need to check out any possible connections between him and Beaumont,' she told him.

'Obviously,' Anna muttered.

Rinaldi spun on her, eyes large. She shifted her gaze to Santos. 'Get her out of here.'

Santos opened his mouth as if to protest, but Anna gently took his arm. 'It's OK. Let's go.'

They squeezed back between the car and the alley wall and walked back along Rivington Street to the Bowery.

'When does it end?' Santos wondered aloud.

'Euphemia thought there weren't any other places like this where the killer could dump someone, but he found one, didn't he?'

With a troubled expression, Santos nodded, then put out his hand to hail an oncoming taxi.

'Interesting,' Euphemia said when Anna called her from the garage later that morning. 'I hadn't heard.'

'You will.'

'And you say the body was dumped in Freeman Alley?'

'That's right.'

'That alley has an interesting history, though very different from those of Amster Yard and Washington Mews. Let's see . . . There's a building on the left as you enter the alley that you may have noticed. It's got an art gallery in it.'

'Yes, I saw that.'

'That building dates back to 1890. It started out as a horse stable, later became a marble and tile manufacturing company, then a chocolate factory. Jimmy Wright, the artist who does those fabulous sunflower paintings, very cleverly bought the building in 1979. He has a studio on the second floor and lives on the third. He rents the ground floor to Jeanne Greenberg Rohatyn for her art gallery. It's called Salon 94 Freemans.'

'What about the dinner theater on the right? The Box.'

'Ah, yes. It has a stage door on to the alley. The Box opened in 2007. That site also has an interesting history. In the mid-1900s it was an African American burial ground. The building went up in 1935 and has been a slaughterhouse, tenement apartments, and a truck garage. A sign company called Spanjer Signs occupied the upper floor for eighty-two years. They moved to Long Island City in 2008 but their sign is still there.

'One of the club's owners is Simon Hammerstein, grandson of the lyricist Oscar Hammerstein, as in Rodgers and Hammerstein. The place is a restaurant and theater, sort of a modern take on the old-fashioned supper club. They do cabaret – vaudeville and burlesque music and shows. It's become one of New York's hottest night spots.'

'What about the restaurant at the end of the alley? Freemans.'

'Opened in 2004. Supposed to look like a Colonial tavern. Full of stuffed animal heads. But don't let that deter you. The food is fabulous. My husband and I love the baked artichoke dip . . . But that's not what you want to know, is it?'

'Not right now, no.'

'Sorry. Now, you said the body had to have been put in the alley between one and two in the morning. So it was either dragged in from Rivington Street or dragged out of one of the places that open on to the alley. The art gallery would have been closed, of course, but I guess it's still possible someone was in there. Freemans is out, I suppose, because it was someone from there who found the body and called the police. That leaves the Box.'

'What do you think the chances are the body came from there?'

'Oh, I think it's completely possible. Anything can happen at the Box.'

A little after noon, Santos stopped in at the garage. 'Got a minute?'

They went to Anna's office. Santos closed the door. 'Couple of interesting things,' he said, taking the guest chair. 'First, police searching Freeman Alley found a five-pound barbell hidden behind a trash can.'

'A *barbell*?'

He nodded. 'There were no prints on it, but Heller says that's what the killer used on Quillan Frank.'

'But why would he have left it there?'

'Maybe because it's heavy and he had to get away quickly. He could have hidden it ahead of time, used it on Frank, and then rehidden it. The second thing I wanted to tell you . . .' He took something from his shirt pocket and placed it on the desk. Anna studied it. It was a round white paper coaster. Printed in the center, in elaborate blue script, were the letters *NMU*.

She frowned. 'What's NMU?'

'Neanderthal MashUp.'

'Come again?'

He smiled. 'It's a pop group. Guess you've never heard of them, but they're huge.'

'And how do *you* know about them?'

'Hey, I'm a hip guy. Actually,' he said with a sheepish green, 'my niece Libby loves them. She's always playing their CDs too loud in her room.'

Anna looked again at the coaster. 'So where is this going?'

'It's where it came from that matters. It was in Quillan Frank's pocket.'

Her eyes grew large. 'You took it?'

'Borrowed it. I'll put it back. Rinaldi and Roche have no use for it. They had no idea what it meant and were ignoring it.'

'So NMU means Neanderthal MashUp, and this coaster was in Frank's pocket. I still don't get it.'

He leaned forward across the desk. 'They appeared at the Box last night. They were a special event. One night only.'

She stiffened. 'Then Quillan must have come out that door.'

'Looks pretty likely.'

'Santos, we've got to go there, see if anyone remembers him.'

He grinned. 'Already taken care of. What are you doing tonight?'

'You have no idea how many strings I had to pull to get these tickets,' Santos said as they walked along Chrystie Street on the Lower East Side. It was a little after midnight. Santos wore black trousers and a hot-coral silk short-sleeve shirt. Anna was in a tight black pencil skirt and a white sleeveless top.

The Box occupied an unassuming two-story yellow-brick building at 189 Chrystie Street. As Euphemia had said, Spanjer Signs was spelled out in shiny silver letters on the top floor.

At the entrance, an unassuming graffiti-covered door, Santos showed their tickets and spoke softly with the doorman, who nodded and ushered them in. They found themselves in an intimate jewel box of a theater that looked as if it had been transported from the 1920s. Its extravagant style was a pleasing hodgepodge – art deco meets Moulin Rouge. Downstairs, rows of spacious U-shaped booths with plush red leather seats ran along the sides, a step up from an ornate parquet floor. People ate and laughed and kissed. On a small stage draped with a heavy mustard-colored velvet curtain, three tiny men in red leotards did wild acrobatics while a tall, scantily clad woman chased them around shouting in French and cracking a whip. From above, people looked down from a wraparound golden balcony and laughed and cheered.

'I see what Euphemia meant,' Anna said, looking around.

'We're supposed to speak to André, the assistant manager.' Santos stopped a busser in bow tie and suspenders and asked where he might find him.

'Upstairs, all the way to the back, door on the right,' she told them, and hurried off.

A curving staircase covered in a sumptuous Persian rug took them to a mezzanine where armchairs stood around a glass display of antique bottles. 'They're bootlegger bottles they found when they excavated the basement,' Santos informed Anna, who looked at him in surprise. 'I did some research. There are also doors from insane asylums, tiles from subway stations in the twenties, and light fixtures from an old Upper East Side department store.' He laughed. 'Your artist friend Clive would love it here, don't you think?'

At the edge of the mezzanine, a New Orleans-style balustrade, generously cushioned for leaning, overlooked ornate antique chandeliers and a mirrored bar, behind which three bartenders wearing polka-dotted ties worked quickly. Up here in the mezzanine a small bar served customers sitting in balcony booths separated by fringed curtains of heavy crimson velvet for privacy.

They headed toward the back. The walls here covered with peeling, mismatched layers of vintage wallpaper depicting cherubs, flappers, Chinese fighting fish . . . and Babar the Elephant. Off to one side stood a magnificent antique marble fireplace.

'Fabulous place. We'll have to come back,' Anna said.

He gave her a surprised look. 'Maybe for a really special occasion. Tables start at six hundred dollars – *if* you can get one – and that doesn't include dinner.'

'Then I'd better bring Daddy,' she joked, and they both laughed.

The door at the back was marked PRIVATE. Santos knocked. A few moments later it was opened by a slim young man of medium height with dark eyes and slicked-back black hair.

Santos introduced them.

'Ah, yes,' André said. 'Now, what is it exactly you're looking for? I'm afraid I don't have a lot of time.'

'Of course.' Santos took from his trousers pocket a blow-up of the photograph from Quillan Frank's driver's license. 'We believe this man was here last night, and that he left by way of the stage door on Freeman Alley. We're looking for someone who might remember him.'

André thought for a moment. 'Left by the stage door . . . That's surprising, because patrons aren't allowed back there. Oh, wait,' he said, raising an index finger. 'We had an incident backstage last night. A couple of guys got back there somehow and were harassing one of the performers. Maybe one of them was your man. Come with me.'

He led them down a back staircase to the first floor, then through a door at the rear into the backstage area. An older white-haired man in a black turtleneck immediately rose from a stool.

'James,' André said, 'wasn't there some kind of scene down here last night? Two jokers bothering one of the artists?'

'Yeah,' James replied immediately. 'I threw them out.'

'By the back door?' André asked.

'Right,' James replied, looking puzzled. 'Why?'

Santos held up the photo of Quillan Frank. 'Was this one of the men?'

James nodded. 'Yeah. Drunk out of his mind.'

Anna's heartbeat quickened. 'What did the other man look like?' she asked.

James thought for a moment. 'That's the funny thing. He was wearing this black fedora that came down low in front of his face, and I'm sure he was wearing a fake mustache.'

'Was he fat? Thin? Tall? Short?' Anna asked.

'Average build, not fat. Medium height.'

'How old do you think he was?'

James gave a little shrug. 'Hard to say. He coulda been thirty, coulda been fifty. Sorry.'

'What else was he wearing?' Santos asked.

'A dark trench coat, which I thought was odd because it was a warm night. But we see everything here.'

André said, 'So what exactly happened?'

'I was sitting here and heard a woman yelling down the hall near the dressing rooms. I ran over there and Gloxinia – she's the star of one of our shows,' he explained, 'she was bent over screaming at these two guys to get out. She was holding a towel around her. I asked her what was going on and she said they'd just barged into her dressing room and the young one tried to kiss her.'

'What did you do?' André asked.

'Well, first I asked them how they got back here. The one not wearing the hat said, "We walked." Wise guy. So I said they were both going to walk right out of here, and I frogmarched them to the door. Gloxinia yelled, "And don't ever come back!" and the young one turned around and said, "It's perfectly all right, madam, we're both studying to be doctors.'"

Anna and Santos exchanged meaningful glances.

'Did the other man say anything?' Anna asked.

'I don't think so . . . No. Come to think of it, he never spoke at all.'

'It's a puzzle,' Anna said when they were back out on Chrystie Street. When Santos gave her an inquiring look, she said, 'The Mews Murderer's four victims must have something in common. We just have to find out what it is. That will lead to the killer.'

Santos frowned in concentration. 'Garry Thomason, Yvette Ronson, Evelyn Thomason, Horace Beaumont, and Quillan Frank. The only link is that Horace was a professor at NYU Medical School, and Quillan was a student there. And of course that Evelyn Thomason was Garry Thomason's grandmother.'

Anna nodded. 'Also that Washington Mews, where the killer dumped Horace's body, is owned by NYU. Otherwise,' she agreed, 'I see no connections.'

'What about age?' Santos said. 'Garry, Yvette, and Quillan were all around the same age, late twenties.'

'But Horace was in his mid-fifties. So no pattern there.'

They walked quietly for a little while. Then Santos said, 'Maybe the killing methods will tell us something. We haven't thought about that yet. Garry was killed with a piece of mirror through the eye. Yvette was stabbed in the heart with a steak knife. Horace was stabbed through the back of the head with an ice pick. And Quillan was bashed on the head with the barbell.'

'*And* the corners of his mouth were cut into a gruesome smile.' She shook her head. 'All different methods, different implements. No pattern there that I can see.'

'Where they lived?' Santos said. 'Garry and his grandmother lived in Washington Heights. Yvette was on West Forty-Sixth Street. Horace lived on West Fifteenth Street. And Quillan's apartment was on East Thirty-Sixth. No pattern there.'

They stopped at a corner, waiting for the light to change.

'The only pattern so far is the mews courtyard alley angle,' Anna said.

The light changed and they started across the street. Anna was thinking about what Euphemia had said about there being no more mews that fit the bill. But she had been wrong. Freeman Alley had suited the Mews Murderer quite nicely.

SIXTEEN

Quillan Frank had rented a room in an apartment on East Thirty-Sixth Street between Lexington and Park avenues. The building was an attractive gray-stucco brownstone with arched double front doors. Anna and Santos entered a small vestibule and pressed the button for 1F.

The intercom clicked to life. 'Who is it?' came a woman's voice.

'Police,' Santos said.

'Oh.'

Through the glass inner door they saw a woman emerge from a side hallway and come toward them. She was tall and had an athletic build, as if she jogged every day. Her lightly tanned face was pretty without make-up, her shoulder-length blonde hair was natural, Anna thought – silky and smooth. She opened the door with a puzzled expression. 'I just spoke to the police yesterday.'

Anna shot Santos a look, wondering what he would say.

'We realize that, but there are a few things we want to double-check.' He showed her his badge. 'I'm Santos Reyes, and this is Anna Winthrop.'

She hesitated, then gave a weary shrug. 'All right. I suppose if it will help catch whoever did this to poor Quillan. Come in.'

She led them down the corridor from which she had come and into a large, airy apartment full of plants and expensive art.

'Nice,' Anna said.

'Thanks. It belongs to my aunt. She's been living in Brazil – she's an artist. These are some of her paintings. Have a seat. Can I get you anything? Coffee?'

They politely declined. Anna and Santos sat on a sofa facing her.

Santos took out a notepad. 'Now, can I just get the spelling of your name again?'

'Sure. Deena – D-E-E-N-A – Armstrong.'

Santos wrote it down. 'How long has Mr Frank lived here?'

'Since January – beginning of last semester. So about eight months.'

Anna asked, 'Are you a medical student also, Miss Armstrong?'

'Please, call me Deena. No,' she said, giving her head a little shake, 'I'm not brainy like Quillan is – was.' Her eyes grew sad. 'I manage a restaurant in midtown.'

'Tell us about him,' Anna said. 'What was he like?'

Deena frowned, thinking. 'A sweet guy . . . though he and I were never – you know, involved or anything. I have a boyfriend. Quillan was quiet, polite, very considerate. He was never any trouble. Most of the time he was here, he was studying. I can't imagine *anyone* would ever have wanted to hurt him, let alone this Mews Murderer.' She shuddered.

'Can you show us his room?'

Nodding, she rose and led the way to a staircase at the far end of the living room. They followed her upstairs and found themselves in a small hallway connecting two large bedrooms, a bathroom between them.

'In here,' Deena said, entering the room on the left.

To Anna it looked as if no one had lived here. A monk, maybe. There was a twin bed, neatly made, and next to it a night table with nothing on it but a small lamp. There was one window with an air conditioner in it, and a closet with shirts and pants neatly arranged.

'He also used this dresser,' Deena told them, opening a drawer. It and the two other drawers contained neatly folded clothing.

The only other piece of furniture in the room was a small desk. To one side of a well-used blotter sat a tall stack of medical text-books, on the other side a pile of ragged spiral notebooks.

The room contained not a single photo or knick-knack. No TV, no radio. No computer, no stereo.

As if reading Anna's mind, Deena said, 'Like I said, he was pretty much all about studying. It's so sad. I'm sure he would have been a wonderful doctor.'

They returned downstairs, sat again on the facing sofas.

'Did Mr Frank have any family, do you know?' Santos asked.

'Yes, his parents live in Florida. The other detectives who were here said they'd been notified. I've never met them. He also had a sister – I think she lives in South Carolina. I've never met her, either. If he had any other family, he never mentioned them.'

'You say he had no family in the city,' Santos said, 'but what about friends? Have you ever met any of them?'

She winced, as if embarrassed for Quillan. 'None that he ever brought here. I certainly wouldn't have minded. I really don't know if he *had* any.'

'No girlfriend, then,' Anna asked. 'Or boyfriend?'

'Not that I know of, no.'

Anna continued. 'I'm going to read you some names, and I want you to tell me if any of them means anything to you: Garry Thomason. Yvette Ronson. Horace Beaumont. Jared Roberts.'

'I'm sorry, no.'

Anna put her hands on her knees, started to rise, then remembered something. From her purse she took photos of Horace Beaumont, Yvette Ronson, and Garry Thomason. 'I don't suppose you've ever seen any of these people – other than possibly in the news.'

'I'm so busy at the restaurant I don't have much time to look at the news,' Deena said, taking the photos from Anna. She didn't recognize either Horace or Yvette. 'Oh,' she said in surprise when she got to Garry's photo. 'I've seen him with Quillan a couple of times.'

They both looked at her sharply. Anna said, 'I thought you said you'd never seen any of his friends.'

'I don't know that they were friends, though I suppose they could have been.'

'I don't understand,' Santos said.

'Both times I was walking down the street and saw Quillan and this man together. They were talking and laughing.'

'But you have no idea who it is.'

'No.' Deena gazed down at the photo. 'Who is it?'

Anna hesitated, then said, 'Garry Thomason. He's another of the Mews— Of the killer's victims.'

'Right!' Deena said, comprehension dawning. 'He worked for the Sanitation Department. And those other names you said – Yvette Ronson and Horace Beaumont – they were victims, too, right?'

Anna nodded. 'Do you know if Quillan kept an address book?' she asked, changing the subject.

'No, he didn't. The other detectives asked me the same thing.'

'An electronic device of some kind?' Santos asked. 'Palm Pilot, BlackBerry, iPhone?'

Deena smiled. 'Quillan said he loved science and technology but hated computers of any size. He said they were distractions. You must have noticed there was no computer in his room.'

'What about those notebooks on his desk?' Anna asked. 'Maybe there are some names and addresses in there?'

'No. The other detectives already looked. They're just Quillan's class notes.'

'So you have no idea why Quillan was with Garry Thomason?' Anna asked, leaning forward, as if asking again might produce an answer. But Deena shook her head. 'You say they were talking and laughing,' Anna prodded.

'That's right.'

'Where did you see them?'

'Let's see . . . both times it was on Lexington Avenue, just around the corner from here. I was going in the other direction. I figured Quillan was heading home.'

'With Garry?' Santos asked.

Deena blushed. 'No, I didn't say that. I – I don't know for sure that Quillan was on his way home, that's just what I thought at the time. I don't know where the other man, this Garry, was going.'

'These two times,' Santos said, 'did Quillan see you?'

She gave this some thought. 'Yes, he did.'

'What did he do?'

'He smiled and waved.'

'So you didn't get the impression he wouldn't have wanted you to see him with Garry?'

'No, not at all. They both looked very relaxed.'

Anna asked, 'What was Garry wearing?'

'Nice clothes. Khakis and a polo shirt, I think.'

'School's not in session now,' Santos said. 'What was Quillan doing for the summer?'

Apparently it hadn't occurred to Deena that Quillan wasn't always attending school. She shrugged. 'I really don't know.'

'Did Quillan like to go to clubs?' Santos asked.

Deena laughed. '*Quillan?* I don't think so. Like I said, he was all about school.'

'Did he like music?' Anna asked.

'Not that I could see.'

'Have you ever heard of a group called Neanderthal MashUp?' Santos asked.

'Of course.' Deena frowned. 'Why?'

'Did Quillan ever mention the group?' Santos asked.

'No. Like I said . . .'

'We know,' Anna said wearily. 'He was all about school.'

'Have you ever seen Quillan drinking? Drunk?' Anna asked.

'No way.'

Out of questions, Anna and Santos looked at each other and rose.

'We appreciate your time, Deena,' Anna said.

Santos handed her his card. 'If you happen to think of anything, remember anything, just give me a call.'

'Right, that's what Detective Rinaldi said.' Deena reached over to an end table and picked up Rinaldi's card.

'No, call *me*,' Santos said, a bit too abruptly, and she looked at him in surprise. 'I mean, call this number instead. You'll get through to us faster.'

'Garry and Quillan knew each other,' Anna said excitedly as soon as they were outside.

Santos walked along beside her, head down, deep in thought. 'Why would they both need to die?'

'Did Garry get killed because he saw or knew something? Had he told whatever it was to Quillan, so that he had to die, too?'

Santos shook his head, shrugged. 'What possible connection could there have been between them? They couldn't have come from two more different worlds.'

'That's what I was thinking when Deena told us about seeing them. A sanitation worker and a medical student?'

'We know Garry had been dealing drugs. Maybe Quillan was one of his customers?'

Anna wrinkled up her nose. 'I suppose anything's possible, but I doubt it – not from the way Deena described Quillan. He sounded like the most straight-and-narrow guy you could hope to find.'

'Yeah, he did, didn't he? So what was he doing at the Box? Who are you calling?'

Anna was punching out a number on her cell. 'Kelly. Maybe she can help us connect the dots.'

'Garry would never talk about his friends,' Kelly said, cutting her French toast. 'He wouldn't even say whether he *had* friends.' She had taken the subway up from Brooklyn and joined Anna and Santos for brunch at Sammy's.

'He never mentioned Quillan Frank?' Anna asked.

Kelly looked at her. 'The guy who was just killed? Why would Garry have mentioned him?'

When neither furnished an answer, Kelly grabbed a crisp strip of bacon and began feeding it slowly into her mouth.

On the way to the coffee shop, Santos had picked up a newspaper.

He opened it to a photograph of Quillan Frank. 'Have you seen this picture?' he asked Kelly.

'Of course. That's him – Quillan.'

'Had you ever seen him before? I mean, before his picture was in the news?'

'No,' Kelly said, looking at Santos as if he were mad. 'Why would I have?' She looked from one to the other. 'What's going on?'

'We spoke with Quillan's apartment mate this morning,' Anna told her. 'She saw Quillan with Garry. Twice.'

Kelly dropped her bacon. 'Really? Where did she see them?'

'On the street.'

'Doing what?'

'Just walking along, talking and laughing.'

'Strange . . .' Kelly said, her gaze wandering as she searched her memory. But she came up empty. 'I'm sure I've never seen Quillan before. And Garry never said his name to me. Quillan was a medical student, wasn't he? What would Garry be doing with someone like that?'

Santos said gently, 'I was wondering if maybe Quillan had been a customer of Garry's . . .'

'You mean for drugs?' Kelly shrugged sadly. 'I suppose it's possible.'

Anna was looking at Santos. She shifted her gaze to Kelly, put her hand on hers. 'Kelly, there's more we've found out about Garry.'

'Like what?'

When Anna hesitated, Santos spoke up. 'We spoke to a woman who ran a shoplifting ring. Garry used to work for her.'

Kelly looked from him to Anna. 'What are you, crazy? Garry, a shoplifter?'

They nodded.

'Who is this woman?'

'Her name is Tally Klaw,' Anna said. 'She's in prison now, Bedford Hills up in Westchester.'

'And you believed her?'

'Yes,' Anna said simply, 'we did.'

'Why would Garry do something like that?'

'To make money. The same reason he sold drugs. Didn't you ever get the impression that Garry wanted things he didn't have, wanted to make more of himself, make money?'

'Yeah, sure. Who doesn't?'

'Well,' Santos said, 'Garry was impatient. These were ways he thought he could get ahead in life, get those things he didn't have.'

Tears ran down Kelly's cheeks. 'Why are you telling me this? To hurt me?'

'Of course not. He was your boyfriend. We figured you'd want to know as much as you can. It's all going to come out. You know about the drugs. Why is this so hard to believe?' Anna's hand was still on Kelly's and she pressed it down harder to comfort her. Kelly pulled her hand away.

'We're wondering if maybe this Quillan could have been connected somehow to the shoplifting,' Anna said.

'How?' Kelly asked.

Anna's shoulders rose and fell. 'Maybe Garry was stealing medical supplies? Maybe Quillan was buying them from Garry to resell? I know it sounds crazy. We're just trying to figure out what the connection was between Garry and Quillan, because by doing that we may be able to figure out why they were killed, and by whom.'

'I can't help you,' Kelly said in a soft voice. She picked up her coffee cup to take a sip, but her hand started to shake and she put it back with a clatter. Then she screwed up her face and buried it in her napkin, silently crying.

'Kelly, I'm so sorry,' Anna said.

'There's nothing to be sorry about,' came Kelly's muffled voice from behind the napkin. 'It's the truth and I have to live with it. It's funny,' she said, lowering the napkin to the table, 'I know more about Garry now that he's dead than I did when he was alive. I loved him . . . but I never really knew him at all.'

Anna drained her coffee cup, tossed it in the trash, and got up to leave the break room. Turning, she found young Tommy Mulligan, a member of her crew, standing in the doorway. 'What's up?'

'Something you need to see.'

'Why are you whispering?'

Putting his index finger to his lips, he motioned for her to follow him. He led the way down the corridor to the men's locker room, peered quickly through the doorway as if to make sure the coast was clear, then motioned again for her to follow. He stopped and pointed in the direction of one of the banks of lockers.

Ernesto, his back to them, had his shoulders hunched over one of the lockers. His arms moved and there was the sound of metal scraping metal. Anna tiptoed forward for a better look. Ernesto had a screwdriver stuck between one of the locker doors and the frame. He yanked it sideways and the steel groaned loudly. He looked back over his shoulder as if to see if anyone had heard, saw Anna, and his eyes bulged. He jumped up, dropping the screwdriver. It hit the floor with a loud clang.

'What do you think you're doing?' she demanded. From behind her came the sound of a shoe scuffing the floor. She turned. 'Thanks, Tommy, I'll take it from here.'

Reluctantly Tommy departed. Anna turned back to Ernesto, who was now standing. 'Well?' she said, moving closer to him. 'That's Damian's locker.'

'*Damian*'s locker?'

'Of course. Damian replaced Garry. But I'll bet you thought it was still Garry's, didn't you?'

Still he stared at her, frozen.

'What were you looking for?' she asked.

He made no response, his gaze fixed on her.

She sighed. 'OK, here are your choices. You can tell me what you were doing, or I can call Allen and let him handle this.'

'What's the difference?' Ernesto said. 'Either way I'm in trouble.'

'Maybe . . . maybe not,' she lied. She had every intention of writing him up. But she needed to know what he had been up to.

He shifted uneasily. 'It's kinda complicated.'

'That's OK,' she said with a forced little smile. 'I've got time. Let's go to my office.'

She turned and led the way downstairs. In her office she sat behind her desk while Ernesto flopped down in the middle of the love seat, legs apart. He looked like a little boy who'd been sent down to the principal's office. He shot a glance at the open door. Anna got up and closed it.

'Well? What were you looking for?'

'A note I wrote.'

She narrowed her gaze. 'What kind of note?'

He lowered his head, embarrassed. 'A love note.'

She blinked. 'To Garry?'

'No! No! To Kelly.'

She lost the little patience she had left. 'I don't want to play this game any more. Tell me what you were doing – right now – or I'm calling Allen.'

'All right, all right. *Calmate*. Calm down. You remember that time Garry and me had that fight?'

'Of course. It was the morning he disappeared.'

He nodded. 'Well, the real reason we was fighting was that I was trying to give a love note to Kelly and he caught me.'

She regarded him suspiciously. 'Kelly never said anything about this.'

'Because she didn't know. I called to Kelly across the garage and held up the note. She didn't hear me, but Garry did. He grabbed the note out of my hand.'

'OK . . . then what happened?'

'He read it.'

'And what did it say?'

'Aw, come on, Anna. I told you, it was a love note.'

For several moments she said nothing, watching him. Then: 'Let's say for a moment that I believe you. Why did you want it back?'

'Why do you think? It's embarrassing. Plus it's against the rules.'

'So is breaking into someone's locker.'

'He's dead! What does it matter?'

'It wasn't in there.'

'What wasn't?'

'Your note. It wasn't in there. The detectives asked me to open the locker the day Garry's body was found.'

'Oh,' he said, clearly feeling foolish. 'Then that's that.' He rose and started to leave.

'No, that's not that. I can't let this behavior go.'

He turned on her. 'You said you wouldn't say anything. You said I could tell either you or Allen.'

'About trying to open the locker. I didn't say anything about your sexual harassment of Kelly.' She shook her head. 'We've got zero tolerance for that here.'

Suddenly he was leaning across her desk, his face a couple of feet from hers. 'Listen, Anna, I really need this job. I got a wife and two little kids at home. You report me and what am I gonna do?'

'You should have thought of that when you decided to keep bothering Kelly. Unless . . .'

He straightened up. 'Unless what?'

'Unless that's not really what was going on.'

He was watching her shrewdly. She was pretty sure the love note story was made up, and knew what he must be thinking. *If I stick to the love note story, I'm going to get reported. But I can't tell the truth because that's admitting I was lying, not to mention that the truth is worse.*

'No,' he said. 'That's what was going on. You win.' He walked out of the office, his fists clenched at his sides.

No, that wasn't what was going on, she was sure of it. But what was? What could Ernesto have been looking for?

Nolan Stewart looked exceedingly uncomfortable as he listened to Anna. When she was finished, he gazed out the window for several moments, then turned to her. 'As you can imagine, this whole matter is bad for NYU.'

She frowned. 'What do you mean?'

'What do you think I mean? Horace Beaumont was a professor in our medical school. His body was found in Washington Mews, *which NYU owns*. Now one of our *students* has been murdered. All roads seem to lead to NYU.'

'So what's your point?' Anna asked bluntly.

'My point,' he said, leaning across his desk, 'is that we're trying to distance ourselves from all of this, and you're just bringing it all back.'

Her jaw dropped. 'Dr Stewart, this isn't some gossip-column item we're talking about. This is murder. You can't simply "distance" yourself from it. And yes, some of these "roads" do lead back to NYU, which is why I'm here.'

'Which brings me to another point I was about to make. Why *are* you here?'

'I've told you. I was Garry Thomason's supervisor. Whoever killed Garry appears to have killed Yvette Ronson, Horace Beaumont, and now Quillan Frank. If I can figure out who killed them, I can figure out who killed Garry.'

'Yes, you've told me all that,' he said impatiently, 'but what I mean is, why *you*? You're not with the police.'

'No, I'm not, but that doesn't mean I can't try to solve these murders. There's no law against that.'

'No, there isn't . . . unless you interfere with police business.'

'Are you saying I'm doing that?'

'I don't know. Are you?'

A slow smile raised the corners of her mouth. 'I get it. You're trying to shoot me down because you're uncomfortable that I'm asking you about Quillan. He's another of those "roads" you don't like.'

'You're absolutely right. I'm uncomfortable about *you* asking me about Quillan. Detectives Rinaldi and Roche have already done that.'

'Then if you talk to me you won't be releasing any more potentially harmful information than you already have.'

He took a deep breath and let it out. 'You're persistent, if nothing else. What is it, exactly, that you want to know?'

'It's very simple. Do you know of any connection between Horace Beaumont and Quillan Frank?'

'No, none at all. Don't you think I asked myself that when we got the news about Quillan? I checked his computer records. He never took a class taught by Beaumont, nor is there any other link.'

'When I spoke to you earlier, you said Professor Beaumont was something of a loner, that no one seemed to know him very well. Have you had any feedback about Quillan Frank?'

'In terms of who might have known him, been friends with him? No. We have a lot of students here. It's not our responsibility to know them intimately, nor would that be appropriate.'

'No one expects the school to know about Quillan's personal life. I'm looking for someone – a professor, another student – who might.'

Stewart drummed his fingers helplessly on the desk, then grabbed a Manila folder and opened it. 'I don't see anyone here . . .' he said, scanning pages and setting them aside. 'No, wait. This might help.'

Anna leaned forward.

'Quillan belonged to one of our clubs, the Arts and Entertainment Club.' He grabbed another folder from behind him and flipped pages. 'They don't meet over the summer, of course, but here's the name and number of the person who headed the club last semester.'

He scrawled the information on a piece of paper and handed it to Anna, the expression on his face making it clear he was relieved she was finally leaving.

SEVENTEEN

After work Anna walked to the Times Square Bookstore, where Ezra Slotkin, who had headed the NYU School of Medicine Arts and Entertainment Club the previous semester, had told her he was working part-time for the summer. The woman behind the information desk told Anna she would find Ezra working in the children's department.

She found him beside a cartload of books he was shelving. He had stopped to leaf through a large illustrated book about Greek gods. He was a big man, and heavy, quite round in the middle. He was also almost completely bald, with a ring of ginger-colored hair around his head. He looked up at her over minuscule glasses perched on his nose. 'Do you need some help?'

'I'm Anna Winthrop,' she said, putting out her hand. 'We spoke on the phone.'

'Ez Slotkin,' he said, shaking her hand, before he checked his watch. 'I can go on break now. Let's sit in the café.'

He got them both coffees. 'So you say you knew Quillan? I didn't quite understand . . .'

'No, I didn't know him.' Where to begin? 'As I told you, I'm a supervisor in the Sanitation Department. A young man who worked on my crew, Garry Thomason—'

'—was the first victim of the Mews Murderer.'

She nodded. 'He died on my watch, you might say, and I'm doing whatever I can to try to find out who killed him.'

'But surely the police are doing that.'

'To the best of their ability, I suppose. But in my experience they often need help.' She pushed some hair back from her forehead. 'I've found out Garry knew Quillan Frank. That's why I wanted to speak to you.'

He drew back in surprise. 'This Garry knew Quillan?'

'I know, it is surprising, but it's true. Quillan's apartment mate saw them together twice – though she didn't know who Garry was.'

'And how can *I* help?'

'You're the only person I can find, other than his apartment mate, who knew him.'

'I knew him, but not well. We attended some club events together
– a few concerts and recitals. He was a nice guy, very easy-going.
Not a complicated person, I'd say.'

'What kind of music did he like?'

Ezra thought about this. 'I don't really know. The events we
attended together were quite varied, from chamber music to hard
rock.'

'Have you ever heard of Neanderthal MashUp?'

He laughed. 'Of course. Why?'

'Do you know where Quillan's body was found?'

'Yes, in an alley off Rivington Street, wasn't it? Freeman's
Lane?'

'Freeman Alley. Did you know there's a dinner theater on Chrystie
Street with a stage door on to that alley?'

He lowered his eyebrows, thinking. 'Wait a minute. Do you mean
the Box?'

She nodded.

'Ah . . . I hadn't realized that. Neanderthal MashUp played there,
didn't it?'

'That's right. Quillan had been in the Box before he was killed.
He was with another man who it appears got him drunk and took
him out to the alley. Do you have any idea who this other man
could have been?'

'Not a clue. I'm sorry. What did he look like?'

'He was disguised. Fake mustache, fedora, trench coat.'

He laughed. 'Sounds like a bad noir film.' Suddenly his face
darkened. 'Wait.'

'Yes?'

'I just thought of something. I have no idea if it's connected.
The Arts and Entertainment Club normally meets only while school's
in session, but we had a special event last Wednesday night – that
would have been two days before Quillan was killed. I had scored
discount tickets to see Steely Dan at the Beacon Theatre. A bunch
of us went, including Quillan.'

Anna nodded encouragingly.

'The odd thing happened after the concert was over. We all gathered outside the theater on Broadway. I suggested that we all go
to this place I like, Big Nick's Burger Joint, a few blocks away.
We were heading toward Seventy-Seventh Street when I saw some
guy approach Quillan. This is going to sound weird, but you made
me think of it when you said the guy with Quillan at the Box was

in disguise. That's the first thing that came into my head when I saw this guy – that he was in disguise.'

'What did he look like?'

'It was dark, of course, so I couldn't see him all that well, but he was wearing a trench coat, which I thought was odd since it was pretty warm. He also had on a baseball cap and big dark glasses.'

'At night?'

He nodded. 'I know. Crazy, isn't it? But hey –' he threw out his hands and shrugged – 'this is New York.'

'So what happened?'

'The guy came up to Quillan at the edge of the group and said something. Quillan stopped. I could tell he didn't know the guy. For a minute I thought the guy was going to ask him for some money. But I heard him say Quillan's name, and then he said, "I'm a friend of Trent's."'

The name on Yvette Ronson's snow globe. Possibly her boyfriend.

'Are you sure that's what he said?'

'Pretty sure, yes.'

'Did he introduce himself to Quillan?'

'No, and I thought that was odd at the time.' Ezra's brows rose. 'Do you think that's the guy Quillan was with at the Box? The guy who killed him?'

'Yes,' Anna said, 'I do. That's why it's important that you try to remember as much as you can about him and about what he said to Quillan.'

Ezra concentrated. 'I can't think of anything else. Except for one thing. After he said that about being a friend of Trent's, he suddenly glanced around and was looking right at me. He stared at me for a second, like he was panicked or something, but then he looked back at Quillan and smiled.'

'Then what happened?'

'Quillan looked at all of us and waved, like he was going to take off. Then he and this guy walked away.'

'Where did they go?'

'I don't know, I didn't watch. Hey, do you think now this creep's going to come after me because I heard what he said to Quillan?'

'Impossible to say. But if I were you, I'd avoid alleys, court-yards, and mews for the time being.'

*   *   *

She bought some flowers on the way home, fat white peonies. As she turned from Ninth Avenue on to West Forty-Third Street, she saw Mrs Dovner and Mr Herman descending the steps of the brownstone, arm in arm. Inwardly she groaned.

Nearing them, she pasted on a smile. 'Hello, Mrs Dovner. Mr Herman.'

Mrs Dovner gave her a superior smile but said nothing.

'What magnificent flowers,' Mr Herman said, then gave a faint frown. 'You're home early.'

'No, this isn't early for me. I work from six to two.'

'Ah,' Mr Herman said.

'They work all hours, you know that,' Mrs Dovner said disdainfully. 'That's why we hear those garbage trucks banging and clanging all night when people are trying to sleep.'

Anna made no reply to that. 'Well, have a nice afternoon.'

'You, too, Anna,' Mr Herman said, and they continued slowly down the street.

Entering the building's vestibule, Anna got out her keys and opened her mailbox. Junk mail, a couple of bills. She tucked them into her pocket and was about to unlock the inner door when an envelope on the floor caught her eye. It was a white, business-size envelope, and on its front someone had printed A. WINTHROP in blue ballpoint pen. Frowning, she tucked the flowers under her arm and bent to pick it up. She turned it over. There was no other writing on it.

She tore it open. Inside was a single sheet of white paper, folded in thirds. She unfolded it. More printing in blue ballpoint.

ANNA
STAY OUT OF THINGS THAT DON'T CONCERN YOU
YOU'RE OVER YOUR HEAD
IF YOU WANT TO FIND OUT WHAT HAPPENS TO RATS IN DARK
ALLEYS, TAKE A LOOK

Her heart was beating heavily. She let the peonies drop to the floor. Clutching the envelope and letter, she ran back out and down the stairs. Mrs Dovner and Mr Herman were nearly at Tenth Avenue. She called their names. They didn't hear her so she ran toward them and called again. They turned, looks of surprise on their faces.

She ran up to them. 'This envelope was on the floor under the mailboxes.' She showed them her name on the front. 'Did either of you see who put it there?'

'I have no idea what you're talking about,' Mrs Dovner said haughtily.

'No, I'm sorry, Anna,' Mr Herman said. 'Why? Is it bad news? I hope not.'

She studied them both for a moment, then said, 'Never mind,' and walked back to the brownstone, stopping short of it at the entrance to a narrow alley on its west side. Far at the back shone the bright daylight of the yard, but the alley itself lay deep in shadow. She looked up and down its length, and saw nothing except weeds poking up through the concrete.

She started down, walking slowly, watching the ground. By the time she was halfway down she had seen nothing out of the ordinary except for the torn gold lid of a Godiva chocolates box. She continued toward the back, and now something came into view. It was on the ground, nearly at the end of the alley. It was darkish, not large. She couldn't make out what it was. She moved cautiously closer.

And gasped.

It was a large dead rat. It lay on its back. Its belly had been sliced open and its guts pulled out – glistening pink intestines, the liver, the heart. She clapped her hand over her mouth.

It was then that she noticed an irregular piece of corrugated cardboard lying on the ground behind the dead rat. Printed on it in the same blue ballpoint pen was the word ANNA. Next to it was an arrow pointing to the rat.

From only feet away came a shuffling footstep, a grunting noise. She froze, started backing down the alley, turned and ran. Only when she had reached the sidewalk did she spin around and look. The large figure of a man came shambling toward her through the shadows. As he came closer she could see that he was a homeless man, in ragged trousers and a long-sleeve striped shirt with the pocket torn off. In his hand was a bottle of whiskey.

'Who are you?' she demanded.

He looked up suddenly, as if only now realizing she was there. 'Eh?'

'What were you doing back there?'

'What do you think I was doin'? Sleepin', that's what.' He gave her a toothless grin, held up the bottle. 'Want a swig?'

Without responding she watched him walk up the street in the same direction in which Mrs Dovner and Mr Herman had gone.

She hurried back inside, grabbed her flowers, and quickly let

herself in. Upstairs, she locked and bolted her door, then dialed
Santos.

Abruptly she replaced the receiver. What was the point? What
could he do? He would only be worried about her, give her a lecture
about playing detective – something she had no intention of stopping. Besides, this was no game. It was serious, deadly serious.
And she was getting closer, this was proof of it. The killer wouldn't
have warned her off if he weren't nervous.

Lost in thought, she went in search of a vase for the peonies. In
the kitchen, as she reached to the cabinet above the sink, she realized her hand was shaking. A few minutes later, as she was setting
down the vase on her dining table, there was a knock on her door.
Praying it wasn't Mr Herman again, she went to the door and looked
through the peep hole. It was a woman who looked around fifty,
with a pleasant round face and short frosted hair. Anna opened the
door.

'Ms Winthrop?' the woman said.

'Yes.'

'I'm Julie Dovner. Iris Dovner's daughter.'

'Oh, yes,' Anna said, surprised, and frowned. 'I thought you lived
in Texas.'

'I do. I flew in this morning to see my mother. Can I talk to you
for a minute?'

'Of course. Come in. Coffee?'

'No, thank you. I shouldn't stay long. Mom doesn't know I'm
up here. I waited till she and Lionel went for their walk.'

Anna had a feeling she knew what Julie had come to discuss,
and she was right.

'Actually,' Julie said, 'it's Lionel I wanted to talk to you about.'

Anna nodded.

'You've met him, of course,' Julie said.

'Yes.'

'What do you think of him?'

'I don't trust him. He seems phony to me, up to something.'

'That's exactly what I think. That's why I'm here, because of
things my mother has been saying. That he was being extremely
attentive, bringing her candy and flowers, taking her out for expensive meals.' She smiled. 'I love my mother, but I also know what
she's like.'

'Yeah, so do I,' Anna said, and they both laughed.

'I imagine she's not always the easiest neighbor,' Julie said.

'You imagine correctly.' Anna frowned as a thought occurred to her. 'What made you come up and see me?'

'After I met Lionel, I told my mother I didn't trust him and thought she should stop seeing him. She told me she could tell you didn't like him either, but she said that was because you're jealous.'

'*Jealous?*'

'I know, it's silly. She said your boyfriend is "a low-life cop" and that you wish you had a man as chivalrous as Lionel. Anyway, when I found out you didn't like him I wanted to know why.'

'It's nothing concrete,' Anna confessed. 'It's his manner. He's . . . smarmy.'

'Good word for him.'

'So what are you going to do?'

'I'm afraid there's not much I *can* do. I've warned Mom to be careful, to watch for ulterior motives. And I spoke to him privately, told him in so many words that he'd better not try anything.'

'Like what?'

'Like getting his hands on her money. She's not rich, but my father left her quite comfortable, and that was a long time ago.' Julie rose. 'Thanks for your time, Anna,' she said at the door.

'My pleasure, Julie. It's good to meet you.'

'Same here.' Julie smiled. 'I can see that none of what Mom says about you is true.'

Anna raised her brows. 'And what does she say about me?'

'You don't want to know.'

Anna had an idea. 'Julie, maybe I can get some information on our Mr Herman.'

'Really? How? A private detective?'

'No, my low-life boyfriend, the cop.'

Julie grinned. 'I'd be grateful, Anna. Let me give you my cell phone number.'

'Can you do some snooping for me?' Anna asked Santos across her dining table that night.

His Szechuan pork dumpling stopped in mid-air. 'You seem to be pretty good at that yourself.'

'Very funny. I'm serious.'

He forced his smile away. 'What do you want snooped?'

'It's who. Mr Herman.'

'Mrs Dovner's boyfriend? Why?'

'Because I don't trust him. I think he's up to something, and
so does Mrs Dovner's daughter. She came to see me this afternoon.'

'I see. Has he done anything that's caused you to distrust him?'

'No.'

'Then what—?'

'It's a feeling we have. He's phony. And let's face it, Santos, no
man in his right mind would be that interested in Mrs Dovner.'

He laughed. 'All right. Got some paper?'

She got him a pad from the kitchen drawer and he took a pen
from his pocket.

'What have you got so far?' he asked her.

'Lionel Herman. He said he lived in Norfolk, Massachusetts,
before moving to New York. He was married to a woman he called
Winnie, but she died. That's why he came here, to fulfill his dream
of living in New York City so he can go to plays, ballets, and
such.'

'With Mrs Dovner.'

'I know, it's bizarre.'

'Got anything else?' he asked.

She thought for a moment. 'Oh, yes, he said he used to be in
finance.'

'Finance.'

'I know, it's vague. I would have asked him questions, gotten
more out of him, if I'd known we were going to check him out.'

'That's OK,' he said, folding the paper and slipping it into his
pocket with the pen. 'This is a good start. Provided, of course, that
what he told you is true.'

She hadn't thought of that. With a mild frown she speared a
dumpling and lowered it into dipping sauce.

When Anna arrived at work on Tuesday, the Art Walk, as it had
come to be known, was completed, running in a circuitous route
along the garage walls from the street to the courtyard. 'What do
you think?' Damian asked. 'I finished it myself last night.'

'I think it's going to work. Thank you.'

He gave her a chivalrous nod and smiled, then headed off to his
truck. Anna went out to the courtyard.

Clive was already there, putting the finishing touches on his
sculpture. 'How are you today, Anna?'

'I'm terrific, Clive. Excited for you.'

He gave her a warm smile before focusing back on his artwork.

She met Allen Schiff in the corridor outside her office. 'Today's the day, right?' he said. 'We let in the crowds?'

'Don't be sarcastic, Allen. I actually think a lot of people will want to see Clive's sculpture once word gets out.'

He shrugged and walked off.

'When do you want to officially open?' she called after him.

'Up to you,' he said with an indifferent wave of his hand, and closed his office door.

At roll-call Anna announced that she was calling a meeting for noon in the break room to go over protocol regarding the Art Walk. There were a few grumbles and then everyone was off.

In her office, she closed the door and dialed Nolan Stewart at Langone Medical Center.

'Anna!' he said with mock cheerfulness. 'To what do I owe the pleasure?'

She laughed. 'I didn't think you could take another visit from me, but I do have a question I wonder if you could help me with.'

'I'll try.' He sounded a bit wary.

'I would like you to please find out if there is a student at the medical school by the name of Trent.'

'What's the first name?'

'That is the first name. It's the last name I don't know.'

'I see. And may I ask why you want to know?'

'It's a long story, but if you really want to know—'

'That's OK, never mind. Let me see what I can do. I'll give you a call back.'

She busied herself at her desk. After about fifteen minutes her phone rang.

'Anna, it's Nolan. I did a computer search for students with the first name Trent.'

'And?'

'And it's very interesting. We do have a student in the medical school, third year, by the name of Trent Roberts.'

'Roberts?' *Jared Roberts.*

'That's right. Home address Bank Street, Princeton.'

'How can I reach him?'

'That's going to be a problem. We're on summer break, as you know. There was a telephone number for him – it's listed as his cell phone – but I tried it several times and it's no longer in service. Nor do we have a summer address for him.'

'Will he be coming back for the fall semester?'

She heard the rustling of papers. 'There's no indication that he won't be. But until then I'm afraid you're out of luck.'

'Is there someone I could speak to who would know him?'

'Let's see . . . We've got the address he was at last semester, but I know he's not there now because that facility is being renovated. Besides which, students aren't allowed to remain in school housing over break. Even if he were still there, he was in a single, so there's no room-mate you might have spoken to, though I suppose there might have been floor neighbors. A moot point now, I guess.

'I tried to reach his academic advisor, but had no luck. She appears to have taken a vacation in France. None of Quillan's professors are available, either.'

'Did he—?'

'Take a class with Professor Beaumont? Already thought of that. The answer is yes.'

Excitement rose in her. 'You say you looked Trent up in your computer.'

'That's right.'

'There would be a photo in his record, correct? The photo used on his student ID card?'

'Yes, of course.'

'I'd like a copy of that photo, if you don't mind.'

'Actually, I do mind. Or to put it more accurately, enforcers of privacy laws mind. But I'll make a deal with you,' he said, lowering his voice. 'I'll get a nice color printout of this photo and send it to you . . . if you promise not to contact me again.'

'I . . .'

'Don't get me wrong, Anna. You're a beautiful and charming young woman – my favorite kind. But the fact is there's nothing else to tell you. I know you want to solve the murder of this young man who worked for you, and that you're following all the trails. But as I'm sure you've noticed, the trails to NYU don't lead anywhere. As I've mentioned to you before, the less additional publicity connecting this Mews Murderer to the university, the better.'

'I understand,' she said with a frown. 'It's a deal. Now, how can I get that printout?'

'It's already in my out-box to be mailed to you. You have a wonderful day, now.'

'But—'

He'd hung up. She'd been about to ask him whether she could come and pick it up. She shrugged. No matter. She'd have it in a day.

Seated at the end of one of the conference tables in the break room, Anna watched the members of her crew wander in. When all ten were seated, some unwrapping sandwiches or twisting the tops off Snapple bottles, she began.

'I want to speak to you briefly about Clive and his sculpture.'

'Oh, is that what that is?' Ernesto blurted out and immediately glanced around the table for a response. There were a few nods and chuckles.

Anna gave him a mild smile. 'Yes, that's what that is. He's been working very hard on it and I expect you to show him respect, especially since he's our guest. Now, thanks to Damian –' he looked up at her in surprise, brows rising – 'we now have a walkway that extends from the garage's street entrance to the courtyard. We will be opening the walkway this morning at ten. People will be using it throughout the day. Therefore, I expect you all to be on your best behavior.'

Terrence ran his hand back through his short, dyed brown hair. 'What do you mean?'

'No swearing. No fighting.' A few gazes slid to Ernesto. 'Drive slowly. The walkway is set up at the perimeter of the garage, but I still expect you to exercise supreme caution. If anyone on the walkway speaks to you or asks you for information, respond politely and help as best you can. If you don't know an answer, direct the person to me. Is that clear?'

Everyone nodded.

'Good. Now there's something else I want to talk to you about. I should have brought it up earlier.' She sat up straighter. 'This has been a very difficult time for us. I don't need to tell you the reporters are still sniffing around. I've seen how you've been dealing with these people – ignoring them or saying "No comment," which are the appropriate responses – and I just want to commend you and encourage you to continue to respond in this way.'

Fred Fox's eyes were a vivid blue in his ferret-like face. 'It's not easy, Anna. These people don't give up.'

'Neither will we,' she said firmly. 'When they realize they're not going to get anything out of us, they'll move on.'

Tommy Mulligan looked doubtful. 'It's been a while and they haven't given up yet.'

There was a rumble of assent around the table.

Brianna spoke up in her husky voice. 'So what *is* going on, Anna? Do the police have any leads?'

'Not that I know of.' *And neither do I have any leads at this point.* 'I'm sure they're doing their best to get to the bottom of this.'

Kelly said, 'Have they got any idea why this person is leaving his victims in these mews?'

Anna gave her head a helpless shake.

Young Pierre Bontecou's expression was earnest. 'I've been reading that this guy kills his victims elsewhere and then takes the bodies to these mews. How is he doing that?'

Anna knew not to talk about the suitcase on the security video. But she did say, 'That's not quite true. The last victim, Quillan Frank, was killed right in Freeman Alley, where his body was found.'

They all nodded thoughtfully.

'At any rate,' Anna said, 'hang in there and keep mum. If a reporter harasses you, come to me. But the stock answer, if you answer at all, is that you're sorry but you don't know anything.'

'We *don't* know anything,' Bill Hogan pointed out.

'Exactly. So this shouldn't be difficult. That's it. Thanks, everyone.' She rose.

At the other end of the table, Kelly and Brianna, who hadn't brought in lunch, also rose. Kelly's face was troubled, her brow furrowed. She shook her head. 'It's sick. Why is everyone so fascinated with these "mews murders"?'

Pablo, who had remained seated, put down his sandwich with a thoughtful look. 'Because these mews are supposed to be the last private places in the city . . . places where things like murder don't happen.'

'Think again,' Damian said, turning suddenly in the doorway. There was a surprising viciousness in his tone. Everyone stopped and watched him. 'We *think* places like that will protect us, block out the world, keep us safe. But the ugliness of the world gets in.' Realizing everyone was looking at him, he quickly added, 'Look at what this maniac has done to these mews.' He lobbed his wadded-up lunch bag into the wastebasket. It hit it with a thump. Then he turned and left, his footsteps clattering on the stairway.

EIGHTEEN

Later that afternoon, Anna was standing near the garage entrance checking on the walkway when Damian and Terrence returned from their route. When she glanced up to their truck's passenger's window, Damian was looking at her, his face expressionless. She turned quickly away and returned to her office.

At a quarter past two, as she left the garage for the day, she saw Damian walking east on Forty-Third Street. His words at the crew meeting rang in her ears: *The ugliness of the world gets in.* On an impulse she followed him, keeping her distance.

Her cell rang. 'Hey.' It was Santos. 'You wanna do something tonight?'

'I don't know. Sure. Maybe. I'll call you back.'

'Wha—?' She closed her phone and quickened her pace, following Damian into Times Square. A man in a red uniform shoved a tour brochure in front of her. She shook her head and hurried down Broadway. At Forty-Second Street Damian turned left and started down the stairs into the subway. She followed.

He had a MetroCard and went quickly through a turnstile. She hurried to a ticket machine and bought a one-ride card. Hurrying through, she saw Damian veer into the tunnel on the right. She broke into a run, turned the corner, and found him again, following him down a ramp and then taking a set of stairs on to a train platform.

He walked to the far end of the crowded space. She positioned herself about a train car's length from him – near enough not to lose him, far enough not to be seen. When, after a couple of minutes, a train roared into the station, she was able to enter the same car he did but by the other set of doors.

She found a seat and sat hunched forward, her hands covering her face as if she were tired. Peeking out, she saw Damian standing at the far end of the car, his back to her, his hand on a pole for support.

She didn't know what she had expected but it was a long time before he finally got out, at Marble Hill – 225th Street. Still keeping her distance, she followed him up the stairs and out on to Broadway.

Here there weren't many people around and she panicked a little, drawing back to put more space between them. He was walking south. Abruptly he stopped and went into a liquor store. He emerged a minute later with a brown paper bag and continued down the street, turning east on West 225th Street. This was a residential area and there were more people around, but still she kept back. When he turned right on to a street called Jacobus Place, she hurried so as not to lose him.

It was a good thing she had. He was already mounting the stairs of a small apartment building. Searching in his pocket for his keys, he went through the front door and was gone.

She looked about her, feeling foolish. Why had she followed him? What had she hoped to find out?

'You lost, lady?'

She turned around. A freckle-faced boy of about thirteen had stopped his bicycle, his feet on the pavement.

'Uh . . .' She smiled her kindest smile. 'Sort of.'

He wrinkled his nose. 'Sort of?'

'I've lost someone. A friend of mine. I know he lives in that building over there, but I don't know which apartment.'

'So why don't you just call him?'

'Because it's a surprise, you see. It's his birthday.'

'Oh. What's his name?'

'Damian Porter. Do you know him?'

'No. But I bet he does.' The boy pointed to a blue-uniformed letter carrier heading their way. 'Hey, Marvin, come 'ere, wouldja?'

Marvin, a balding middle-aged man with a pot belly, waddled over. He smiled charmingly at Anna and gave the boy a look of irritation. 'Is something wrong, Patrick?'

'Lady here says she's a friend of Damian Porter in that building, but she doesn't know his apartment number.'

Marvin looked at her with mild suspicion. 'If you don't mind my asking, if you're his friend, why don't you know his apartment number?'

'He's never given it to me as part of his address,' she said quickly. 'He says his letter carrier is so good that he doesn't need apartment numbers – he knows everyone's apartment numbers by heart.'

Marvin blushed. 'I guess that would be me. It's true, actually. If you gave me a list of all the tenants in that building, I could give you all of their apartment numbers. I could do the same for all the buildings on my route.' He frowned. 'I really shouldn't give them out, though. You know, official policy, privacy and all that. You could call him,' he suggested.

'She can't do that,' Patrick said. 'It's his birthday and she wants to surprise him.'

Marvin looked her quickly up and down, no doubt imagining the surprise. 'Lucky man, lucky man.' He laughed. 'You don't look like a stalker or anything. I think it would be all right this time. Apartment twenty-three.'

'Thanks so much,' she said on a grateful breath.

'Sure thing. No birthday present?'

She raised and lowered her eyebrows suggestively. He blushed again, looked down.

'Damian is a new friend for me,' she said. 'Have you known him long?'

Marvin's face grew serious. 'Patrick, get lost.'

'My pleasure, you big fat creep,' Patrick said, and took off, giving him the raspberry.

'Brat. I didn't want to talk in front of him. You know about what happened to Damian, right?'

'No,' she said, shaking her head quickly. 'He's so private. But I want to get to know him better.'

'Right,' he said thoughtfully. 'It's very sad. Way I heard it, he and his wife and a two-month-old baby were living somewhere in Queens. One Sunday morning he went out to get the paper and some bagels, and when he came back his apartment was on fire.'

'How awful. Were they hurt?'

He nodded. 'Killed.'

'Did the whole building burn?'

'No, that's the thing. It wasn't a building, it was a single apart-ment that used to be a stable for horses. You ever seen that kind of thing?'

She nodded.

'That old dry wood went up like kindling.'

'How do you know all this?'

'From Mr Cantalupo in eighteen. Damian told him.'

'And now Damian is alone.'

'Well, no,' Marvin said brightly, 'he's got you, right?'

'Yes, sure, right. I didn't know any of this.'

'I'm sure it hurts for him to think about it, let alone talk about it.'

She nodded. 'Thank you, you've been very kind.'

'Not at all. I hope you two have a great birthday celebration.' He stood watching her.

Suddenly she realized he was waiting for her to go into Damian's building. 'You know, now that I think about it, I feel funny not bringing a present.' She smirked. 'I mean, a more *traditional* birthday present. Is there a store around here where I might pick something up?'

He thought for a moment. 'Yeah, over on Broadway there's a big Hallmark shop. It's right near the subway. They should have something.'

'Great idea. Thank you, Marvin.' He blushed yet again.

She walked quickly back on to West 255th Street. Approaching Broadway, she thought about what Marvin had told her and was overcome with sadness. No wonder Damian had said what he did in the break room. No wonder he was so strange. Anyone would be after suffering a tragedy like that. She resolved to cut him more slack, treat him more kindly.

As she started down the subway stairs Santos called again. She laughed. 'I'm sorry I kind of blew you off.'

'Yeah, what was up with that?'

'I was preoccupied.'

'You want to preoccupy yourself with some dinner?'

'I'd love it.'

'Great. I feel like Indian. Paratha at twenty-eighth and Lex? Around six?'

'Perfect. See you then.'

The subway platform was deserted. It occurred to her that it wasn't out of the realm of possibility that Damian might come back down and spot her. She found a place near the very end of the platform behind a wide support that shielded her from view. Then she waited, her back to the support, hoping the train would come soon. She strained her ears for the familiar rumbling sound but there was only the eerie silence of the platform with its warm, fusty air. There was a dank smell, with the faintest tang of urine.

A faint scraping sound came from behind the support. She jumped, thinking it might be a rat, and peered cautiously around.

She gasped. Damian stood only inches from her, still in his Sanitation uniform, smelling of alcohol and sweat, his expression blank. Instantly his hands were gripping her upper arms, pulling her even closer to him. He pushed her up against the support. 'Why didn't you come up, babe? That's why you followed me, isn't it?

I knew I was right about you.' He nuzzled his face hard into her neck and she felt his hot breath on her skin. He pulled back a little, but only to grab the back of her head with one hand and pull her roughly to him. He kissed her, hungrily, sloppily, breathing hard. She felt his other hand exploring between her legs. She clamped them tightly together but he was strong and pried them apart.

'Why didn't you just say what you wanted?' he said, pulling back a little to look at her. 'Why'd you have to play games? We're two adults, aren't we?'

He kissed her again, even rougher this time, and now she felt his teeth tugging painfully at her upper lip. She twisted her head away, squirmed, tried to free herself, but now he had her arms pinned to her sides and her legs immobilized with his own. She screamed.

'Yeah, you scream, baby. You're gonna be screamin' hard when I'm finished with you.' His arms went around her waist like a vise and he buried his face in her neck again, breathing deeply. She screamed again.

'Hey! What's goin' on over there?'

Damian froze, then turned. A man in his twenties stood halfway down the subway stairs. 'I'm calling a cop!'

Damian laughed. Anna broke free and ran. When she emerged on to Broadway the young man was nowhere in sight, and neither was a cop. She flagged down a passing cab and jumped in. She looked to her right out the window and saw Damian come up the subway stairs. He saw her and started to laugh. The taxi took off. She burst into tears.

It was her own fault, Anna decided. What had she been thinking? Santos would tell her she was lucky something worse didn't happen to her. Something worse . . . like dying?

Because she *had* learned something. Damian and his wife and child had lived in a mews in Queens. But the ugliness of the world had gotten in, as he had put it at the meeting. It was in a mews that his life had, in a way, ended. Had the tragedy so twisted him inside that he had become a killer himself, who left his victims in mews and courtyards and alleys to symbolize what had happened to him?

She had asked the cabbie to take her directly to the restaurant where she was meeting Santos. The fare was astronomical but she didn't care, and even gave the man a generous tip.

She made a point of smiling as she entered Paratha, but as soon as Santos saw her his own smile disappeared. He stood up as she approached the table, took her hands in his. 'What's wrong?'

'Who said anything was wrong?' she said brightly . . . and started to cry.

He took her in his arms. 'Anna, what happened?'

She sat down, asked for a drink, and told him everything.

When she was finished he was looking at her gravely. 'You're lucky something worse didn't happen to you.'

She burst out laughing.

'That's funny?' he said.

'No, of course not. It's just that I knew you would say that.'

He had to smile. 'I see. So we're already like two old married people, each knowing what the other is going to say, what the other is thinking.'

Already.

'You're right, of course,' she said. 'It was a stupid thing to do. It was the way he said that about mews not protecting you and ugliness getting in. I knew there was something behind it. And I was right.'

'True. But you still have no proof that he's the Mews Murderer.'

'No, but he's the closest we've come. He needs further investigation.'

He smiled. 'Spoken like a true detective. I'll tell you what. I'll check him out, see if anything comes up on him. Speaking of which,' he said, removing several stapled sheets of paper from his pocket, 'I did some research on our Mr Herman.'

She sat up straight, waiting.

'It seems he was telling you the truth, as far as it went.'

'What do you mean?'

'It's true that he was married to a woman named Winifred who died last year. It's also true that he lived in Norfolk, Massachusetts, but it wasn't in a house or an apartment. It was in a prison. Bay State Correctional Center, to be exact.'

Anna's eyes widened. 'For what?'

'Wire fraud. He was in finance, all right. He was a broker and investment manager. Seems he diverted about two million dollars from clients and investors, who included a woman in her nineties with Alzheimer's disease. He took her entire life savings.'

'How long was he in prison?'

'Six years and six months, followed by three years of supervised release. He was also ordered to pay almost nine hundred thousand dollars in restitution. He got out of prison two years ago.'

Anna had her hands pressed flat on the table as she leaned forward. 'Santos, we have to tell Mrs Dovner.'

'Wouldn't it be better if you called the daughter, told her all this, and then let her tell her mother?'

'Yes, I suppose you're right. I'll call her as soon as I get home.'

He handed her his notes, which she put in her purse. Then she took up her menu. 'I'm starving.'

They ordered two dishes to share and some of the bread called naan, which Anna liked so much she could have made a complete meal out of it.

'And now,' Santos said after the food had arrived, 'I have something else to tell you.'

She looked up.

'I found this out from my friend Margolin, who heard it from Roche. When they searched Evelyn Thomason's apartment, guess what they found in the freezer.'

'Ice,' she joked.

'You're right,' he said. 'It was a diamond necklace. A very valuable one.'

'No!'

'Yes. It was in a plastic zipper bag inside of a small padded envelope. Also in the envelope was a note. It said – and I quote –' he took a folded sheet of paper from his shirt pocket and read from it – '"G. See what you can get. Thanks, man. EB."'

'Who's EB?'

'No one has any idea.'

'EB . . .' she said, munching on naan. 'EB . . .' Then her eyes grew wide. 'I know who it is. Ernesto Balcazar.'

'That guy on your crew who had the fight with Garry?'

'The very same. There's something I haven't told you yet.' She filled him in on catching Ernesto trying to break into Garry's locker, and the explanation Ernesto gave her. 'But now I don't believe a word of it.'

'What are you going to do?' he asked.

'What do you think I'm going to do? I'm going to talk to Ernesto.'

Anna called Julie Dovner as soon as she got home. Julie was silent as Anna delivered her information.

'You'd better speak to your mother right away,' Anna said.

'Absolutely. I can't thank you enough for this, Anna.'

'No thanks necessary. I'm just glad we found this out before Mr Herman could do any harm.'

Half an hour later, Anna heard slow, heavy footsteps and the banging of a cane on the stairs outside her apartment. She opened the door and saw Mrs Dovner's flyaway hair appear in the stairwell from below. Anna went out to greet her, knowing what was coming.

'Good evening, Mrs Dovner.'

'Don't you "good evening" me, missy,' Mrs Dovner said, short of breath, mounting the top stair. 'How dare you call my daughter and talk to her about me? My life is none of your business.'

'Would you like to come in?'

'No, I would not like to come in!' Mrs Dovner shouted, waving her cane. 'I want you to tell me why you did that.'

'I'll be happy to, but I think it would be better if you came inside,' Anna said, casting a glance at the stairs up to Mr Herman's floor.

But Mrs Dovner remained stubbornly anchored to the spot.

'All right,' Anna said patiently, and lowered her voice. 'Julie and I were worried for you. We had a bad feeling about him and I asked my boyfriend to check him out. I'm sorry you don't like what he found out, but I thought you would be glad to know the truth.'

'Well, I'm not,' Mrs Dovner snapped. 'Because I don't believe it, not a word of it.'

'You don't?'

'Nope. I know you don't like me, any more than I like you. You're just trying to hurt me, to take away whatever happiness I've been able to find in my lonely life. Well, it's not going to work. Keep your big fat nose out of my business!'

'Ladies?'

They both turned. Mr Herman stood on the stairs in a pale-blue dressing gown and leather slippers. 'Is everything all right?'

They both stared at him. Finally Mrs Dovner said, 'Everything is fine, Lionel, except that some neighbors don't know how to mind their own business.'

He looked at Anna shrewdly. 'What do you mean?'

'Nothing,' Anna put in quickly, then turned to Mrs Dovner.

'I apologize. I meant well. Goodnight.' She went back into her apartment and closed the door.

Some people just didn't want to be helped.

Approaching the garage on Wednesday morning, Anna saw that a sign had been set up at the beginning of the Art Walk: ENTER HERE TO VIEW CLIVE BEATTY'S SCULPTURE. PLEASE DO NOT LEAVE THE WALK.

She smiled, happy for Clive.

She found Ernesto in the break room. 'My office,' she told him, and headed back down the stairs. When he arrived in her office he looked outraged.

'What now, Anna?'

'Shut the door and sit down.' When he was seated she said, 'I'm going to give you another chance to tell me why you were trying to get into Garry's locker.'

'I told you. To get a note I wrote to Kelly.'

'That's a crock and you know it. You want me to guess what you were looking for? OK. A diamond necklace.'

His eyes grew large and round. He said nothing.

'You gave it to Garry to fence for you, am I correct?'

For a long time he looked down. Then, almost imperceptibly, he nodded his head.

'Where did it come from?'

He mumbled something.

'What? I can't hear you. Speak up.'

'My brother Jimmy took it. He's a janitor in a fancy department store in New Jersey.'

'And he gave it to you to give to Garry to fence for both of you.'

He met her gaze. 'Jimmy and me – we had no way of getting rid of it. I knew Garry used to be part of a shoplifting operation under Tally Klaw. I thought if anybody would know a fence, he would.'

'So you asked him to see what he could do.'

'That's right.'

'And he had no problem doing it? He didn't hesitate?'

'Actually, at first he said "no problem" and took the necklace, but the next day he said he'd changed his mind. He wasn't in that kind of business any more, he said. He was going to give the necklace back to me. But he never did, because a few days later he got murdered.'

'So you went to Garry's grandmother's apartment, somehow got her to let you in, strangled her, and searched the place. But you

didn't find it. That's why you were trying to get into Garry's locker
– maybe he'd hidden it there.'

He pulled back in alarm. 'What? What are you talking about?'

'You know what I'm talking about. You figured it was in that
apartment and you were going to get it back.'

'You're crazy, Anna. I'm no killer.'

'You're a liar and a thief, but not a killer, is that correct?'

'Well . . .' He frowned at her. 'Yeah. So where is it?'

'Where is what?'

'My necklace.'

'Gone, as far as you're concerned.'

He got up, glared at her resentfully. 'You know, Anna, you ain't
no detective. I don't know who you think you are, trying to figure
out who killed Garry, but I got news for you. It ain't none o' your
business. And neither is this. Besides which, you can't prove any
of it. Not against me, not against my brother.'

'Maybe not, but I'm going to get you fired. I don't want you
here. Sanitation is an honorable profession and there's no place
for someone like you in it.'

'Oh, I get it,' he said, as he turned at the door. 'It's a place for
rich girls who want to play blue-collar, even though they could buy
their own sanitation department with their daddy's money.'

She just looked at him, shocked. There was a triumphant smirk
on his face as he walked away.

NINETEEN

D amian wasn't at roll-call. Anna didn't expect to see him
again, which was fine by her. She would start her report
on him immediately.

During the morning only a trickle of people availed themselves
of the Art Walk, but as word began to spread, the trickle became
a steady stream. People on their lunch break strolled in, in pairs or
small groups, laughing and chatting. Some lingered to speak with
Clive or compliment him on his art or his recycling efforts or both.
Anna popped her head in at noon. 'So how's it going?'

He looked up, beaming happily. 'Fantastic. It's an artist's dream.
I can't thank you enough.'

'Don't thank me, thank Allen. This was his idea.'

'I already have thanked him. Really, I'm grateful to you all.'

At that moment a woman with two small children, a boy and a girl, appeared at the end of the walk. 'You see this man?' she said to them. 'He's an artist who uses things people have thrown out to make his art.'

'It's ugly, Mommy,' the little girl said.

The woman looked at Clive in embarrassment. 'I'm so sorry,' she said with a little giggle.

'That's OK. Everybody's a critic.'

They all laughed.

'Well,' Anna said to Clive, 'it looks like you're in good shape. Can I get you some lunch?'

'Thanks, but Brianna is bringing me a sandwich.'

She left him to chat with the woman and her children. Afterward, as she crossed the garage, Gerry Licari came up to her. 'You're not gonna believe this. CityWide News is coming at the end of the day to tape a segment on our resident Andy War-haul. *Haul*, get it? Like hauling trash?'

'Yes, I get it, Gerry,' she said, inwardly rolling her eyes. 'That's great news. I'm delighted for Clive. Who knows where this might lead for him?'

'Yeah, but do you have any idea what that's going to mean for *us*? People are going to be streaming in here like Disney World.'

'Not a problem. We've got the walk!'

Gerry wandered away scratching his head.

Anna had just finished the first drafts of her reports on Damian and Ernesto when her phone rang. 'Hey, Anna.' It was Allen, sounding artificially matter-of-fact. 'Can you come see me when you get a sec?'

'Sure, Allen,' she said, frowning, and went down the corridor to his office.

'Have a seat.'

'What's up?'

'I'll get right to it. Damian Porter has filed a complaint against you.'

She blinked hard. 'A complaint of what?'

He looked at her with a combination of shock and embarrassment. 'Sexual harassment.'

She opened her mouth to speak, then closed it because she wasn't yet sure what to say.

'You have no response to that?' he said.

'No – yes, of course I do. It's nonsense.'

'Is it?' He sat down in his desk chair, swiveled to face her, his hands clasped between his knees. 'He says you followed him home yesterday afternoon. Is that true?'

'Uh . . . yes.'

'*Yes?* Why on earth would you do that?'

Where to begin? 'Allen . . . you didn't know this, but I've been trying to get to the bottom of who killed Garry. I had a meeting yesterday—'

'Whoa, wait, hold it. You're trying to "get to the bottom" of Garry's murder? Forgive me, Anna, I hate to break this to you, but you're not a cop. You're a sanitation supervisor.'

'I don't appreciate your sarcasm, Allen.'

'And I don't appreciate one of my supervisors playing detective when she should be working.'

'Who said I wasn't working?' she said, her voice rising. 'I think you'll find I always get my work done. You've never complained about it.'

'All right, all right, let's calm down. I apologize. Finish what you were going to say.'

She took a deep breath. 'I had a team meeting at lunch yesterday, and at the end Kelly said she couldn't figure out why people are so fascinated by the mews murders. Damian said it was because mews and courtyards are supposed to be safe places where the ugliness of the world can't get in, but that it does. It was the way he said it – I knew there was something behind it. So I . . . I followed him.'

Allen's jaw dropped slightly but he made an obvious attempt to control himself. 'OK. And what were you hoping to achieve by doing that?'

She shook her head. 'I didn't know. It was an impulse.'

'So what happened?'

'As it turned out, I did find out something interesting. Damian had a wife and baby who were killed in a fire in their apartment, which was in a *mews*.'

'So you think that means he's the murderer?'

'Maybe. Not necessarily. But it's the closest we've come to a motive, isn't it?'

He waved his hands, not wanting to talk about that. 'Who told you that about him?'

'A letter carrier.'

'Where did Damian go when you followed him?'

'To his apartment.'

'And what did you do then?'

'I went back down to the subway to go home. That's when he attacked me.'

'He did *what?*'

She explained. 'He must have seen me and followed me back down to the station. He grabbed me, started kissing me. It was awful. I screamed and someone came down and said he was getting a cop.'

'Did he?'

She shrugged. 'When I got up to the street, the man was gone and there were no cops around.'

'I see. Then let me ask you something. If you knew where he lived, why didn't you find a cop yourself and take him back to Damian's apartment? I know why,' he said before she could answer. 'Because then you would have had to admit you'd been following him. I'm surprised at you, Anna. You've never done anything like this before.'

Not that you know about.

'Damian is completely within his rights to file a complaint against you.'

'You've got to be kidding! *He* attacked *me!*'

'I understand that. But it's a separate issue, isn't it?' It was more a statement than a question. 'You have every right to file a complaint against him . . . though somehow I doubt you will.'

'That's where you're wrong. When you called me I was just finishing my report recommending his termination. Following someone is one thing – I wasn't breaking any laws. Attacking someone is quite another.'

He was looking at her shrewdly. 'Why would he attack you, try to kiss you?'

'He said he thought that was why I'd been following him, to . . .'

'And why would he think that?'

'Because there had been several incidents – times when he flirted with me, claimed I'd been flirting with him, too.'

'Had you?'

'Of course not! Allen, I'm a professional. I'm not in the habit of flirting with members of my crew. Not to mention I've got a boyfriend.'

Abruptly he swiveled back to face his desk. 'A professional, eh? I don't know, Anna. I really don't know. You can go.'

She rose, trying to think of something to say, but no words came to her. Frustrated, she marched out of his office. Back in her own office, she called up the computer file containing her report on Damian and deleted it. Then she called Santos and told him what had happened.

'Are you all right?' he asked, concern in his voice.

'I'm fine. Just embarrassed that I followed him – though that doesn't excuse his attacking me.'

'I was about to call you about him,' Santos said. 'I did a back-ground check on him, as promised, and nothing came up.'

'All right. Thanks.'

'We all make mistakes, Anna. Your judgment got a little cloudy, that's all.'

'What's that supposed to mean?'

'Well, you have to admit you've become kind of obsessed with this whole Garry thing.'

'*Obsessed!*' Heat rose to her face. 'Santos, "this whole Garry thing" is a murder. A young man's life was taken away. You're a cop. I thought you'd understand that. Maybe I also thought it because you've been *helping* me!'

'Anna, calm down. I'm sorry. I didn't mean—'

She hung up on him. Then, barely holding it together, she reached for a file at the corner of her desk. It contained paperwork on Damian. She'd given it a cursory glance when he started at the garage the previous month. Now she examined it carefully. She realized there was no indication of what Damian had been doing before coming to Manhattan Central 13. Gathering her courage, she picked up the file and went back down the hall to Allen's office. He looked up. 'Yes? Is there something else?'

'I need some information on Damian.'

'You've got to be kidding.' When she just glared at him he said, 'What information?'

'Where was he before he started here?'

'What do you mean, where was he?'

'What garage?'

He shook his head. 'He wasn't with any garage. He's new with the Department.'

She raised her eyebrows in surprise. 'Interesting. What was he doing previously? He's got to have put something down.'

Allen took a long, irritated breath. 'You're unbelievable,' he said, turned in his chair, and yanked open a file drawer. He flipped through the folders, pulled one out, and opened it. 'Here we go,' he said, moving his finger down the top page. 'He was a custodian in an apartment building.'

'Where?'

'At 537 West Forty-Eighth. Let's see . . . that's between Tenth and Eleventh avenues.'

Her heart began to beat faster. 'That's a block down from New Amsterdam Mews.'

It made perfect sense. Damian could have slipped out of his building, hidden behind New Amsterdam Mews, grabbed and killed Garry, and returned to his building until nightfall, when he would have returned to the mews and dumped Garry's body in the middle of the courtyard. It all fit except for one thing. Why Garry?

Allen was staring at her, waiting for her to elaborate. But she wouldn't. Instead she asked, 'What are we going to do about him?'

'I've already taken care of that. I'm transferring him to another garage. There's no way you and he could work together after what's happened. Now I need to find someone else – something I have absolutely no time for.'

There was nothing else to say. She could feel his gaze on her as she left his office.

A short time later, Anna exited her office, started down the corridor, and stopped. Blinked. A man stood in the dim light. No, it couldn't be. *Mr Herman?*

'Hello, Anna,' he said before she could speak.

'What are you doing here?'

'I'd like to speak to you.'

'So speak.'

'May we go into your office? You don't have to worry, I'm not going to kill you or anything.'

Why had he said that? She gave him a sardonic smirk. 'I'm not worried that you're going to kill me, Mr Herman. Take my life savings, maybe, but kill me . . . no.'

He hurried past her into her office and she followed. 'Can you shut the door, please?' he asked.

'No, I can't. Now say what you came to say.'

'All right,' he said, dropping into her guest chair. 'I don't know why you took such an immediate dislike to me, Anna, but you did and you seem determined to do me harm.'

'Do *you* harm! It seems to me you're the one doing people harm.'

'I don't deny that what I did was wrong, but I've paid my debt to society, paid the restitution the court ordered. Now it looks as if I'm to go on being punished.'

'Cut the drama, Lionel. No one wants to punish you. We just want you to go away.'

'Oh, really? And who is "we"?'

'Julie Dovner and I.'

'And what about Iris?'

'Iris is an old fool, which is doubtless why you've targeted her.'

He gave a disdainful chuckle. 'Targeted. *Now* who's being dramatic?' He looked directly at her. 'You listen to me. I have given neither you nor Julie Dovner any reason to think my intentions with respect to Iris are anything but honorable. I'm fond of Iris. We enjoy each other's company. Iris is an adult who can make her own decisions. That's all there is to it. What you're doing – spreading venomous information about me – is no less than slander.'

'That's where you're wrong. Slander is when the venomous information isn't true. This venomous information is all too true.'

'But you're spreading it in an effort to hurt me. I think my attorney would see that as slander.'

'As I said, I'm not trying to hurt you. I just want you to go away.'

He rose. 'Well, I'm not going to. I have the same rights you do, and unless and until I have done something wrong, you have no reason to malign me. That's what I came here to say. I'm sure my attorney would be only too glad to fill you in on the legal details.'

'Don't you threaten me, you pompous little crook. Get out of here before I throw you out.'

He walked to the door, turned, his eyes narrowed to slits. 'Don't say I didn't warn you, Anna.'

And he was gone. When Anna went out to the corridor, Brianna was standing there. 'Anna, who was that?'

'My upstairs neighbor. He wanted to speak to me.'

'But why *here*?'

She shrugged. 'This *is* a place for garbage.'

* * *

The CityWide News van arrived at three o'clock. Anna had stayed late to watch. She was heading out to the street when Allen called her name. She turned.

'I want you to deal with these news people.'

'All right.'

'Don't let them stay too long.'

'Why not?'

'Because this is a sanitation garage, not a museum,' he snapped. 'The more they make of this, the likelier other jokers like Clive will try to do this. Speaking of which, I want him out of here ASAP.'

'Allen, we can't just kick him out. You promised him people could come in and see his sculpture. The walk has only been open for one day.'

'I'll give him a week, tops. Then he's outta here. It's just a big ugly pile of junk anyway.'

She watched him go. She'd never seen him in such a foul mood. When she got to the street the news reporter was heading across the sidewalk toward her. It was Arlene Volchok. 'You're expecting us, right?'

'Absolutely,' Anna said, returning her smile. 'I'll take you to Clive.'

'Can you give me some quick background on this guy?' Arlene asked, walking alongside Anna as they followed the walk. The camera crew trailed noisily behind.

'His name is Clive Beatty. He started out creating his sculpture on the sidewalk outside the garage. As you'll see, he uses only discarded items – it's really interesting. He was drawing quite a crowd. Our district chief, Allen Schiff, offered him the use of a courtyard at the side of the building. That way, Clive could have a quiet place to finish his piece, and then we would allow the public in to see it when he was ready. We constructed this walk so that people could get safely from the street to the courtyard.'

'Interesting . . .' Arlene said with a thoughtful frown. She looked at Anna. 'This courtyard . . .'

Oh, no.

'. . . something happened there, no? I remember! A woman was found murdered there. She worked on your crew, right? Had an ankh carved into her chest. They never did catch the Ankh Killer, did they?'

Anna gave her a tight little smile. 'What happened in the courtyard is behind us now. What you're here for is a happy thing.'

'Mm.' Arlene looked at Anna again. 'I know about you, don't I?'

'Yes, we met on Ninth Avenue last Friday.'

'No, I don't mean that. I just realized who you are. You're that
rich deb who decided to slum it and work in trash.'

Anna stopped. 'Excuse me?'

'Oh.' Arlene's eyes widened. 'Sorry. I have such a big mouth
sometimes.'

'Yes, you do,' Anna said pleasantly. 'Here we are.'

Anna went into the courtyard first. Clive had wet and combed
his hair and looked very sweet. He greeted Arlene and her crew
enthusiastically.

'All right,' Arlene said to her camera crew, suddenly all business.
'I want to interview him in front of this thing.' She turned to Clive.
'I'll ask you some questions about it and also about you, OK?'

'Sure,' Clive agreed quickly.

At that moment a skinny teenage boy in torn jeans and a black
tank top appeared on the walk. Seeing everyone, he hesitated.

'Who's that?' Arlene asked Anna.

'I imagine he's here to see the sculpture. Isn't that right?' she
asked him.

He was chewing gum. He nodded. 'Yeah, but I could come
back.'

'No,' Arlene said, grabbing him by the arm and pulling him into
the courtyard. 'It's perfect. I'll interview you after Clive. You up
for that?'

'Sure!' He suddenly remembered what he was wearing. 'But is
this OK?'

'Perfect. What's your name?'

'Taylor Moore.'

'OK, Taylor Moore, you stand over here till we're ready for you.
Anna, I think we'll begin with you.'

'Me?'

'Yes, I want to interview you first, didn't I mention that?' When
Anna shook her head, Arlene said, 'You OK with that?'

'Sure.' Who knew what Allen would say if he were interviewed?
She quickly finger-combed her hair.

Meanwhile, the camera crew had finished setting up. 'Ready
when you are,' one of the men told Arlene, who grabbed a microphone and came up close to Anna.

'I won't be introducing any of you on camera,' she said. 'We'll run your names in the caption.'

'Go,' the man with the camera said.

Arlene instantly broke into a dazzling smile and shoved the camera in front of Anna's face. 'How does the Sanitation Department feel about artists like Clive who demonstrate that there are far more creative ways of using refuse than dumping it in a landfill?'

Anna hesitated, momentarily taken aback. 'Obviously we think he's making an important statement, or we wouldn't have invited him to work here in our courtyard.'

Arlene tilted her head searchingly. 'Oh, come on, Anna, didn't you just want to get him off the sidewalk because the neighbors were complaining?'

Anna's jaw dropped. 'No! Uh – cut! Stop the tape.'

The cameraman obeyed, lowering his camera, and looked to Arlene for instruction.

'What do you think you're doing?' Arlene asked Anna.

'Try that again and you're out of here.'

Arlene gave Anna a little snarl, then turned to Clive, who had been waiting politely beside his sculpture. Arlene walked over to him and turned to the cameraman. 'OK, go.' The blinding smile reappeared. 'This is quite a remarkable piece of work. How did you decide what to use in creating it?'

Clive's hands were shaking. 'Well,' he said in a trembly voice, 'I roam the city looking for interesting things people have thrown out. I pick objects that I think will go well together.'

Arlene cast a dubious glance at the sculpture. 'And you thought these things would go well together?'

'That's right.'

'What statement are you making with this piece, Clive?'

Clive thought for a moment. 'Only that there is beauty every-where, even in things the world has discarded.'

Arlene nodded slowly, looking deep. 'Stop,' she told the cameraman. 'OK, bring the kid over here. Lose the gum,' she told him. He took it out of his mouth and held on to it. When the camera was running again, she asked him, 'What do you think of this sculpture?'

'I think it's cool.'

'Do you think it's art?'

'Sure. I mean, it's real, you know? It's not some painting hanging in a fancy museum. It's from the streets. It's the way the world really is.'

'Thank you,' Arlene said with a warm smile. Then it was gone. 'That's it,' she told her crew, and they all started out. Anna followed them.

'When will this air?' she called after Arlene.

'Tomorrow at six,' she called from the passenger window of the van, and it took off.

'How did it go?' came Allen's voice from behind her.

'Very well,' she said brightly. 'I think it painted both Clive and the Department in a good light.'

'Whatever. I'm leaving now.' He walked out, clearly still angry at her.

She checked her watch. It was a few minutes after five. Taylor had wandered out and was already halfway down the block. Anna rolled the two posts at the end of the walkway into the garage and closed and locked the door.

Crossing the cavernous space, she welcomed the quiet. There was no movement in the garage, all of the sanitation workers on duty still out on their rounds. She went to her office and grabbed a stack of mail she hadn't had time to process. A Manila envelope with 'Langone Medical Center' in the upper left-hand corner caught her eye. She sliced it open. Inside were two sheets of paper. On the top sheet was scrawled *Trent Roberts. Regards, Nolan Stewart*. The bottom sheet was a large computer printout of a color photograph. Anna gazed down at it, blinked hard.

It was Garry Thomason.

She called Nolan Stewart but got his voicemail and decided against leaving a message. She would speak to him in the morning.

How could this be? Garry Thomason was also Trent Roberts, a medical student? It made no sense.

Baffled, she went about wrapping up her work for the day. Clive would need to leave the garage soon. She went out to check on him, and also to congratulate him on his interview.

She found him using a trowel to dab white plaster on to a rough corner of the sculpture. When he looked up he was beaming. 'Thanks so much, Anna.'

'For what?'

'For stopping that barracuda from making a mockery of us.'

'It was my pleasure.'

'Anna, is it true what she said? That you only put me back here because the neighbors were complaining?'

'I won't lie to you, Clive. That is why Allen put you back here. He just doesn't get what you're doing. But everyone else I've spoken to thinks it's amazing. We're proud to have you here.'

'Well, whatever the reason, I'm grateful. If I hadn't been invited to use this courtyard, I would never have gotten all this publicity. People coming in on the walk . . . being on the news.'

'Bottom line, it was definitely a good idea. You were able to work in peace. It was up to you to decide when people could look, and when you wanted to keep out the world.'

Concentrating on his repair, Clive laughed. 'I'm afraid nothing keeps out the world, Anna.'

She frowned, unsure what he meant, and watched him work, his face up close to his creation as he smeared on the plaster. The sculpture was easily twice his size, with its wide cinder-block base and towering split mannequin in the middle.

He'd seen her gazing at it. 'So what do you think of it now that it's finished? Still not your cup of tea?'

She smiled. She realized she'd never really *looked* at it before, never taken it all in. 'First impressions?' she said. 'Striking. Imposing. Disturbing.'

'Go on. I love it.'

She laughed, concentrated harder. Cinder blocks . . . a man cut in half . . . roses . . . twisted wires . . .

'Well?' He was looking at her.

She couldn't answer him. She felt faint. 'It's . . . just wonderful,' she finally got out, working tremendously hard to keep the smile on her face. She looked at her watch. 'Ooh, I'd better get going. You're probably leaving soon, too, no?'

'Yeah, I'd better. I just want to finish this repair. Thanks again, Anna. For everything. You're a good friend.'

'Don't mention it.' She turned and followed the walk back to the corridor. She forced herself to walk slowly into her office, then gently closed the door. Seated behind her desk, she picked up her phone and called Santos's cell.

'Anna,' he said as soon as he picked up, 'I'm sorry. Please forgive me. You know how much I love you.'

'Sh-h,' she whispered.

'There's something I need to tell you,' he continued. 'I was about to call. It's important.'

'Sh-h!'

'What? What's going on? I can barely hear you.'

'I know who it—'

Her office door burst open like an explosion, banging hard on the wall. In the doorway stood Clive, a stony expression on his face, the plaster-covered trowel in his hand.

TWENTY

Clive lunged across the room, the trowel held out before him, and deftly knocked the receiver out of her hand. She screamed, jumping back.

'Anna! Anna, are you there?' came Santos's voice from the earpiece.

Clive ran around the desk and stabbed at her with the trowel. She jumped out of the way and its tip caught on her shirt, tearing it. Now he had her up against the wall. He raised the trowel to cut her neck but she grabbed his arm with both her hands and grimaced as she tried to push him away. Simultaneously she stomped on his foot. He let out a cry of mild irritation and relaxed long enough for her to remove one of her hands from his and grab the lamp from her desk. She drew it back and smashed it into his face, the bulb shattering, tiny shards of glass going into his eyes.

He let out a cry of pain, closed his eyes and hunched over. Frantically she scanned her desk for something else to hit him with. She picked up her steel pencil cup and with all her might brought it down on his head, pens and pencils flying, then did it again. He grunted, still feeling at his eyes from which blood ran.

Her cell phone began to ring in her pocket as she ran out of her office, down the corridor, and out to the entrance area to the nearest means of escape, the door where the walkway ended. Her phone still ringing, she began to fiddle with the lock but as she did Clive appeared from the corridor, blood running from his eyes, the trowel still in his hand, and ran toward her. With a cry of frustration she abandoned the door and ran toward the large truck door. It was closed. To open it would be a slow process.

The only way to go was back into the garage. She made a mad dash toward the building's back wall. In her pocket her cell suddenly stopped ringing as the call – no doubt from Santos – went to voicemail.

Clive's footsteps pounded behind her. She ran faster but suddenly she felt him grab her by the back of her shirt and pull her to him. She spun around, kicking at him, then clawed at his bleeding eyes. He cried out in pain and let go. She took off again. Ahead of her was a long line of parked collection trucks. Quickly she ran behind one of them and crouched against the wall, watching the floor under the truck. Suddenly his feet appeared and walked slowly by. She froze.

'Where are you?' he demanded. The sound of his footsteps receded as he walked along the row of trucks.

Carefully Anna took her cell phone from her pocket and dialed Santos. He answered instantly. 'Anna, what's going on? Where are you?'

She was afraid to make a sound. 'Garage,' she whispered.

'Are you in danger?'

'Yes.'

'I'm on the way.'

Suddenly Clive's feet reappeared and she jumped. Her cell phone slipped from her hand and clattered on the concrete floor. Again she froze. Abruptly Clive stopped. 'There you are, smart girl.'

She took off, keeping low as she ran between the trucks and the wall, stopping when she had nearly reached the entrance to the courtyard. Glancing back, she saw Clive appear in the space between the trucks and the wall. She darted a few feet forward between two trucks, getting out of his line of vision.

'Yes,' he called out, and from his voice she could tell he'd gone back out to the open space in front of the trucks. 'You're very clever, Anna. Too clever. But then, that's why I'm here, isn't it? To keep an eye on you. You almost made it. I would have left in a few days. I even tried to warn you to keep your nose out of it, but even the little gift I left for you in the alley didn't deter you.'

He began to walk, his footsteps nearing. 'I guess you've figured out by now that courtyards don't save you. The dark, ugly, traitorous world gets in. It finds you.' Now he was crying, his voice growing higher. 'He was my whole world, Anna, do you understand that?

He was everything I lived for. Then *they* took him away from me,'
he said with sudden viciousness. '*They* turned him against me. So
they had to die, do you see that, Anna? Because if I couldn't have
him . . . neither could they. Ah, there you are.' He was peering down
the space between the trucks, looking right at her. He started toward
her, the trowel at his side.

She ran back along the wall. 'Help!' she screamed, and her voice
echoed in the cavernous garage. But she knew no one had heard
her. She and Clive were alone.

'Anna! Anna, where are you?' came Santos's voice.

'Santos!' She ran between two trucks back out into the open
space of the garage. Santos stood at the far end, his gun drawn.
Behind him, the truck door stood open. She darted across the
space toward him. Behind her, Clive burst out from between two
trucks.

'You!' Santos shouted. 'Stay where you are!'

Anna rushed to the beginning of the corridor as Santos stepped
deeper into the garage. As she turned to see what was happening,
Santos moaned, 'Oh, no . . .' She spun around.

Clive lay on his back on the concrete floor, dark crimson blood
pumping from a gash in his throat. Blood covered the trowel he
still clenched in his hand.

Santos was on his cell even as he approached Clive. 'I need a
bus! Sanitation garage on Forty-Third between Seventh and Eighth.
Hurry.'

Far to Anna's left, where Santos had been standing, the figure
of another man appeared. Anna gasped, felt faint again.

It was Garry.

But of course it wasn't. The young man who looked exactly like
Garry walked forward, past Santos, and gazed down at Clive lying
on the garage floor.

Clive gazed up at him through his bloody eyes as his life ebbed
away. With a great effort he moved his lips. His words were faint
but clear. 'Why? I loved you, son . . .' Then his eyes rolled back in
his head and his body went limp.

High in the girders of the garage ceiling, a pigeon fluttered its
wings for a violent moment, then grew still.

TWENTY-ONE

They couldn't take their eyes off him. In a booth at Sammy's, Anna and Kelly watched Trent Roberts. In appearance he was identical to Garry. The difference was in his manner. Whereas Garry had had a rough way of speaking, Trent was refined, well educated, polite.

It could be that way with identical twins.

'I've given a lot of thought to the best place to begin,' Trent said, sipping his coffee before carefully replacing the cup in the saucer. 'I've decided it's when our parents met.'

Santos, seated next to Trent, nodded encouragingly. Though Trent had given a statement to Rinaldi and Roche, neither Santos, Anna, nor Kelly knew what he had said.

'I didn't know the complete story until today,' Trent said. 'Garry learned a lot from Evelyn. I got some information out of Jared. But it wasn't until Anna and Kelly filled in the remaining gaps for me that I knew everything.'

He took a deep breath, then began.

'It was 1982, and Woodhull Hospital in North Brooklyn was still new. In the psychiatric ward, two patients met and fell in love. Adam North was twenty-two. Roberta Thomason was nineteen. Each had recently suffered a psychiatric breakdown. It was several months before they were released from the hospital. They decided to live together.

'Adam was an orphan, a former foster child who bounced from home to home. Roberta, an only child, lived with her mother, Evelyn, in Washington Heights. Neither Adam nor Roberta had any money. Adam moved in with Roberta and Evelyn.'

'Did they get married?' Santos asked.

'No. But in all other respects they were husband and wife. I believe they intended to marry, especially because Roberta had become pregnant with twins.'

'You and Garry?' Kelly asked.

Trent shook his head sadly. 'No. Roberta had a late-term miscarriage.'

Kelly frowned in bewilderment. 'I don't understand. Then who—?'

'Wait,' Anna told her. 'Go ahead, Trent.'

'Roberta and Adam were devastated. Early in 1983, Roberta entered Woodhull Hospital, which she had gotten to know pretty well during her months there. Posing as an employee, she stole newborn identical twins – Garry and me.

'Roberta and Adam named my brother Garry. They named me Peter. They were ecstatically happy. Amazingly, they had completely eluded the police. They began raising Garry and me as their own children.

'But their happiness wasn't to last. When Garry and I were four months old, Adam discovered that Roberta was having an affair with another man she had met at Woodhull. In the living room of Evelyn's apartment, as Roberta held Garry and me on her knees, Adam confronted her. Evelyn was in her bedroom napping.

'There was a horrible scene. Roberta denied everything, which made Adam even more furious. In his rage he grabbed a knife from the kitchen and stabbed her. Moments later Evelyn, having heard Roberta's screams, hurried in. In a panic, Adam grabbed one of the twins – me – and fled.

'Evelyn had to think fast. Leaving Roberta where she lay dead, she rushed Garry to her next-door neighbor and close friend, Imogene Small. Then Evelyn returned to her apartment and called the police. When they arrived, she told them she had returned from running errands and found her daughter dead. She suggested to the police that any of a number of men Roberta had been seeing could have killed her. She made no mention of Adam . . . and no mention of me and Garry.

'Evelyn loved us. For all intents and purposes, we were her grandchildren. If the police found out about Garry, they might ask questions that could lead back to the day Roberta stole us from the hospital. Evelyn had lost me. She couldn't lose Garry, too.

'And so she raised him herself, telling him his parents had died in a car accident when he was an infant. Only one person knew the truth: Imogene Small, who had kept Garry hidden from the police.'

Anna nodded. 'She was blackmailing Evelyn. But once Evelyn had lost Garry – the only person she lived for – she no longer cared if the truth got out. So she left a note for Imogene saying there would be no more payments, that Imogene could do what she wanted.'

Kelly turned to Trent. 'What happened to you and Adam?'

'Adam was as desperate not to lose me as Evelyn was not to

lose Garry. Adam found a place where he and I could hide from the world – an idyllic, hidden mews on Bank Street in Princeton, New Jersey. The world was an ugly place, Adam said often to me, a place we must keep out. In our mews apartment, a secret, hidden, sequestered world within a world, we were safe.

'Adam created new identities for himself and for me. He became Jared Roberts. I became Trent Roberts. I would be told my mother died of cancer when I was a baby.'

Santos asked, 'Did he ever tell you that you had a twin?'

'No. Nor did Evelyn ever tell Garry.' Trent took another sip of coffee. 'Adam had no marketable skills. But he had to support us. So he drew on an as-yet-untapped artistic ability and supported us as a street artist, the person everyone watches but never gets to know.'

'In Princeton?' Kelly asked.

'No, New York City, but never the same place twice. That's how we lived. He was a good father, as good as any father could be. He was devoted to me. I was his world. But I was never allowed to have friends, never allowed to talk about my life or my home or the man I believed was my father.

'I did well at school and was able to attend Princeton on a full scholarship. After graduation, I worked for three years for a local law firm. But I had decided there was something I wanted to do with my life. I wanted to become a doctor. My dream was to go to medical school in New York City. One day I worked up my courage and told him.'

'How did he react?' Anna asked.

'Like I'd dropped a bomb. He had a mix of emotions. He was devastated at the thought of my moving out – I'd never lived away, even during college. But on a practical level, he was terrified that Garry and I might see each other. He knew Evelyn had raised Garry and had no reason to believe she didn't still live in New York City. Even in a city as big as New York, we might run into each other. You hear about that kind of thing happening all the time.

'But I insisted, told him I was going to do it whether he liked it or not. I promised him I wouldn't abandon him, that I loved him. So he relented – praying, I'm sure, that the unthinkable would never happen. I enrolled in NYU School of Medicine. I got loans to pay my tuition. I lived in school housing and came home frequently to see Jared. In New York I started dating a lovely girl named Yvette

Ronson. She had come to New York recently from Minnesota and worked in a daycare center.

'Then the unthinkable happened. On the morning of Friday, July sixteenth, I walked out of Yvette's building on West Forty-Sixth Street at the exact same moment that Garry walked up to the building to get the trash. We looked at each other and stopped dead. We couldn't believe what we were seeing – mirror images of ourselves. The likeness was too strong to be a passing resemblance. We were identical twins, there was no doubt about it.'

'What did you do?' Kelly asked.

'It was surreal. I introduced myself. Garry introduced himself. We knew we had to talk – a lot. We made a date to meet that night. Over dinner we compared our stories and realized something very bad happened shortly after we were born. We agreed to see what we could find out. Garry confronted Evelyn. He screamed at her—'

'*Half my life* . . .' Anna said, and the three of them looked at her. 'That's what Mr Goldblum heard Garry shouting at Evelyn. Now it's clear what he was saying. We thought he was referring to something that had affected half of his lifetime. What he was actually saying was that by keeping his twin from him, Evelyn had, figuratively speaking, stolen half his life.'

Trent continued. 'Evelyn broke down, confessed everything.'

'Did she want to meet you?' Santos asked.

Trent shook his head sadly. 'Garry asked her. She said she couldn't bear it. Garry told me what Evelyn had confessed to him. I went to Princeton and confronted Jared. I told him I knew what he had done . . . and that I had met my brother. I told him not to worry – I wasn't going to turn him in – but he would never see me again.'

'How did he react?' Anna asked.

'He went insane. Because, really, he was insane. He begged me not to leave, pleaded with me. He reminded me how much he loved me, how he had raised me, protected me . . . of the private, protected world he'd created for us in the mews, a world where the world hadn't been able to hurt us. I told him he'd simply been hiding from the police.

'I told him I had my own life now, other people who cared about me. I had my girlfriend, Yvette. I had an instructor who had taken a special interest in me, Professor Beaumont. And I had a buddy, a fellow medical student named Quillan Frank. We went to movies, lifted weights at the gym together. And, of course, I had my brother. I left the mews, not looking back.'

Trent asked for more water, and didn't continue until the waiter had refilled his glass. He took a sip, set down the glass.

'I know now that Jared completely fell apart. His life had been pulled out from under him. The one person he'd lived for was gone for ever. As I've said, he was insane, but he'd managed to keep it masked for twenty-seven years. Now that insanity came out in full force.

'These "other people" I had told him about – this was all *their* fault. It was *they* who had taken me away from him. Well, if he couldn't have me, neither could they. He would never hurt me, but he *could* prevent Garry, Yvette, Professor Beaumont, and Quillan from having me. He would murder them, one by one, each in a very special way.

'Garry was the mirror image I had seen that horrible fateful day on West Forty-Sixth Street. Therefore, Jared killed him with a shard of mirror through his eye.' Kelly winced, looked down. 'I'm sorry,' he said. She shook her head to indicate that it was all right.

Trent knit his brows, thinking, and looked at Anna. 'Jared must have known you'd solved murders before. You were a threat to him. He had to keep an eye on you. So Clive Beatty, the "trash artist," was born. By setting up shop outside the garage, he could watch you, know where you were. When you invited him to move his art into the courtyard, he must have thought it was too good to be true. The irony of moving into a courtyard would not have been lost on him.

'There in the courtyard, Jared commemorated Garry's death by adding a secret symbol to his sculpture. A mannequin cut in two – twins.' Trent took a deep breath. 'My poor beautiful Yvette was next. She had captured my heart. So Jared stabbed her in her own heart. On his sculpture he represented the murder with red roses, a symbol of love.

'Horace Beaumont had captured my mind. Jared drove an ice pick into Horace's brain, then added a computer to the sculpture to symbolize his death. Quillan and I had met at a gym, laughed together as friends. Pretending to be a mutual friend of ours, Jared invited Quillan to see Neanderthal MashUp at the Box. He got Quillan very drunk, took him backstage, and intentionally made a scene so that they would be thrown out the back door. There in Freeman Alley Jared had hidden a barbell and a knife. He killed Quillan by smashing the barbell into his head, then enlarged his mouth into a grotesque smile to represent our laughter. Back in the courtyard, two cords twisted together, a symbol of friendship, would represent his death.

'But the symbolism most meaningful to Jared was where he dumped the bodies – in mews, a courtyard, and an alley, representative of the place where he had believed the world couldn't penetrate . . . until it came crashing in.'

Anna asked Trent, 'When did you realize Jared was the Mews Murderer?'

'After Yvette was murdered. It was the only explanation. I had to do something, but even though I had done nothing wrong I was afraid to come forward. So I anonymously tipped off the police, gave them our address in Princeton. Then I disappeared. Jared would know I had given him up. I thought he might very well come after me.' Trent gave a mirthless laugh. 'I needn't have worried. It seems now that it would never have occurred to Jared that I would do something like that to him. It had to have been someone else, and he decided that person was Evelyn, that somehow she had obtained his address and given it to the police.

'He went to her street to look at her building. Evelyn saw him from her window. She called you, Anna, and said, "I've seen him." You thought she meant Zeus, whom she'd said she was afraid of, but it was Jared, a ghost from the nightmarish past, whom she'd seen and was terrified of.

'Jared went up to her apartment. Maybe he told her he knew Garry and I had met and he wanted to talk to her. We'll never know. But he must have promised he wouldn't hurt her. She made the fatal mistake of believing him. He strangled her and fled.

'It wasn't until three days after Quillan was murdered,' Trent said with regret in his voice, 'that I finally decided I had better go to the police in person, try to help them. This afternoon I went to the Midtown North station house.'

Santos nodded, looked at Anna. 'When you called me from the garage, Trent was with me. Fortunately, Rinaldi and Roche happened to be out in the field. Trent told me his story and we rushed over. I was going to arrest Clive.'

For a few moments they sat in silence. Finally Anna spoke, tears in her eyes. 'I feel for all of Jared's victims, of course, but Kelly and I *knew* Garry. To die after surviving Iraq, just when he was turning his life around . . .'

'It's true,' Trent said. 'He'd made some bad choices – the drug dealing, the shoplifting. All in a misguided attempt to bring him the money Evelyn had never been able to provide on her late husband's death benefit. Garry told me joining the army was his first step in going straight. He'd intended to continue on this new path once he was discharged. But he never had a chance.'

Anna looked up as a thought occurred to her. 'Now that you know the truth about your past, are you going to try to find your real parents?'

'Yes. I've been thinking about it. I'm certainly going to try.' Trent smiled sadly. 'It's the least I can do for my brother.'

When they emerged from Sammy's, a police cruiser was parked at the curb, and detectives Rinaldi and Roche were getting out of it. Santos let out a low moan.

'I heard that,' Rinaldi said, then turned to Trent. 'You're going to have to come to the station and answer some more questions. You up for that?'

'Sure. Might as well get it over with.'

'I don't know what it is with you,' Rinaldi said to Anna, shaking her head in wonder. 'You're like a cat with nine lives. You do realize that several times while you were *investigating* this case, you could have died.'

'Yes. But I didn't, did I? And now I've solved it.'

Rinaldi let out a bark of laughter. 'Solved it! That's debatable.'

'No, it's not,' Anna said, holding her ground. 'If I hadn't suddenly realized the significance of the objects in Clive's sculpture, he would never have come after me. So I flushed him out.'

Rinaldi threw up her hands and turned away. Roche did the same thing.

'I expect you at the station within the half-hour,' Rinaldi called back to Trent.

'What a perfectly awful woman,' Trent said, his eyes on the receding car.

'True,' Anna said. 'But we're used to her by now. Let's walk to the station. We'll still get there in plenty of time.'

The two men nodded and they started along West Forty-Fifth Street.

'Here's a short cut,' Santos said, stopping at a dark alley between two apartment buildings.

Anna and Trent exchanged a knowing look.

'I think not,' Anna said.

TWENTY-TWO

Anna and Santos hurried down the stairs, eager to hit the road. Today they were heading out of the city to attend a family party in Greenwich in celebration of Will's thirty-third birthday.

As they reached the foyer, Mrs Dovner's door opened and she stood quietly watching them.

'Good morning, Mrs Dovner,' Anna said cheerfully. Santos smiled and nodded.

'You were right,' she said flatly.

'Beg your pardon?' Anna said.

'About Lionel.'

They both walked up to her.

'What do you mean?' Anna asked.

'I knew you didn't like him and you were right. He's a crook. He wined me and dined me and said he was fond of me, all to get me to invest my money with him. Well, I did, and as soon as my check cleared, he was gone.'

'What do you mean, "gone"?'

'Don't you know what the word *gone* means? He left. Doesn't live here any more. Took off. See for yourself.'

Anna and Santos climbed the stairs to the third floor. The door to Mr Herman's apartment was ajar. Anna pushed it open. The place was completely bare. Santos was shaking his head sadly as they returned downstairs.

'I'm so sorry, Mrs Dovner,' Anna said.

Mrs Dovner took a crumpled tissue from the pocket of her housecoat and dabbed at her eyes. 'I'm such an old fool.'

'No, you're not, Mrs Dovner. You trusted him. There's nothing wrong with that. He's the one who betrayed your trust. Have you called the police?'

'The police?' she said, and shot a glance at Santos. 'What on earth could they do?'

Santos said, 'Maybe a lot. Like catching him. Let us help you.'

*   *   *

When they arrived at Anna's parents' house, everyone was in the family room, talking and laughing. Anna gave her brother a kiss and wished him a happy birthday. Santos shook his hand and wished him many happy returns.

Gloria hurried over to Anna, smiling broadly. 'Wait till you see Mom and Dad.'

'What do you mean?' Anna asked.

'They're like lovebirds. Mom has moved back. You were so right. I'm sorry, Anna. It was wonderful what you did, taking Daddy to that AA meeting.'

'I only took him to one. If he's gone to more, that's all his doing.'

'Indeed I have gone to more,' came their father's voice behind them, and they turned. Jeff looked healthier than Anna had seen him look in years. There was a brightness in his eyes she couldn't recall ever seeing. 'I go every day,' he explained. 'I intend to do my ninety days and then keep going.'

'So the meetings are all right?' Gloria asked.

'They're more than all right. I've already made two new golf friends. We go to the clubhouse and drink iced tea.'

'Isn't it wonderful?' said Tildy, walking in from the terrace where she had been playing with Will's daughter, Nina. 'Thank you, darling,' she said to Anna, and kissed her on the cheek.

'Santos,' Anna heard her father say in a low voice. 'I wonder if I could have a word with you.'

'Of course, sir,' Santos said, and followed the older man into the den. When Santos re-emerged twenty minutes later, he was smiling.

'What was that all about?' Anna asked him.

'Your father apologized for unkind things he's said to and about me in the past, and asked for my forgiveness.'

Anna's eyes welled with tears. 'Step nine, if I'm not mistaken. Is that all he said?'

'No. He also said he would be honored to have me as his son-in-law some day.'

She smiled up at him. 'Some day?'

'Some day soon,' he said, lowering his head, and their lips came together in a gentle, lasting kiss.

AUTHOR'S NOTE

One of the pleasures of writing the Hidden Manhattan mysteries is learning about actual secret places in New York that I can share with you. I always try to explore these places in person, and would encourage you to do so if you find yourself in New York. There's nothing like really being there.

Amster Yard, Washington Mews, and Freeman Alley are all real places that you can visit. New Amsterdam Mews is the product of my imagination.

If you have discovered any secret places in Manhattan, I'd love to hear about them. You can e-mail me at evanmarshall@optonline.net.

To learn more about the secret places in my books, visit my website at www.EvanMarshallMysteries.com.

Evan Marshall